A SOLDIER'S PENANCE

JERRY AUTIERI

1

"Optio Marcus Varro, hero and conspirator."

Varro whispered into the darkness of the camp, staring at his sandaled feet lost in the gloom. The camp was silent but for the chirping of crickets and rippling of tents with the cool breeze. Thousands of soldiers and horses and twenty war elephants were encamped on this hill. Yet when Varro closed his eyes after dark, he could imagine himself alone. Silence pressed the sleeping camp like a strong hand clamped over the mouth. No sound escaped.

"Listen, Optio, the girl has what's ours and we're simply taking it back."

Falco stood an arm's length before him. Yet behind the row of tents where the hastati slept, he was little better than a paler outline against the black. The unmistakable sarcastic note of his harsh whisper irked Varro. He and Falco were childhood friends, and when in private they behaved as equals. Still, he struggled with his new rank and did not welcome Falco's disrespect.

Varro stared past him to the main roads where torches fluttered orange light over well-trodden paths. Though he was second in command after Centurion Drusus, he had no excuse to be out after dark. If the centurion or others of the command group realized Varro had slipped away, he would be desperate for an excuse. Yet the roads were empty. He and Falco expected only a single shadow to slip between the tents and join them.

"I know," Varro said, acknowledging their shared cause. "But it still doesn't feel any better to me. It's as if we're doing something criminal. We are, actually."

A snort was Falco's answer. Varro saw his pale gray form shift in the darkness. Though his heavy brows were erased in shadow, Varro also knew they were drawing together and pulling deep lines across Falco's thick face. His arms swished across the fabric of his white tunic as he folded them across his chest.

"Stealing back from a thief is no crime. Besides, she's a slave," he said. "We can do whatever we want with her."

"Consul Galba's slave," Varro said. A shudder rocked him, and he considered it a bad sign. How often had the goddess Fortuna blessed him, he wondered. He would need her once more, yet doubted she favored plots carried out in secrecy and darkness.

"But still a slave," Falco said. "If she gets hurt, it's no worse than breaking one of his fancy chairs. Besides, a little pain would serve well to remind her what she is."

Knowing he would get nowhere with Falco, he also folded his arms and continued to watch for Curio. He was the final conspirator, brought in to Varro and Falco's plot because he had learned their secret and demanded a share for his silence. Yet he was a valuable partner who seemed to know someone in every century. Without his connections, they might not have ever arranged this night's adventure.

"There are no stars," Varro noted, looking into the black velvet night hanging over them. "It's not a good sign."

"Thankfully we don't have to sail a ship. Stop looking in the sky. Why would starlight be a good sign? You're just nervous and you're passing it to me like a cold."

"Sorry, I'll feel better when this is all done." Varro turned back to watching the roads. They had only just met as planned, yet he felt as if he had been watching all night.

He rubbed the back of his neck. All this subterfuge for that damned chain. He had claimed it from an Illyrian bandit chief. He had pulled it from his corpse, a prize of braided gold as thick as a strong man's thumb. That chief had a sister who was captured and made a slave to Consul Galba. The consul doted on her, no doubt for her beautiful face and winsome figure. She somehow learned that Varro and Falco had split her brother's chain and hid the sections in their packs. The slave had not only been brazen enough to steal it then rub it in his and Falco's faces, but also had sworn to kill Varro in revenge for her brother.

The plan to retrieve it was brutally simple. She had to keep the chain on her person. So they would lure away the other slaves that shared her tent, then capture her in the night. Finally they would threaten to kill her if she did not return the chain. She could not appeal to the consul for help since she had stolen the chain, which was Varro's rightful battle spoils. He would worry about her death threats later.

He did not like this plan. Under no circumstances would he kill the girl, though Falco seemed easy enough with that idea. Though she was simple property, murdering for gold sickened him. A little over a year ago, he would not even raise his hands in self-defense. Now he would threaten a girl with death? He would have to become some kind of beast to do such a thing. Therefore, the whole plot relied on his questionable acting abilities.

"We're ready."

Curio's sudden appearance jarred Varro out of his worries. The short man simply emerged from the shadows and spoke. Falco hissed at him.

"I almost shit myself, Curio. Don't sneak up on us."

"I wasn't sneaking. The two of you are asleep on your feet." Curio sighed and his short silhouette pointed toward headquarters. "We've got a long enough window to do what we need. Two of the slave girls are entertaining the consul. Our girl got a break tonight."

"Did you arrange that?" Varro asked. He followed Curio's gaze across the road, but the orange haze of torchlight hid the command tents at the center of camp.

"No, but you can still thank me." Curio's whisper was bright with self-satisfaction. "I've done some asking around about Galba's habits. He likes our girl as a singular experience, and he seems to have a bit of a schedule. So it wasn't hard to figure out that tonight is our lucky night."

"And every night is Galba's lucky night," Falco said, followed by a wistful sigh.

Varro shook his head in admiration. "You seem to know too much about everyone, Curio."

Though obscured in shadow, Varro still imagined the grin on his short friend's face.

"Let's be quick. Galba's guards might catch us sneaking into the slave tent. But I'll be the distraction to let you two inside."

Though Varro outranked his two companions, he took his orders from Curio. This style of underhanded work seemed suited to him, whereas Varro knew he lacked imagination in this regard. He would have simply confronted the slave and demanded she return the chain. But the value of that chain meant someone higher up, possibly Galba himself, would find a reason to withhold it. So now he tucked his head down and followed Curio into the light of the roads on his way to reclaim his prize by threats and trickery.

Stepping into the golden circle of light felt to Varro as if it had set him aflame. It marked him and revealed his treachery to anyone watching. Yet he wanted that chain, as did Falco and Curio. So he dashed across the road into the welcoming darkness. The three gathered together in silence.

The main road into the parade ground and headquarters was too well lit to follow. The guards at Galba's tent would spot them long before they could reach the smaller tent where his female slaves lived. Curio gestured they should follow the row of tents to their right. Varro glanced across the way, to the row of tents opposite. His bed was there, along with Centurion Drusus and the others of his command group. They were all asleep, as he was supposed to be. He squeezed his eyelids together as if trying to force the worry out of his head.

Curio sped off and Varro followed with Falco trailing. Guards at each gate looked out beyond the camp. Inside, only Galba and the tribunes had guards to watch over their sleep. The rest of the army did not warrant anyone's attention, and Varro was glad for it. He lifted his feet high as he ran so the hobnails of his sandals would not scratch against the dirt and awaken a light-sleeping centurion in one of the tents he passed.

They collided together where Curio halted them at the end of the row. Consul Galba's tent was larger and brighter than all the others. To Varro and likely any other regular solider, the so-called tent might be bigger and better appointed than their actual homes. Two soldiers in muscled bronze pectorals and black plumed helmets stood guard. They were likely wealthy principes, young and strong and selected especially for this duty. They stood in bright torchlight cast from torch stands set around the entrance.

"A watchful pair," Falco said, leaning out of the dark. His breath was warm against the side of Varro's face. "And the slave tent is in full view. How are we getting inside?"

Varro grunted his doubt as well. The smaller slave tent, still larger than what Varro slept in as an optio, sat next to the consul's tent. While it was closer to Varro than the consul's tent, no one would fail to see them entering.

"A bit of confusion in orders," Curio said. "You're my optio. Let's just say you sent me out here to relieve one of the guards. You can back up that story if you must. They just need to look away for a moment, then you're inside. After you get the necklace, I'll meet you around the back of the tent. I'll pull up the rear wall for you to slip under."

"Why not just do that to enter?" Varro looked again to the guards. While anyone on guard duty remained alert for danger, these two seemed as if they were awaiting it.

Falco clucked his tongue but Curio explained with measured patience.

"Because it'll take a few pulls to dislodge the stakes, and the girl inside might be alerted."

"And crawling in on our bellies will give her a chance to bash our heads," Falco added, less patiently. "Do you really need another knock on your head?"

Varro touched the crown of his head, feeling the rough patch of flesh still tender months after Gallio had brained him with a stone.

"But what if something goes wrong?"

Curio's expression flattened. "You're right, Optio. Let's go back now. We'll just have to grab her when the consul is not looking."

They stared at each other, lingering at the edge of darkness. He wished there was another way, like sneaking into her tent during daylight to search for the necklace. She must have it hidden inside. Yet in daylight the command center teemed with men on every sort of task. No one approached the consul's tent without notice.

"All right, it'll be quick enough," Varro said. "But we're just going to scare her. No real violence. Do you understand, Falco?"

"We can't scare her unless she believes we're serious. Look, we've talked this to death. We'll give her a good fright and she'll collapse. Gods, we're here now. She stole from us and threatened to murder you. Why do you need so much convincing?"

"Shut up," Curio hissed. "You're getting too loud. Waking to a knife at the throat will be frightening enough. You won't need to do more. She'll give up the necklace, I'm sure. Now, let's begin."

He vanished back the way they had come. Varro and Falco crouched in the shadows, staring at each other. Falco's eyes were lost beneath the shadow of his heavy brows. A thick orange stripe of torchlight quivered on the side of his head. Falco seemed confident, but Varro knew he was just as nervous. They dared much, but then again, the rewards were worth it.

At last Curio reappeared at the far end of the parade ground. He walked with purpose toward the guards, pretending to wipe sleep from his eyes as he did. The two guards standing watch noted him immediately and stepped forward to greet him.

Curio ambled up and looked at the two guards towering over him. He gave a sheepish smile.

"Reporting for duty," he said in a small, tentative voice. He seemed to shrink as he spoke.

"Duty for what?" One of the guards stepped forward and grabbed his sleeve. "You've no business here that we know."

Falco tapped Varro's shoulder. Without looking away from the two occupied guards, he stepped out into the light.

Had he been thinking, he might have dressed better for this underhanded work. Instead, he wore his white tunic that now felt like a blazing beacon in the night. Each step forward felt like a scream for attention. His heart raced and his breath was short and hot.

Yet Curio kept the two guards distracted. He argued with them, pulling away from the one holding his sleeve. This drew them forward and positioned their backs so Varro's brilliant tunic would not catch their peripheral vision. Falco kept pace with him. The two reached the flap of the tent in four strides, and both knocked the flaps open into the dark interior.

Varro slipped inside, careful to draw the flap shut once more. The interior again plunged into darkness, then his heart flipped. How were they going to see anything? He had not considered this need and now he hung paralyzed on the other side of the closed tent flap. The sides of his neck throbbed. They were both blind. He felt Falco's shoulder against his. Neither moved.

Curio's argument echoed outside, but was muffled and indistinct. Varro imagined his own racing heart was louder. Suspended in the darkness, he dared not breathe. At his hip, he carried the pugio his mother had gifted him, blessed at the temple of Mars and carried by his uncle when he was a young man on campaign. It was like a leaden weight on his belt, for now he must draw it and threaten this slave with its edge.

At last the arguing outside ended. Curio must have seen they had entered and now retreated. If the guards were as competent as they appeared, Varro expected them to check the surroundings. He doubted they would look inside the tent, but they might hover outside to listen for something amiss. So when Falco motioned ahead, Varro seized his wrist and yanked him still.

Whether the guards checked or not, Varro did not know. Neither did he know how long he waited, as nerves made every moment stretch beyond counting. Yet he realized now that for a slave tent the air carried a pleasant scent. It was some sort of flower that itched his nose. He feared sneezing, but of course that was only his imagination. Flowers had never caused him to sneeze before.

At last Falco broke out of Varro's grip. They both took tentative steps forward. By now the dim light filtering through the seams of the tent flap granted sight again. Their blindness was replaced with a kind of half-sight. The girl slept atop a low bed piled with furs. A white sheet was pulled up to her neck against the cold.

This was the correct girl, too. He recognized the shape of her head and the thin arm pinning the sheet to her body as she slept. Her brown hair had grown to her shoulders, much longer than the boyish cut she wore when he first met her. In fact, back then he had thought her a boy.

Falco drew his pugio, then frowned at Varro to do the same. The dim lines on his face wrinkled as he nodded to him.

Drawing the pugio into his hand, it felt cold and angry. Perhaps he offended Mars by using this blessed weapon for such evil. This entire operation had so unsettled him that he had failed to think through any of these details. He was ready to forego the gold and leave this moment.

Crouched over and stepping carefully across the pounded earth floor, he and Falco converged on the sleeping girl. As he neared, Varro saw her brows drawn tight and her mouth bent as if her dreams disgusted her. Falco crept to the foot of the bed, and Varro stood over her.

With a shared nod, Falco pinned her legs which did not immediately awaken her. She stirred and mumbled then the sheet ruffled as she tried to move her legs.

Varro clamped his hand across her mouth and leaned across her body. He set the cold pugio blade at her neck and pricked her skin which shined gray in the feeble light.

Her wide, doe-like eyes fluttered open. She blinked then tried to sit up, only to discover Varro pinned her flat. Her scream blew out as a muffled, wet blast against Varro's palm. He crushed down on her while driving the blade against her skin.

"Shut up," he hissed, leaning closer. "You make a noise and I'll end your life now."

The girl stared at him, two huge eyes framed by the sprawl of her hair and Varro's hand. He hated the fear and loathing he saw directed at him. But she had started this trouble, and he had to end it.

"Don't move," he said. "Falco has your legs. You remember him? You stole our necklace."

Her eyes narrowed and she growled an answer beneath his hand. Her breath was hot in his palm.

"Good," he said. "Now, we'll let you sit up. Don't do anything stupid. There are no guards to come help you. Even if there were, you'll not live to see them. Everything is really simple, actually. Just return what you took from us, and you'll be left alone. I don't want to have to kill you."

"Don't tell her that." Falco shook his head, then leaned closer. "I'll kill you if he won't. So just be nice and give us the necklace."

She quailed at Falco's hissed threat and her eyes again widened with fear. She nodded, her smooth chin sliding under Varro's rough hands. He kept the pugio firm, but feared she would note the trembling of his hand. He sincerely wished she would let this go without a struggle.

Falco swung her legs off the bed while Varro guided her up. The rope net holding the mattress creaked in the wood frame as she adjusted her position. Varro still held his hand over her mouth and pugio at her neck. But his position was awkward now with his standing and her sitting.

"I'm going to take my hand away, and you'll tell Falco where the necklace is. We'll take it and be gone." He waited to see if she understood. But the whites of her big eyes just glared at him. So he relaxed his hand to test her reaction, and when she did nothing he let if fall away.

"Fool," she said, matching their whispers in her broken Latin. "Other soldier already took it. Too late."

He snapped his head up to look at Falco, who stared back in amazement.

"Other soldier?" Varro asked. "Who? When did he come?"

She sneered at him. "Big soldier. Long ago. Like you come now but alone. It's gone."

"She's lying," Falco said. "That's not true."

"Not lying. Big soldier showed me big knife, then took gold from there. See?"

Her hands were free, Varro realized as she pointed behind him. He knew it for a ruse and would not turn around. Yet Falco leaned ahead to see into the darkness.

"What's that, then?"

The girl yanked Falco forward by his tunic. Already off balance he crashed into Varro as she pulled back from the edge of his blade.

A real criminal could have killed her before she could escape.

Yet Varro realized she knew he did not have the will. Somehow she understood Varro would not kill her no matter what he said. Predators like her sniffed out weakness.

As he stumbled back from Falco rolling into his feet, she recoiled on her bed with a sneer of triumph then opened her mouth to scream.

2

In the faint light, Varro glimpsed the slave girl kicking back on her bed and sending furs and sheets sliding to the floor. The wall of the tent bulged as she pressed against it. The whites of her eyes were like two points in the dark fixed on Varro.

Falco grunted as he recovered from being thrown off balance. Varro had stepped back, but his foot landed on something unstable. He slipped and thudded to his side and expelled the air from his lungs. He landed in soft furs, perhaps other bedding. But in the darkness he had no idea what had spared him a worse crash.

The girl's scream cut to silence. What might have alerted every soldier in a hundred yards of the tent ended as little more than a wren's chip.

Falco had leaped atop her and now pressed his hand over her mouth. She was prone beneath him, still on her bed with the furs and sheets spooled out to the floor.

Struggling to his feet, Varro realized he had dropped his pugio. Looking down, he could not penetrate the gloom.

The girl's muffled struggles drew his attention away. Falco had wrestled her upright. She thrashed against his grip, but his size and strength outmatched her. She shook her head against his hand and beat at his shoulders.

He thrust the girl into Varro, who instinctively caught her.

"Keep her quiet," he whispered. "I'll get the truth out of her."

Varro pinned both the girl's arms to her back with one arm. His other hand again crushed her mouth shut. She spit into his fingers and tried to kick Falco. But Varro felt anger at her revealing his weakness which lent him a cruel strength. She would not escape him again.

Though merely an outline in the dark, the rage emanated from the tense lines of Falco's muscles. He raised his pugio as if to plunge it into the girl's neck. It hovered a finger's breadth from the base of her throat. An errant gleam of light flashed in his eyes as he poised to thrust the blade home.

"No more lies. You've got one chance to tell the truth. Show us the necklace or you die."

The girl began to sob and shook her head. She was trying to speak, but Varro would not remove his hand. She might trick them once more.

"I swear it, girl." Falco pulled back as if ready to stab her. She squealed in response. "It's as easy as just pointing to the hiding spot. Come on."

Again she sobbed and slackened in Varro's grip.

"I think she's telling the truth," Varro said. "We've got no time. Someone is going to hear this. Let's go."

"Not so soon, Lily." Falco's low voice was full of threat. "She needs some encouragement."

"Don't hurt her," Varro said. "She doesn't have the necklace. This is pointless."

"We'll see about that."

Falco placed the tip of the blade at the pit of her neck. She pressed back into Varro, who braced his legs to steady her.

Then Curio popped up in the darkness, emerging from beneath the tent wall.

He collided with Falco and sent him stumbling forward.

And sent the razor-edged pugio sliding into the throat of the girl Varro restrained in his arms.

A horrible, wet gurgle rose up as Varro staggered back, still holding the girl. He stood still, staring at Falco's frozen outline. The girl's struggles ebbed as hot blood bubbled from her mouth and between his fingers. It seemed hours with everyone in the tent suspended in the darkness, each likely praying as hard as Varro that the girl survived.

But a gruesome hiss leaked her final breath. She collapsed against Varro, slack and lifeless.

She slipped out of his arms, crumpling to the shadowed floor. Her head slumped over her chest, revealing her slender neck. Her pale skin shined as silvery gray in the darkness. Varro blinked at her leaning heavily against his shins.

"You killed her," Varro said.

"Curio, what did you do?" Falco's voice barely registered as a whisper.

"You two were making so much noise," Curio whispered back. "Those guards are not fools. They're bound to come check out what's happening in here."

The three of them hovered around the dead girl. Varro had seen his share of dead bodies. Yet no mangled corpse was more horrible than the murdered girl leaning against his legs as if begging for protection. Had he not braced his legs, she might still live. But he had killed her.

He was a murderer.

"All right," Falco said, rubbing his hands over his face. "We need to get the body out of here."

No one responded to that statement. Varro continued to stare dumbfounded at the corpse pinning his feet to the spot. Her flesh was still warm. Maybe she had not died after all.

"But there'll be blood on the floor," Curio said. "And how are we going to carry a body through camp? Where would we put her? And we'll all get covered in blood."

Falco groaned.

Then Varro heard a shuffling outside the tent flap. He and the others crouched as if to run, but remained still and staring at the flap.

Heat drained from Varro's hands. They were about to be caught. Perhaps that was best. He should face punishment for murder, after all. She might be a slave, but she had been a helpless woman in his control. This was what his great grandfather had warned him against. Once you turn to violence it never ended and made you into a beast.

"We should surrender ourselves," he said, letting his voice rise above a whisper.

Before he could say more, Falco grabbed him close and covered his mouth with a vicelike grip. They shoved into the shadows, and the girl's corpse collapsed into the spot Varro had opened.

Was this how she felt, he wondered? Such a horrible, terrifying way to pass from life, and he was to blame for it. He surrendered to Falco's overbearing strength. He had no will to resist.

They held still. Falco's heart beat against Varro's arm. Curio hung in the faint light beside the girl's bed. They all watched the flap, where a shadow hovered against the heavy cloth.

"Is everything all right in there?"

The voice was tentative and nervous, more like he was checking on a rich man's daughter than a slave. Curio turned to Falco and Varro, his small face a gray globe in the dark. Falco shook his head but Varro had no idea what the two were communicating. He offered no resistance, and thought of nothing other than the body piled on the floor between them.

The shadow lingered and no one moved. Nothing could warm Varro's hands and feet, or quell his racing heart. He felt as if he would black out.

With no answer offered, the shadow drew back.

Then Curio sneezed.

Of course, the forgotten scent of flowers still hung in the air. All Varro smelled now was spilled blood. But Curio's sneeze had been violently unfeminine.

Falco wrenched Varro down to the floor, shoving him into the dark corners of the tent. Curio leaped into the girl's bed and gathered the spilled furs over himself.

"Who's in there?"

The voice was sterner now, and the shadow grew crisp against the tent flap. Varro found himself holding his breath, and guessed Falco and Curio did as well.

"Are you all right?" The guard repeated himself, again seemingly confused as to what to do. Another voice more distant and indistinct spoke to him. The shadow narrowed, then seemed to be pulling away.

"I'm going to open the flap," he said suddenly. "If you're awake, forgive the intrusion."

Falco's arms clamped down around Varro's torso, but it seemed less an attempt to restrain him and more like a scared boy clutching his straw pillow. As the flap rustled and peeled back, Falco's grip tightened.

The exterior light cut into the darkness as smoothly as Falco's pugio blade had punctured the girl's throat. Golden light slid like an opening wound across the floor. Varro stared in horror as it flowed to the girl's bed. She lay dead just beside it atop furs she had worn to bed. While her nightclothes were dull gray and hid her well, the white flesh of her legs was like twin lanterns. Varro knew anyone looking inside would see them.

The light swept onto the bed, where Curio now cowered under the white sheets. Varro could see one of his sandals peeking out at the end of the bed. While he was the right size to replace the girl in her bed, his sandal would betray them.

The light continued to cut slowly across to the rear wall. Then a shadow moved through it, thankfully obscuring more detail.

"Are you asleep?" The voice was low and deep. Varro did not move. He could not move with Falco crushing the breath from his lungs. They huddled in the darkness while the shadow hovered in the flap. Curio remained under the furs, his sides rising and falling as if he were in sleep. It was good acting, Varro thought, but should he sneeze again they were finished.

Worse yet, Varro saw a black puddle of blood oozing out into the slice of light cutting across the floor. His eyes flicked wide at the realization that the guard could not help see the sheen on its surface.

"A bad dream, then?" The voice again formed a question. Curio did not respond, but shifted to pull his foot under the furs. It seemed to be the answer the guard expected.

The flaps again closed, hanging loosely against each other. The guard's shadow bobbed away and left a thin line of light behind from the poorly closed entrance.

After long moments, Falco's grip relaxed.

Curio popped his head from beneath the furs.

No one spoke. Even Varro had time to recover his wits. While the guilt of this slave's murder would be a lifelong scourge, he was no longer so willing to surrender himself to justice. The consul would have him executed. He could not atone for this crime if he died now, and would spend eternity burning in Tartarus.

They pulled apart. Falco wormed aside until he could get to his feet. He paused with each movement, ever looking toward the flap. Curio swiveled on the bed and set his feet down. He sat like a man who had lost all his possessions, head held between both hands.

Once he and Falco had regained their feet, they met over the body of the slain girl. She had shifted to her side, and now curled up as if asleep.

Falco began gesturing that they should pick her up and shove her beneath the tent wall. But Varro agreed with Curio. They could not carry her through the camp. There was no avoiding evidence of her murder, and no one would believe she had escaped in the night. Varro felt that the best they could do was to leave her in place. He pulled down Falco's gesturing hands then drew him and Curio closer.

They leaned in, their heads touching in the dark. Varro smelled their fear-soured breaths as he gave a weak whisper.

"Suicide."

Falco leaned back with a smile, mimicking a clap of his hands. Curio nodded and set to work.

They arranged her on the floor, taking Falco's pugio and placing it into her hands. Her corpse was still fresh and pliable, but if left overnight it would stiffen in place, or so Varro hoped. They propped her onto her knees and set the pugio back into the wound. Now he hoped it seemed as if she had knelt beside her bed and took her own life. What else could a slave do with a stolen pugio?

This loathsome task completed, Varro nodded to the others that they should exit the tent where Curio had emerged. Falco shook his head, holding up his palm. Varro knew he wanted to search for the gold chain. He again yanked the hand down and shook his head. Curio had already ducked out of the tent.

"It's why we did all this," Falco said, pulling Varro close to hear his whisper.

"She doesn't have it, and you can't see anything. Don't get us caught now. The guards are alert."

He tucked his head down fearing their exchange had been heard. Yet the guards did not come, though both stared long at the loose tent flaps. At last, Varro pulled away from Falco then slipped beneath the tent.

Cool and fresh air greeted him. Curio had retreated to the same row of tents where he had originally gathered all of them. Varro scrabbled to his feet and scurried to join him. He heard Falco scratch against the earth as he too exited the tent.

Once all together, they looked to each other. Both Curio and Falco were pale and sweaty. A spray of blood had stained Falco's tunic. Varro pointed to it.

"The two of you clean up and get back to your tents. Let's hope no one noticed your absences. I'll get back to my tent. I've got to clean my hands first." He stared at his hands, the blood showing black in the errant light. "We'll talk more tomorrow."

He nodded toward the rows of tents they hid behind. Men slept there, and any more conversation might awaken them. Right now, Varro wished he could fly away to anywhere but here. He wished Philip of Macedonia would attack the camp this moment. The best he could do for solace was to hide himself under his sheets and pray their ruse succeeded.

The three broke up without a word. They shared grim nods and vanished into the dark. Varro had a short walk to his tent, but he had to find water to wash himself. The latrine was the best he could think of and so first visited it to scrub his hands with cold water in a clay bowl. He threw the water into the latrine, then left for his tent.

He slipped into the front, expecting Centurion Drusus to be awake and staring at him. But the bearlike Drusus was wrapped in his blanket and snoring off to the left. The others of the command group, the tessarius, signifier, and tubicen, all slept equally sound. A narrow path unraveled between them to Varro's opened bedding at the rear of the tent. He had not even done the basic work of making it seem as if he were still under his blankets. Anyone half-roused from sleep could have discovered his absence. Heat rose on his cheeks.

Removing his sandals, he carefully stepped between the sleeping men, stooping over and once more holding his breath. Reaching his bed, he felt the relief a drowning man might feel for latching onto the side of a boat. He yanked the wool cover up to his chin and wrapped it tight.

Drusus sputtered in his sleep then rolled over. The other three lay still, their covers rising in time with their measured breathing.

Varro rested on his back, eyes closed. The visage of the dead girl slumped against his feet floated through his mind. The wet thump of Falco's pugio sticking into her neck echoed through his thoughts. He wanted to scrape the memories from his mind, but he doubted he ever would. The slave did not even have a name, yet he had killed her. Certainly he had detested her and she had threatened to kill him. Yet it had all been idle threats, and now he had done something too heinous to consider.

How many beatings had he endured at Falco's hands and would never fight back? He had devoted himself to peace to keep his vow to his great-grandfather. Yet in one year the army had excised that spirit from him and replaced it with a murderous streak. What more evidence of his debasement did he need other than tonight?

He shifted in his bed, never finding a comfortable position and doubting he would find sleep to match. However, as the hour wore on, he settled into his covers and the draining experiences of the night began to weigh on his eyelids. As his waking mind darkened, he relented on his self-hate. Perhaps he was dealing too harshly with himself. He had never intended to hurt her, much less kill her. It was all a terrible accident, one he should atone for but certainly should not cause him to despair for his soul. Maybe sleep would help him think more rationally in the morning, or so he hoped.

With a yawn he flipped onto his left side. Something pressed against his hip and startled him awake.

It was his belt, which he had forgotten to remove. Attached to it was the sheath for his sacred pugio.

And it was empty.

His eyes snapped open. His throat closed in terror. The pugio his uncle had carried on campaigns, gifted to him by his mother, and blessed at the temple of Mars—that pugio lay on the floor of the murder scene lost in darkness and ready to be discovered in the light of day.

3

Sunlight stained the roof of the tent orange and Varro felt unable to rise from his bed. The others were already awakened since he heard their tired mumbling. He realized numbly that Centurion Drusus had kicked him. A dull ache lingered on his thigh. He blinked up at Drusus's creased, round head hovering over him.

"Good morning, Optio. If it's not too much trouble, you ought to think of getting up. It'd be a shame for me to throw you ass-first out of the tent."

"Sorry, sir." Varro threw aside his blankets and sat up. The others were already dressed and exited the tent. Drusus sniffed then followed, leaving him isolated in the stale air of the small enclosure. It smelled of sweat-damp wool. He heard low voices murmur around the exterior of the tent. The deep grumbles of Drusus and the others at the front were clearer. He heard the centurion complaining about bad dreams while handing out breakfast.

Varro knew about bad dreams. Would that his night had been one long nightmare. Yet his belt and sheath remained empty. He had stripped it off during the night and tossed it aside. Now it curled atop his sandals, also carelessly dropped into the corner where the rest of his gear was stacked.

"What are you doing in there, Varro?" Drusus batted the tent flap, dislodging a cloud of brown dust. It shined as it floated through the shaft of thin light slipping between the flaps.

"Here I am, sir." His voice sounded loud and thick in the tent. He prepared himself, clapping on his belt and sword, then lacing his sandals. He made enough noise to confirm for Drusus that he was not seated on his bed in utter despair.

The empty sheath felt unnaturally light against his side. He considered removing it, but realized an absence would be more obvious than an empty sheath. He planned to retrieve his pugio at the first opportunity. In the meantime, he could stick another in this sheath. No one but him would know the difference.

All night he had debated sneaking back to retrieve it. That extra weapon would likely alert Galba to the fact the slave had been murdered. Yet it could also just be another pugio she had stolen. Varro could not be sure how others would perceive its presence beside her dead body. So he did not risk returning. Besides, he still faced the same problem of being unable to light up the tent to search for it, not after the guards were on alert.

Stepping into the bracing air, Varro greeted the men of his command group. Centurion Drusus chewed on black bread and palmed a clay cup of wine. He offered the hunk of bread to Varro, who surprised himself with still having an appetite. It was hard and cold, and tasteless without vinegary wine to dip it in. But he ate it gratefully as Drusus studied him.

"Sir?"

"Nothing, Varro." Drusus shook his head then drank from his mug. "You'll see to the men's drilling today and full-gear march this afternoon. I've got payroll to handle. I'll be tied up all day with it. Not my favorite part of the job, but the boys have to be paid. You too, Varro. First pay as an optio. How does it feel?"

Drusus smiled, broad and friendly. The others were stooped over their own hunks of bread and wine mugs, but each offered him a knowing smile.

"It feels great, sir. Money is important."

Everyone laughed, though Varro had spoken out of innocence. He did not see the humor.

"Of course it is," Drusus said, wiping the back of his wrist across his mouth. "Your civic crown is nice, and now Optio Tertius is in your debt for life. But it's all worthless if you're poor. And that's how all we infantry end up if we're not careful. So mind your coins like you'd mind a beautiful lover. That's good advice for all you boys, too."

With lectures given and a grunt of general dissatisfaction, Drusus left them for headquarters. Varro stared after him, chewing the hard bread. The next mouthful went down hard and nearly stuck in his throat. Soon the girl's corpse would be discovered, if it had not been already. Would Drusus be walking past the tent and look in on the mess Varro had made? He suddenly felt terrible shame at letting down Drusus. For he had enough faith in his capabilities to promote him to optio at an age when most soldiers were still learning the basics.

Having received his orders and Drusus's expectations, he could not linger in carrying them out. He had to behave normally and not draw suspicion. Curio's performance from last night was bound to bring him attention. Having gone to bed wondering how to excuse it away, he now had an idea born with the new day.

Fetching his vine cane from the tent then leaving the others behind, he set out for his century of hastati. The main road leading to headquarters was already busy with messengers and soldiers crossing between tents. Varro did not linger, but could not resist looking toward Galba's tent. A queue of men waited outside, but nothing else seemed unusual. Perhaps the other slaves had not been sent back to their tent yet.

His first instinct was to find Falco and Curio and reconvene. They needed to coordinate their stories, as at least Curio would be called to account for his actions. There was also the matter of Curio's loyalty. He was most likely to be called into suspicion, and might succumb to pressure from Galba to confess. It seemed the likely move if murder was suspected, which might yet be avoided.

Varro did not have the guile needed to ensure Curio looked out for all their interests rather than his own. He genuinely liked Curio, but he always seemed to know something he should not. Falco said it was just his mannerism. Despite initially despising Curio for forcing himself into a cut of the gold necklace, Falco had come around to accepting him as one of his own. But Varro remained unconvinced Curio didn't know more than he let on.

He followed a longer route to the row where his century camped. This led through the rows of triarii and principes, the older and experienced soldiers in his legion. He took an unexpected delight in the raised brows of these soldiers when they realized his rank. He also enjoyed the staid but sincere nods from fellow optios among them.

His own men were less respectful, either out of envy or just due to his being green. No one had given him cause for formal punishment yet. But certainly that day must come, and Varro had to prepare for it.

"Optio Varro." One of the triarii from the tents lining the path called to him as he passed.

His hands turned as cold as the night before and his throat tightened. He heard hobnailed sandals scraping the dirt as the man approached. He turned and found a tanned, wrinkled man in a brown tunic.

This was his old team leader who had supervised him and Falco on a construction team in the elephant pens last winter.

Varro recognized him as an old veteran of the war against Hannibal. His name was Aulus Aquila, and he waved Varro closer even has he scurried up to him.

"Well have a look at you," he said. "Promoted to optio and a civic crown to top it off."

Aulus clapped him on the shoulder, but remembered himself. Though a triarus, he was not equal to Varro's rank.

"Don't worry," Varro said, feeling relief drain through his feet like bathwater flowing off his body. "I'm not used to it either."

"Well, still, I meant to congratulate you earlier, sir."

They chatted about the arrival of spring and hopes that Philip would have had time to think about his defeat all winter. But the conversation stumbled and at last Aulus drew closer with a conspiratorial glance over his shoulder.

"So now that you're an optio, I suppose you've heard?"

A bloom of heat like an ember erupted in Varro's stomach. He struggled to keep his voice from rising. "About last night? Terrible business, I agree."

Aulus pulled back with a frown. "Last night? No, sir, I don't know what happened last night. I'm talking about the veterans. You've not heard, I take it."

Varro shook his head, determined not to give himself away any more than he already had. His cheeks warmed but he tried to match Aulus's sly look. The old soldier leaned in closer.

"I like you and Falco," he said. "You're good men. And you're a good soldier, but getting closer to an officer. So you might get pulled into this. There's talk among the Punic War veterans and it's not good. All of us have been on campaign too long. We were promised we'd be on our way home by now, but the fucking Macedonians won't even give us a stand-up fight. So there's a lot of—talk—about taking things into our own hands. You understand my meaning, sir?"

Varro nodded, though he was not completely certain what sort of talk Aulus indicated. He seemed satisfied that his message had been delivered and stepped back with a sharp salute.

"Congratulations again, Optio Varro. Just thought you'd want to know so you can stay out of it. But of course you keep that between us, sir."

They parted with Varro offering his thanks. He noted two of Aulus's fellow triarii watching him with hooded eyes. Why he had been given this warning about—talk—he could not say. Aulus might have unspoken intentions for him. But Varro had other worries this morning. He continued on the path toward his men.

He felt it too obvious to head straight for Falco and Curio. So he began at the end of his row, stopping to chat with his men and inspect their progress. He informed them of the march at the end of the day, after drills. Most took the order in stride, but halfway down the row one soldier moaned overlong.

"A full-gear march after sword drills again, sir? Then more drills to follow. Are we going to defeat Philip by drilling him to death?"

The man had sandy hair in tight curls and pale eyes that radiated challenge. His beard was like soft down around a pouty mouth. The haughty twist of his smile informed Varro that he had deliberately made a public challenge.

With everything else on his mind, his first instinct was to ignore the comment and move on. His feet shuffled ahead, but he caught himself. Others watched though they tried to hide their curiosity. So he narrowed his eyes and folded his arms behind his back, vine cane flicking in imitation of his old Optio Tertius. He ordered the soldier to stand at attention. He obeyed, but with a minute delay, further challenging Varro.

"Are you certain you don't want to rescind your statements?"

"Sir?" The soldier cocked his head. "I'm sorry, sir. But I do not understand that word."

Varro knew he had to lash the man across the face with his

vine cane. He wanted to do it, but then he would waste more time with the aftermath. So he leaned closer.

"Well let me help you learn what I meant," he said. "Get all your gear right now and march the perimeter of camp until we're ready to start sword drills. That's at least an hour away. When that time comes, you can tell me if you learned the meaning of what I asked. If you have, and you rescind your statements, then you'll join us for drills. If not, I'll lash you bloody raw until you do. For it is my opinion that you know full well what I've said and are deliberately making trouble. So fetch your armor and your pack then start marching."

The soldier's bravado faltered and he saluted before Varro excused him to get his gear. He then pointed at the next closest soldier.

"You watch him and make sure he doesn't stop. If I find that he has, you'll be joining him for lashes." Varro further imitated Tertius in appointing one of the man's friends to ensure his punishment. He left without waiting to see the outcome. Doing otherwise would make it seem he had no confidence his orders would be carried out.

Even though he was the officer in charge of these men, his heart still pounded from the stress. Subtle jabs and comments that he had let go in the first weeks of his appointment had now bloomed into open challenges. His error would be hard to correct, but he had to take immediate action or else lose the respect of these soldiers. He noted how the rest of the men after this incident responded clearly and with respect. They were no longer his friends, but his subordinates. Both sides had to realize this.

At last he came to his old contubernium. Curio and Falco squatted outside the tent, each picking at wine-dipped bread. The formerly underaged recruit Cordus, at last turned seventeen in January, stood beside them staring off into the distance. The others were in the tent, chatting as they repaired their sandals or other gear. They sat in the shadow and did not see Varro's approach, which agreed with him.

The three former friends stood to attention at Varro's arrival. At least he could count on them to offer no trouble. Falco's heavy brow filled his eye sockets with shadow. Yet his nerves were betrayed in his bouncy stance like a child eager to run. Curio's face was pale but his cheeks were stained red as if seeing Varro shamed him. Only Cordus seemed unaffected.

"We'll start the day with sword drills, and have a full-pack march to follow. Cordus, pass that along to the others in there." He waved at the tent and Cordus nodded but did not act. "I mean now, Cordus."

He blinked at the odd command, as the others were within hearing distance. Varro wanted a moment with Falco and Curio. After Cordus ducked into the tent, he looked expectantly at them.

Falco shrugged at the unspoken question, then looked to Curio who slowly shook his head.

Varro nodded in understanding, then carelessly looked away.

"So no alarms raised," he said. "It's still early, but it's a good sign."

Both Falco and Curio smiled. None of them could say much in public, but at least Varro was certain neither had been visited by Galba's representatives.

"Curio, I need you to get me a new pugio. I don't want to requisition one." He turned to the side to display his empty sheath. Falco sighed.

"You say it's blessed, but the fucking thing is cursed. Lost again?"

"It's not lost," Varro said. "I know where it is. I just wouldn't want to be found without one, if you understand. Now, Curio, how fast can you get one?"

"No worries, sir," he said with a smile. "I'll have one by the afternoon march."

Falco looked at him in astonishment, but Varro simply offered his thanks. He had not been wrong about Curio. Varro wondered about his civilian life, which must exist at the gray edge of legality. He left them to complete his rounds.

The morning passed and Varro conducted sword drills. He had only a single year of experience with the gladius, much like all the men he supervised. Usually Centurion Drusus would attend these drills and offer both Varro and the soldiers advice. But Varro was on his own today and preoccupied. He simply watched out for men taking advantage of his distraction to relax. Most were sly enough to put forth minimally acceptable effort.

The longer the morning wore on, the more assured Varro felt that his coverup of the accidental murder had succeeded. By now Consul Galba would have learned the fate of his favorite slave. In truth, how much could he have felt for her? This was not a slave of many years, but a recent captive from the summer. She was pretty, but a consul could attract the most beautiful women of Rome. He would be dismayed she had taken her own life, but would not miss her.

With his campaign stalled and his consulship ending, he had greater concerns. Varro expected he would have lost face in Rome for not finishing Philip when he had the chance last winter. Now his successor would have to complete his task. Galba would not have the time to fret over a dead slave when his rivals in the senate would be seeking to humiliate him.

So Varro breathed a sigh of relief, and once sword drills ended, he allowed the men a short rest before gearing up for the march. He used this time to meet Falco and Curio alone. They all expressed relief that so far nothing had come of the previous night.

"But what bothers me," Falco said. "Is no one has questioned your orders to Curio."

"That has probably been forgotten in the chaos of finding a dead body next to the consul's tent."

Falco frowned. "If anything, a dead body following such an unusual mix-up should have generated more attention. But I guess we're clear for now. We still have to find out what happened to our necklace. It'll probably turn up when they search the girl's tent. It's going to be doubly hard to get it back if Galba snatches it. Now I hope she was telling the truth, since that gives us a chance, at least."

Varro rubbed his face. He did not want to argue this point. He decided the necklace would never be found. Falco had stolen two rings from King Philip's hands when they had captured him briefly last winter. Curio did not know about them, meaning both he and Falco were still wealthy. But Falco was relentless. They had no more time for discussion, as the men were already assembling for march and stealing looks toward Varro.

Before they broke up, Curio brushed against Varro. Something cold and hard pressed to his hip, and he slipped it into his palm. Curio continued on, and Varro deftly stuck the new pugio into his sheath. He looked about and no one had noticed the exchange, not even Falco.

The rest of the day went as planned and never a word came from Galba or anyone else. Once the sun dropped to the horizon, he had dispensed an entire day of duties. He left Curio and Falco with a general feeling of success. He regretted celebrating a terrible crime, and swore he would find a way to atone. But now he had a chance at that atonement, whereas to be called before Galba would likely end his life shortly thereafter.

Back with the command group, he prepared for the evening meal and updated Centurion Drusus on the events of the day, including the punishment he had assigned. Drusus listened intently and nodded appropriately. Nothing seemed amiss with him. Varro resisted asking if he had heard any news. When Drusus offered him nothing, he went to bed confident of avoiding suspicion.

As he drifted off to sleep, he jerked back to wakefulness when a brilliant globe of light appeared at the tent entrance and someone batted the cloth.

"Optio Varro," a rough, commanding voice said. "By order of the consul, present yourself immediately."

4

Everyone in the tent with Varro shot upright at the explosive command. The globe of yellow light cut sharp outlines of three men beyond the flap. The cozy warmth of Varro's gray blanket vanished as icy fear crawled into his limbs. He stared at the light, wishing this was all a nightmare and that he was asleep. But the scene was clear. His tent-mates turned to him one by one, their eyes wide with confusion and shock. Only Drusus sat up, leaning on his thighs and staring ahead without expression.

"Optio Varro, please comply."

The hard, deep voice left no room for delay. He answered as he pulled on his sandals and strapped his belt across his tunic. He stepped between the others, pausing beside Drusus. While everyone else regarded him with shock, the centurion did not meet his gaze and stared ahead as if watching his century retreating from battle.

So he did know about the girl's murder, and suspected him. His sagging posture and stunned expression said as much.

Varro ducked out of the tent into the globe of light. The heat of a blazing torch struck him across the face, and the yellow light blinded him. The woody smoke itched his nose, making him think of how Curio had sneezed and attracted the guards. Of course, the guards would remember such a thing too.

He had been a fool to be so optimistic.

The man before him was about his height, perhaps ten or more years older with a beard so dark and thick that no shaving could tame it. Thick, abrupt eyebrows furrowed over lively eyes that glittered with the torchlight. He wore an expression of impatience, as if Varro's delay had wasted his entire evening. Two other soldiers flanked him, one holding the torch aloft.

All three dressed in heavy chain shirts and wore polished bronze helmets with black horsehair plumes. Varro noted they were all fully armed, and the two guards rested their hands on the pommels of their swords.

"I am Centurion Fidelis, First Legion First Century of Principes. You will obey my commands." The centurion scanned Varro from his toes up. "Bring your pugio. Don't retrieve it yourself. Tell my men where it is, and one of them will fetch it."

"It's just inside the tent, sir. With my gear by the only empty bed." Varro hoped the quivering of his voice did not betray the icy fear wrapped around his heart. That the centurion asked for the pugio meant he suspected Varro had left his at the scene or that it was used on the girl. He would soon discover the centurion's intentions as his man already exited the tent with the stolen pugio.

Rather than offer it to Varro, he extended it to Centurion Fidelis. He grabbed it with a frown and thrust it under arm. "Follow me."

The two soldiers flanked Varro as he followed the centurion toward Galba's tent. The main road to headquarters was empty, as normal for after dark. Yet Varro had a strange sense of eyes peering out from the dark gaps in the tents he passed. He did not turn to either side, instead focusing on the back of Centurion

Fidelis's head. His black horsehair plume swayed as he strode up the center of the road.

Despite his circumstances, Varro admired the supreme pride and confidence that Fidelis displayed. His motions were like that of a hero, strong and deliberate. Each stride ahead was as if he were bounding across the Tiber. His shoulders did not slope nor did his back hunch. The chain shirt seemed weightless to him.

The consul's tent drew closer. The two guards flanking the entrance did not seem to be the same as the night before. Varro could not be sure, as they were of the same sharp and sturdy stock. They did not look at the approaching party, even as Varro studied them. He expected them to throw the tent flaps wide, but they remained motionless.

Instead, Fidelis turned to the tent where the slaves were kept. The flaps were pinned open and a low light burned within. He stopped before it and extended his strong arm with palm out.

Varro followed instructions, stepping into the tent he had sneaked into the prior night. The scent of flowers remained, stronger than before. Three clay lamps burned at various spots inside, one sitting on the wooden bed frame where the girl had been.

He tried not to take in everything he could not see last night. Instead, he stepped inside and avoided the furs and sheets on the floors, and he did not look to the other small beds which appeared shoved out of place. If he studied the area too intently he might give himself away. Instead, he looked to Centurion Fidelis standing in the open tent flap. He nodded to both his men, who remained posted outside. He entered, and the flaps closed behind him.

They stared at each other for long moments. Varro noticed two vases of white flowers flanking the interior entrance. These were fresh and their scent cloying. He did not know flowers, but his mother or sister would have told him their name and season. To Varro, such things were frivolous.

Fidelis glanced to the vase to his right and smiled.

"Take a good breath. I find the fragrance refreshing in such a crowded tent."

"I don't have any opinion on flowers, sir. These are white ones, and that's all I may say about them."

"Inhale, Optio. Maybe you will appreciate them better after you do." He smiled like he was stepping on Varro's feet and knew it.

Varro sniffed, and once Fidelis corrected the weak attempt, he drew another breath through his nose until his chest puffed. His nostrils stung and he felt mucus rise in answer to the irritation, but he did not sneeze.

"Sir, respectfully, may I ask why I am here? Certainly not to smell flowers."

"In fact, you are here to smell flowers, Varro. Thank you for cooperating."

"Gladly, sir. Then I may go?"

Fidelis's smile widened. He had a rugged, handsome look of a man accustomed to winning. Varro imagined him as a champion chariot racer or some other celebrity that women would fawn over.

"Not yet, and maybe not at all. You have some questions to answer for me."

"Of course, sir." Varro stood to attention and looked past the centurion. His heart raced and head throbbed, but he determined he would not show his fear. While he deeply regretted the accident that led to the slave's death, he was not about to throw his life away for it. He could repent, and would find a way to do so.

"Relax, Optio. I want you to look around this room and tell me what you see. Do you know the purpose of this tent?"

"It was used by Consul Galba's slaves."

Varro now turned around and cast his eyes over the scene. Of course he understood that Fidelis was trying to trick him into revealing a detail he could not know without having been present the night before. He would not fall for this. He avoided looking to the spot where the girl had fallen. That would be unreasonable since it was nearly underfoot. Instead, he looked to the beds and the furs, then the tent poles and the small chests shoved into the corners. He wondered if the gold chain was in one of them.

"There is nothing to see, sir."

"Come now, Varro. Are you so unobservant? These two beds are askew. Look at the dirt. They were violently shoved aside. But look more carefully. These are light beds, hardly worthy of the name. I could flick them over with one finger. Yet see how deeply they gouged the dirt. Someone heavy fell on these, pushing them aside."

Varro looked closer and nodded. "That seems likely, sir."

"What makes you certain it was someone and not something?" Fidelis stepped beside him, arms crossed.

"Well, I'm not sure, sir. That's just a manner of speaking. There could be a number of reasons why the beds were moved like this. How should I know what happened?"

Fidelis narrowed his eyes at Varro.

"How should you know? Well, that's for me to find out, Optio. Come now, I've asked you to look around and you've barely glanced at anything. Why should that be?"

"Sir, if I may speak freely, you are making me nervous. You've summoned me in Consul Galba's name after dark to meet in a slave tent. Then we smell flowers and imagine why beds have been moved. What is this about? I think an explanation is reasonable."

"One of Consul Galba's slaves was murdered last night. He has tasked me with finding out who did this and why."

Varro did not need to feign shock by much. "That is terrible news. So, you want my assistance in determining what happened?"

"Yes, I do." Fidelis pushed against Varro, the cold and hard links of his chain shirt abrading Varro's exposed shoulder. "I want your confession, Optio Varro, and I want your motive. You can make things easier on both of us if you'll just be forthcoming."

A wave of fear threatened to crush Varro and squeeze out a full confession of all he had done. But he loved life and did not want to die like this. For surely Galba would see him dead for killing his favorite slave, even if accidentally. So he pressed back from Fidelis and met his dark eyes.

"Sir, you are accusing me of this crime? We are here alone, with no witnesses. This is hardly procedure. If I am to be tried, then let it be before the consul and in full daylight. Not in this shadowed tent with me unarmed and you battle-ready."

Fidelis laughed and clapped his hands together. The sharp slap rang in Varro's ears.

"All right, Varro, everything you said is true. I know you're involved somehow. But you're not going to confess, after all. And I admit I've been having a bit of fun at your expense. So let's address your concerns. First, witnesses."

Fidelis turned toward the closed flap and shouted a name. "Sulla, come inside."

The flap flipped open, and one of the guards entered. He had been holding the torch, but now ducked inside with empty hands. His chain shirt caught orange points of light from the clay lamps. He saluted then looked coolly at Varro.

"Sulla, you were on guard outside the consul's tent last night. Tell us what you experienced."

"Yes, sir."

Varro twitched at the deep voice, which he recognized from the night before. This Sulla had been the guard that had chanced to peer inside.

"First, we were approached by a soldier, Camillus Curio. He claimed Optio Varro sent him to relieve the guards at Consul Galba's tent and to assume the duty himself. Of course, this order was not in procedure. Anyone should know consul and tribune guards are not switched out unless expressly ordered by themselves. Curio argued the point, but left after we threatened to arrest him."

Both Sulla and Fidelis looked to Varro, who said nothing or else risk revealing too much. He was not sure if Curio or Falco had been previously questioned. Maybe he was the last, or the first. In this case, he decided to say as little as possible. Sulla resumed his narrative.

"We checked around the tent after Curio left, but found nothing amiss. Though shortly after that, I thought I heard something from this tent. There was only one of the women in here, but I thought I heard several voices. I listened for a while and called out, but no one answered and I heard nothing more. That is until someone sneezed."

Fidelis smirked at Varro. "My guess is the flowers irritated your nose. But then maybe you were not alone, Varro?"

Rather than rise to the bait, he stared ahead. Unless ordered, he would not speak more. He prayed Falco and Curio did the same during their questioning.

"The sneeze didn't sound like a woman's," Sulla said. Now he touched the back of his head and frowned. "But my mother sneezes like a man. So I thought maybe that might also be true for the woman in here. Still, I had to check. I know we've been told not to even look at these women, sir."

Fidelis closed his eyes and raised his palm. "It's fine, Sulla. You were doing your duty, which is what the consul expects of all his men. You had to look inside. What did you see?"

"I didn't dare open the flap all the way. What if she was awake and told the consul I tried to sneak up on her during the night?

But I let in just enough light to see her bed right there." Sulla pointed to the frame and net bed with its ball of white blanket and furs. "She seemed to be sleeping and rolled over. I figured she was having a bad dream, and that was what I heard. I should've gone inside, sir. I know that now. But then, I didn't see anyone with her, and if I was caught in there alone I wouldn't want the punishment. So I closed the flap and let her be. I didn't hear anything more."

"So you saw the girl's face," Fidelis asked.

"Not her face, sir. She was under the blankets. I just saw her roll over and pull the blanket tighter."

"And nothing else struck you as unusual at that time?"

"No, sir." Sulla paused and looked as if he should admit his next statement. Fidelis rolled his hand, indicating he should continue. "Well, sir, we heard nothing after that from the tent. But I swear I heard more voices somewhere nearby."

"And you didn't check these out?"

"No, sir. My partner heard nothing. But now I'm sure I heard at least two voices, maybe three. Whispering to each other."

"And so you heard nothing more from this tent all night, until the time the other women returned in the morning?"

"That is correct, sir. They started screaming and we found the girl dead on the floor."

Fidelis turned to Varro and folded his arms.

"So you sent Curio to distract the guards while you slipped in here to murder the consul's slave."

"Sir, I was in my tent all night, as I'm sure Centurion Drusus must have already told you." He remembered his opened bedding and hoped his centurion had remained asleep. "Does someone claim to have seen me here?"

The smirk on Fidelis's face dropped as he unfolded his arms.

"Explain your orders to Curio."

Varro looked down, placing his hand on the back of his neck. "Well, it is embarrassing, sir, now that I have to explain it. But

Curio and I were in the same contubernium. He can be an ass at times and I've often thought of giving him a spot of trouble as repayment. So I made up an order for him to relieve the guards at Consul Galba's tent. It got him up in the middle of the night and embarrassed him. I knew we had a long day of drills and marches ahead and he'd not have a good night's sleep. I suppose I thought that was clever until all of this happened. Now I feel stupid."

Fidelis curled his lip and looked at Varro as if he were covered in dung.

"You're his optio. You can give him a hard time for any reason. If you wanted him awake all night, just ask your tessarius to put him on night guard duty."

Varro shook his head. "I wanted him to fall asleep and then wake him. Like I said, sir, it was stupid of me, but at the time I thought I was just giving him a hard time."

Whether this lie stuck or not, Varro gave an innocent smile to Fidelis. At least now he had an excuse for the heat on his face. He hoped Curio didn't say anything different. But Varro figured no matter how Curio spun his excuse he could not stray from his original story that Varro ordered him to relieve the guards.

"Very well." Fidelis pulled Varro's pugio from his belt, where he now held it. The hilt looked worn and dark, so unlike the well-cared-for pugio his mother had gifted him.

"There were two of these at the murder scene. Whoever did the act staged it as if she had killed herself. But that cannot be. For one, no more noise was heard after Sulla investigated. It is hard to believe she would not have cried out when she stabbed her own throat."

He handed Varro his pugio, which he accepted with a nod. The weight of it was assuring to him. Had that sheath remained empty he would appear far more guilty today.

Fidelis turned and picked something from the girl's bed directly behind him. He turned back then held forward Varro's pugio. Its oiled and honed blade caught the lamplight. Varro nearly reached out for it.

"This one was found lying on the ground as if dropped by accident. It was not even near her body. Whoever owned this weapon took tender care of it. Look at that edge." The white line of the pointed blade gleamed as he twisted it. He set it back down on the bed frame, then picked up another pugio.

"This one was in her hands and stuck into her neck. I believe this weapon killed her. Do you notice anything about this one?"

"The blade and grip are covered in dried blood, sir."

"Correct!" The sudden shout caused Varro to snap back as if the weapon was a poisonous snake. "But here is the curious thing. The outside of the girl's hands had no blood at all. If she had spilled enough of her own blood to run over this entire pugio, why should her hands be clean?"

Varro stared at Fidelis, who once again gave him a knowing smile. Of course, he thought, he had pinned the girl's hands behind her back. His throat tightened but he managed a quizzical smile.

"I wouldn't know, sir. Perhaps her hands fell away once she had stabbed herself."

"Her hands continued to grip the blade in death. The blood was only on her palms. Not even a fleck on the outside of her fingers. Very strange. Optio, would you draw your pugio, please."

Suddenly the weight of the pugio was not so assuring. He slowly drew it from the sheath, horrified to see that it was an old blade with a dull edge. Fidelis shook his head.

"That is not even a serviceable weapon. What are you doing with it?"

"Well, sir, I don't have much use for the pugio in my current position. I have not attended to it like I should. I will make amends, sir."

"I can't believe Drusus lets you get away with gear like that."

They stared at each other in silence. The other soldier, Sulla, added the weight of his stare to Fidelis's.

"Why do you insist she was murdered, and that it was me, sir? She killed herself and somehow her hands did not get as bloody as you would've liked. So she had two weapons. I don't understand why that matters."

"Are you not listening?" Fidelis drew closer, his white teeth clenched together as he sized up Varro. "The guards were distracted on orders from you. They heard multiple voices from this area. The tent space has signs of a violent struggle, and an extra weapon obviously dropped. Then there are the blood stains."

He stepped aside and showed Varro the spot where the girl had died. The ground was fresh where others had removed the pools of blood. But blood splatter showed on the ropes of the girl's bed netting.

"Did she stab herself standing up?" Fidelis asked. "How else would blood land here if she were kneeling on the floor away from it?"

"Blood can splash, sir."

"Yet is can, but take a look at this and tell me if it is splashed blood."

He pulled Varro closer and pointed him at the edge of the tent wall that Curio had pulled up. The ground there was disturbed from their passage and bloody fingerprints dotted the cloth wall.

"That's right, Varro. Those are from someone's bloody hand lifting the tent wall to sneak away after killing the girl. But here's one better."

Fidelis now pointed to white sheets that were spread out on the girl's bed. To Varro's horror, bloody footprints were stamped all over it. The brown stains recorded the dancing struggle and their frantic efforts after her death.

"The fools who did this not only failed to convince anyone she had killed herself, but also left their footprints behind. There has to be at least two different feet here, maybe three. But there is one excellent print right here."

While most prints crossed over each other, Fidelis tapped a perfectly formed footprint. Every hobnail had left its mark within the defined outline of the sole. Varro's jaw clenched and his heart raced with fear. Fidelis seemed to sense it, and spoke with quiet threat.

"That's right, a perfect print. Now all we have to do is see if your foot fits."

"Sir, that does not prove anything at all. Many feet will generally fit that shape."

"You're right, Optio. But take a closer look. There are three hobnails missing. What are the chances of not only your foot fitting that print but also missing the same three hobnails? I'd say that's very low."

Varro could feel Fidelis's clammy breath on his neck as he leaned even closer. The hard links of his chain shirt pressed against his forearm.

"Take off your sandals, Optio, and let's find out."

5

The wavering light of the oil lamps, the cloying scent of fresh flowers, and the roiling fear in Varro's gut left him nauseated. Fidelis stood with his arms folded. He glared at Varro, his short and thick brows arched in expectation. Sulla, the guard who had heard the struggle, now stepped closer. The crowded tent space heated up from the bodies of three men and from the tension. Sweat beaded on Varro's forehead.

He looked at the mess of footprints on the impossibly white sheet. The brown stains were a jumble, with sections of prints clear. But one footprint showed better than all the others, as if stamped off to the side to serve as a reference. From the look of it, it seemed the heel had borne most of the weight, as the outline shaded off at the toes. But it was a complete and crisp picture of a left foot. Three hobnails were absent in a roughly triangular pattern. One was vacant at the base of the middle toe and two more toward the heel.

"Optio, I ordered you to remove your sandals. I want to see the hobnails."

Varro nodded, struggling to control his breathing as he knelt to unlace his sandals. Each lace rasped through the fretwork, the only sound within the tent other than Varro's labored breathing. He pulled the first one off, then the next. His soles felt cold against the dirt of the tent floor. He set aside the sandals and stepped back.

Fidelis selected the left one. He then placed the sandal onto the print. Varro and Sulla both leaned in to see the result.

The sandal sat in the middle with a thin margin around the edges. Varro's foot was too small for it. He could have screamed with joy. The print had come from Falco's foot, and with luck he was not yet under suspicion.

Still Fidelis turned over the sandal to review the sole. He picked at it with his thick fingernails, then studied it from different angles. At last, he shrugged.

"Clearly not your footprint. A pity these other prints are all jumbled." He flipped the sandal over again, tapping out small clods of dirt. "Any blood left has been worn away, too."

"There was no blood on them, sir," Varro said, now more confident. "As I said, I was asleep in my tent all night."

"So you claim." Fidelis extended the sandal to Varro, who took it. "I will verify that with your tent-mates. For now, you are free to go. Tell no one of our discussion except your officers, and then only if they ask."

Varro accepted the sandal, then knelt to relace both on his feet. As he did, he glanced at his pugio resting on the bed frame. He wished for a way to retrieve it, but he had been lucky enough for one night. Besides, it seemed a fitting punishment. Perhaps Mars withheld the blessed weapon from Varro for using it for such an ignoble purpose.

He stood up and saluted Centurion Fidelis. His heroic jaw tensed and he seemed about to speak. Varro hesitated and at last Fidelis rubbed his face.

"You're connected to this somehow," he said. "I have not come this far without learning to see a lie when someone drops one at my feet. I don't like losing."

The centurion folded his arms and Sulla followed. Both frowned at him as if he were gutter scum. But Varro had won this contest, and felt braver for it.

"Don't worry, sir. You've not lost yet. You will find the culprit before long. It's just not me."

"What I don't understand," Fidelis said, looking past Varro. "Is why you did it? There must be some greater evil she knew about you, and you wanted that silenced. But what could she have known?"

"Sir, I realize the mischief with Curio was ill-timed. But it does not mean either of us had anything to do with this murder. Maybe the real killer simply took advantage of the confusion we caused. I regret my actions, sir. But I am not the killer you are looking for."

Fidelis fixed Varro with one eye as his frown deepened. "We'll see about that. You're dismissed."

The walk back to his tent seemed twice as long as it should have been. His mind hummed with thoughts of what to do next. He wanted to find Curio and determine what had happened with him. As long as Falco remained free of suspicion and no other witnesses came forward, there would be no conclusive proof they had killed the slave. Fidelis may have guessed the basic truth of the matter, but he could prove nothing.

He found the men in his tent asleep, even Centurion Drusus. Perhaps they were awake, but just feigning sleep for Varro's benefit. They were good, competent men whom he respected. So he again wove the path to return to his bed, setting his sandals and pugio aside. Then he slipped under his sheet and stared up into the dark.

His mind turned on what he should do next. The only plan that made sense was to do nothing different. If he went to Curio, Fidelis would undoubtedly learn of it and confirm his suspicions.

He would still have to interact with Curio if called to as part of his duties. But otherwise, he would need to work through Falco to communicate. Yet if he met too often with Falco, then that would arouse suspicions as well.

With all these possibilities swimming through his head, and despite the tensions of the night, sleep still crept upon him.

The next morning he awakened refreshed but still no less worried about Fidelis's investigation. Had Curio been questioned overnight? Would there be guards awaiting him outside the tent? He was the first awake, though Drusus threw aside his covers and sat up with the coming dawn. He turned his round head to Varro, and offered a sleepy nod. He then stretched and began to dress for the coming day.

That felt worse than if he had barked a curse at him. While the others might know nothing, Fidelis had obviously spoken with Drusus before he started questioning. At least Drusus should acknowledge this. Behaving as if nothing were happening made Varro worry something worse would follow.

Yet they dressed, ate breakfast, and planned the day ahead just as always. He asked nothing about the unusual summons. At last, when they were breaking up to their duties and the rest of the camp was now bustling with soldiers starting their day, Varro pulled Drusus aside.

"Sir, I'm certain you have questions about last night."

Drusus's expression flattened and his eyes seemed to drain of color.

"Not at all. You deal with Centurion Fidelis, and if he or the consul have questions for you then it's all on you. Leave me out of it."

"But, sir, you are my commanding officer. I thought you should know—"

"I know, Optio." Drusus's words came out sharp and short. He stepped closer and lowered his head along with his voice. "I know

Consul Galba's slave was killed during the night and that your name has somehow come up along with Curio's. The consul is as mad as a speared boar. He was quite taken with that girl. So he must be wondering why anyone would kill her. Is it a threat? Is he going to be next after his favorite lay?"

Varro blinked and shook his head. "Sir, the men love the consul. Why would anyone want to kill him or his slave?"

Drusus stared hard at him. "Let's not discuss this anymore. You'd do well to stay away from Curio, or else Fidelis is going to get ideas. He's a good man, and the consul has great faith in him. But he's a stubborn bastard, and a glory-seeker. Do your job and let Fidelis work out his own answers. Don't hand them to him."

Varro opened his mouth to ask another question, but Drusus shook his head. They parted to attend their duties. Varro would again walk the rows of his soldiers and assign tasks as Drusus had outlined earlier. Drills and other work would fill a normal day, but Varro wondered how such a day would end. He drew a breath and set out down the main path.

He welcomed the routine. It soothed his nerves and rested his mind from worries that Fidelis might have squeezed Curio until he told everything. He also found it easier to behave as the sour, short-tempered optio the men expected him to be. When he came to the soldier he had forced to march the camp perimeter, he found him far more respectful today. Varro did not address him, but continued on until reaching his old contubernium.

Falco and Cordus were cleaning their hands and scrubbing their faces in a wooden basin. The others were scattered around the tent, either tending their gear or engaged in other menial tasks. Since Varro did not call them to attention, no one did more than greet him. He tried to be casual about seeking Curio, but he did not find him.

Falco stared at him, trying to gesture him aside with his eyes. But Varro was too wary for that. He shook his head and announced the plan for the day. Yet Falco continued until Varro gave in to his own fears. He nodded them ahead as he moved on toward the next tent. Falco hurried alongside him.

"They've taken Curio," he said in a desperate, hushed breath.

"Centurion Fidelis and two others?" He tried to smile and look ahead as if discussing the weather. But his heart flipped in his chest.

"Yes, did he get you too?"

"How long has Curio been gone?"

"All fucking night. No one knows where he is. Gods, Varro, he's going to give us both up. We've got to—"

"We've got a long day ahead," Varro said overloud, stopping to face Falco. He hoped to silence his fears, no matter how well founded. He then leaned in and whispered. "Stay away from Curio. You left a footprint at the scene. Replace the hobnails on your left sandal and use old nails. Do it right away. And just remain calm. I'll find a way out of this."

Falco backed up, eyes wide beneath his heavy brows. He seemed to have shrunk during their talk. But Varro closed his eyes and offered a gentle nod. If they all lost heart, then they would surely fold under scrutiny. He had to ensure Falco was confident, even if he himself was not.

"I'll get right on it, sir." Falco spoke louder and saluted. Only Varro would be able to read the subtle gleam of fear in his eyes.

The rest of his inspection passed as if in a dream. Fidelis had taken Curio and he had not returned. It could mean so many things. Varro wondered if he might be tortured into a confession. Would the army do something like that? For all its vicious punishments for the least of infractions, the army ran on procedures and laws. Torturing a Roman citizen for the death of a slave, even the consul's, would be too much. But Fidelis seemed to be a true competitor, and he had chosen Varro for the competition.

All morning Varro hoped Curio would return, but he

remained absent. At last, Varro and Drusus led the century in sword drills. Varro took more of Drusus's ire than the men.

"What are you looking for, Optio? The drill is not happening in the fucking sky. It's right here. Pay attention to the men."

His rebuke drew snickers and gloating smiles from the soldiers. But Varro was too distressed with the possibilities of Curio's absence. He knew Falco was as well. He dropped his wooden practice sword and took a sharp blow to the back of his legs from Drusus's vine cane.

"What is wrong with my century today?" His face had turned scarlet. "One more green mistake like this and I'll have you all marching in full gear to the top of Mount Olympus. Do you understand?"

The drill had paused for Drusus's outburst, and the men shouted affirmation in one voice. Yet a number of eyes shifted to Falco and then to Varro himself. For a moment he forgot he was the optio and shrank back from their glares. But he shook his head, then turned to the nearest man. He slapped his own vine cane across his scutum shield with a hollow whack.

"You heard the centurion. Stop gawking."

Varro folded his arms at his back and flicked his vine cane as he studied the pairs of men. He took pains to stay away from Falco and his old contubernium. Wooden swords thumped on wooden shields. Men grunted and cursed at the exchanges. Drusus shouted corrections and complaints, his mood worsening each time.

Then Curio joined the century.

He trotted up in his gear, practice sword in hand and shield on his arm. His face was flushed and he looked out of breath. Varro's feet went cold. He expected Fidelis to be right behind Curio, but the wide field had only other centuries conducting their own drills. Across the camp an elephant trumpeted.

Drusus gathered Curio to him, saying nothing, then pointed

out a man he could join for practice. With an odd number of soldiers due to Curio's absence, one group had three men who alternated rounds. Curio now picked up with the waiting man and they began practice.

Varro turned aside as Drusus's head swiveled toward him. He did not want to seem overanxious. But he would now have an excuse to meet Curio. His feet shifted as if he were going to run to him, but better judgement kept him with his current pair. They sweated as they circled each other, each looking for the opening in the other's defenses. Varro stood with arms locked behind his back and watched. To his surprise, he had learned more about sword fighting from watching hundreds of these practice matches every day. When the drills were settled, he and Centurion Drusus would practice and invite the men to watch. As such, Varro expected his own abilities had improved.

He gradually shifted from group to group, hoping he would not betray his anxiousness to reach Curio. To further enhance his nonchalance, he backed up toward him and never looked directly. Now he turned and found Curio hacking away at his partner's scutum.

"Curio, you're not chopping down a tree!" His criticism was automatic despite his nerves. It was the right response, as it stopped the drill. Curio lowered his sword and his partner peeked from behind his shield. He glared at Curio but said nothing.

"Sorry, sir." Curio did not face him but stared into the distance. "I'm not feeling like myself today."

"I can see that," Varro said. He intervened so that Curio's partner stood behind him. "What's the matter?"

Curio stared ahead without answer, then his eyes shifted to meet Varro's.

"It was a long night, sir. Two long nights in a row. I'm tired. Too tired. I may have said some things to upset an officer. So I'm frustrated with myself, sir."

Their eyes locked and Varro read the pain in Curio's eyes. He must have said something to incriminate them. Fidelis must have kept him up all night to wear out his endurance, and then extracted everything he needed to know.

"Well, don't take out your frustrations on your partner," Varro said, keeping his voice steady. "I assume what you said to this officer was quite serious?"

"I'd rather not discuss it here, sir." He nodded to his partner.

Varro rubbed the back of his neck and grimaced. "You two carry on. But make it a drill and not a log-splitting exercise. If you fought like that in a real battle, you'd not make it out alive. I shouldn't have to tell you that, Curio."

He left them to resume their drill. Strangely, he felt relieved knowing this game between him and Fidelis was now over. All that remained was for the consul to determine their fates. Going before Galba a second time would not end well, particularly when the consul was personally aggrieved. The men of the legion lived or died at his word. He would only want to learn the reason for the crime, if Curio hadn't revealed that already. Their executions would follow.

What could he do now? He decided to enjoy his final hours of freedom. There was no place to run, and he had no desire to flee. He regretted the girl's death and all the ruin that greed had brought him. He did wish for a way to send the ring stolen from King Philip back to his mother. She would need money for her future. Without any other male heir in line, she would probably have to sell the farm unless she found another husband. Remarriage might be impossible given the disgraces of her dead husband and son. He put the concern aside, focusing on these final hours before Fidelis got his orders from the consul to round up his criminals.

So he worked his way among the men. He didn't yell out corrections, but offered compliments instead. These seemed to unsettle the men more than if he had striped their hamstrings with his vine cane. He watched Falco bungling his drills, being knocked down and disarmed by even the most feeble attacks. Curio's arrival must have unnerved him even worse. What would he do if he knew Curio had given them up?

This concerned Varro more than their eventual fate at Galba's hands. He did not want Falco's final hours to be full of shame and violence. Despite many years of hating the man, Varro now loved him like a brother. A strange thing to believe, considering a little more than a year ago he had wished Falco an early death. Perhaps this was his wish coming true. In any case, he would try to keep them apart. Without a doubt, Falco would attack Curio for giving them up, and thereby make his eventual punishment even worse.

A runner dashed into Varro's view. His stomach tightened as watched the runner locate Centurion Drusus and lean in to deliver his message. The messenger did not seem to care about hiding his communication, as Varro could hear the indistinct voice across the field. Drusus nodded throughout, then the messenger saluted and ran off.

Drusus blew his wooden whistle, halting the drill and gathering the attention of the century.

"Drill's over," he said, his dark face taut with angry lines. "Get cleaned up. Consul Galba is holding an assembly."

Varro's peaceful acceptance shattered into icy shards that pierced his extremities. He felt his eyes bulge and dry against the breeze as he looked to Curio and Falco, who both stared back with the same glassy-eyed expression.

The consul was skipping the trial and going directly to punishment.

6

Varro followed at the rear of his century. They exited the field beneath a heavy gray sky. Cold breezes pushed at the back of Varro's feet, hastening him along. To his surprise, all the other centuries in the field were also filing back to their tents. They were black lines of men radiating out in all directions. While Varro's column remained silent—tense with the uncertain fears that must be a reaction to Drusus's and Varro's strange demeanors—echoes of friendly banter came from the other lines.

Drusus led them to their tent row, where he gave orders to dress for assembly. The men smelled of sweat, but would have no time to wash. Varro's duty required him to walk the tents and hasten the men. Yet he found himself unable to concentrate and simply passed tents without comment. Drusus instead followed up, bellowing for speed.

"How long does it take to strap on a helmet and pectoral? My grandmother could do it faster than any of you."

Galba had to be in a fierce mood to conduct his punishment before both legions and the tribunes. Perhaps it was due to Varro's recent lauding as a hero. The men would enjoy seeing him fall, for there is nothing sweeter than the misfortunes of the successful. Many of his own former companions did not think he deserved the rank of optio. In fact, besides Drusus and Falco, Varro could not name a single person who seemed to agree with his promotion.

However much as he wanted to meet with Falco and Curio before this assembly, he resisted. For there was always a chance he could be wrong about Galba's purpose. He could think of nothing else to bring them all together this morning, but perhaps something else warranted an army-wide assembly.

Once all the hastati of the tenth century of the tenth maniple were in order, Drusus led them to the parade ground. If he knew Varro, Falco, and Curio were heading toward their last hour alive, he gave no sign. Other than to check that Varro had assumed his proper place in the column, he did not look twice at any of them.

Other columns flowed toward the parade ground surrounding headquarters. Varro could not help but look toward the tent where his fatal mistake had taken place. It seemed so small and insignificant, a white box bobbing with the cool breeze. Yet it had shaped the end of Varro's life. He felt tears stinging his eyes, and he looked away.

The century took up their allotted position in the rear of the gathering audience. Only the velites stood farther back. A small platform had been set where Galba would eventually address them. Would he call Varro to stand upon it then accuse him of murdering his favorite slave?

A chilling thought struck him. What if Curio had lied to save himself? The sudden fear turned the ice in his stomach to fire. As the century shuffled into position among the other soldiers, he looked for Curio. He stood beside Falco, though the two were unnaturally rigid and stared ahead as if expecting the worst.

"You little bastard," he muttered. He probably told Fidelis that his optio put him up to distracting the guards then blamed him and Falco for the murder. Why would he not try to save himself? Fidelis seemed more intent on bringing Varro down, and Curio was astute enough to realize this himself. He would just feed the centurion the lies he wanted to hear.

Varro determined that if Galba intended to shame him before his execution, he would shout out the full and complete truth. Curio would not get away with his betrayal. He now found himself glaring at the back of Curio's head. The rest of the world fell away in a wreath of gray haze.

The assembly formed quickly, with every solider pressed in tight to hear Galba's eventual address. The consul's arrival was presaged by servants placing a step at the base of the stage and several guards clearing men back who had settled too close.

With so many others in the way, Varro could only see the top of Galba's helmet when he arrived on the scene. At least a dozen other heads surrounded him, most not wearing helmets. He did not need to struggle long to see the details, for Galba mounted the stage. Before he addressed the men, he assisted another man onto the stage. He was perhaps the age of Varro's father. He wore a formal toga with a purple stripe to mark his senatorial rank.

Galba held up his hand for silence, though it was unnecessary. Though thousands of men pressed into the semicircle around the stage, the only sounds were an occasional cough or the clink of bronze. Everyone knew to maintain strict silence to allow Galba's address to be heard. It seemed even the elephants in their pens silenced their quarrelsome trumpeting while the consul took the stage.

Varro held his breath, waiting for Galba to lead in with a sorry speech about his beautiful slave and her horrid end. Then with dramatic flair he would point out Varro. Centurion Fidelis would appear out of nowhere—for Varro could not locate him in this crowd—then drag him through the throng while his former soldiers jeered at him, spitting and cursing as he passed in shame.

But this did not happen.

Galba simply stared at his men. Even at this distance, where his expression remained indistinct, his posture of admiration was unmistakable. He nodded his head and appeared to wipe a tear from his eye.

Here it comes, Varro thought. Now you're going to cry over your dead slave. Let's get this done.

Galba lowered his head and appeared to regain control of his emotions. The breeze had kicked up, sending the red plume of his helmet fluttering over his shoulder. As he shook his head, the bronze helmet shot glaring sunlight like javelins at his audience. But at last he raised his head and spoke in his full, commanding voice.

"My fellow Romans, I have known no greater honor than to have served as your consul this past year. Time has flown, and the end of my term comes all too soon. While there is much ahead to be done, I wish to reflect on all that has been achieved. You have delivered a sharp rebuke to Philip of Macedonia. You have sent him fleeing for safety, sneaking away like a coward in the night. You have defeated his best soldiers, destroyed his walled cities, and ruined his allies. I've no doubt that you will finish what we have begun together, and that I shall meet you good heroes of Rome one day soon in our beloved city."

He paused to stare out like a grandfather admiring a family gathering. Varro recognized it as a moment to applaud. The audience took this up with vigor, clapping and cheering no matter how stretched Galba's truths had been. For his part, Varro clapped to work off the nervous energy coiling within him. His eyes shifted to Curio and Falco. They too applauded and cheered, perhaps overmuch. Yet being in the last rank of the assembly no one but Varro noticed. The velites had gathered to the rear and left of their position, leaving their backs open to the rest of the camp.

After Galba basked in this applause, he again raised his hand to continue his speech.

"Many of you are not aware of all the efforts conducted away from your sight to make this transition as smooth as possible. Due to the vagaries of travel, it is not always possible to pinpoint when my successor would arrive. As some of you may realize, your new consul arrived only last night. He is here with me now, Consul Publius Villius Tappulus."

Consul Villius stepped forward, his white toga as flawlessly brilliant as the noontime sun. Varro could not see the details of this man, other than he was shorter than Galba and less robust. He held himself with the supreme confidence of a politician accustomed to standing at the pinnacle of the social order. Polite applause greeted him and he extended his hand to the thousands of men who would live or die by his choices.

Varro noted that of all the soldiers applauding, a swath of thousands either kept their hands folded underarm or else offered applause so tepid it was more of an insult. These must be the Punic War veterans his old team leader, Aulus, had warned him were growing weary. He grimaced at their bold indifference to their incoming leader. Not even their centurions exhorted them to be more enthusiastic. In fact, they held their hands underarm as well.

Consul Villius either did not see this or ignored it. He instead confirmed his assumption of command.

"I thank Consul Galba for his glorious service and am humbled at the magnificent force he has left in my care. I will strive to live up to his high standard. Now, in this five hundred fifty-second year since the founding of the city, on this day the fifth kalends Iunius, I assume my role as your consul."

Spontaneous cheers rose up. A year ago, Varro might have

genuinely added his voice. But he had become cynical enough to realize this warm welcome was expected and part of army procedure. The average soldier did not care who stood at the top as long as he believed he would not be maimed or killed under that leader.

Varro had been wrong about the cause for the assembly. With Galba leaving, the entire affair of his slave's murder might be set aside. For Consul Villius had only arrived last night, meaning when Galba started his investigation he expected more time. But no camp was large enough for two consuls. He would be leaving on the ship that had delivered Villius, and would likely leave behind any thoughts of his slave.

Varro could have shouted with joy along with the others. But he used the moment to step behind Falco and Curio, who followed along with the rest of the assembly in cheering Villius.

"What did you tell Fidelis?"

He spoke in a harsh but hushed voice into Curio's ear. Falco whirled to look at him, his false smile vanished.

"That you ordered me to relieve the guards and nothing more."

Curio's face turned red and he stared ahead, clapping hard with everyone else.

Varro checked to be sure none of the others listened. He had made it seem he just leaned in for a quick word. No one paid him any attention.

"You were gone all night. What was that about?"

"He kept me awake. Trying to exhaust me so that I would let something slip. But I said nothing."

Falco elbowed him. "Then why is your face red? Are you fucking lying?"

Curio whirled on him, his teeth bared like a wolf. "I lied all fucking night. But I'm not lying now. I haven't slept in a day. Maybe that's why my face is red, you oaf."

"All right," Varro said, trying to ease the tension. Others

glanced at him, and he had to pull back or else draw too much attention. "I think we're out of trouble now. Galba's no longer consul. Just act normally, and we'll be good."

Falco grumbled but turned back to the new consul. Varro stepped back before anyone grew curious.

Villius and Galba shared a love of their own voices. Both gave windy speeches, Galba of his glorious exploits over the past year and Villius of all the glory yet to come. Varro listened to it all, and watched Curio wavering on his feet. He was about to pass out, and it did not seem an act.

At last they were dismissed, again to cheers of welcome for Consul Villius. Galba also waved to his departing men, but Varro noted that no one acknowledged him other than those within the possibility of his vision. Such was the fleeting light of fame, he thought. It doubled his warm feelings of safety. No one cared about pleasing yesterday's consul. The whole affair of the girl's accidental death would vanish with the consul himself.

Drusus led them back to their row with the same precise discipline. With midday arrived and a new consul in charge, the remainder of the day was declared a time of rest. Special wine would be dispensed with the evening meals. It was an astute ploy, Varro thought. Maybe the wine would buy some smiles from his reluctant Punic War veterans.

With a half day of leisure ahead, Varro was free to mingle with his men. Drusus warned him to keep order, and not to hesitate to hand out work if anyone showed too much energy for mischief.

During the late afternoon as Varro lingered at the end of the row, a familiar voice called out from behind. His reaction was immediate, born from long obedience.

He turned to find Optio Tertius smiling at him, a dozen feet away.

His old optio looked healthier than he had in months since he had nearly been killed at the Eordaea Pass. Varro had been awarded the civic crown for his efforts to save his old optio's life, and had been promoted to the same rank to fill the vacancy Tertius left.

For he would never be an optio again. His injured arm had to be amputated due to a wound turned bad. His arm stump was still now wrapped in a white bandage.

"I wanted to say goodbye," Tertius said as they closed the distance between them.

"You're leaving with Galba?"

"There's not much call for a one-armed optio." Tertius lifted the stump and smiled. But the smile turned to a grimace. "Gods, I can still feel it at times, and it hurts worse than it ever did. Anyway, Galba is taking back some of us wounded. I'll be on his staff for a little while at least. We'll see what happens when we reach Rome. Everything can change."

Varro smiled and felt an awkward need to apologize, though he could not think of for what.

"You don't need to treat me like a father," he said, referring to Tertius's obligations for having named him for the civic crown. Tertius laughed in response.

"Why not? My own father is dead. Listen, I'd not be speaking with you if it wasn't for what you did. You're a brave man and you'll make a fine optio. Maybe more than that one day. I owe you my life and so my life is yours. Enjoy your crown, since no one will want to give you a second one."

"Optio Tertius, why did you recommend me for one?"

Tertius's warm smile faltered, but he held it firm. "Because you deserved it. And it'll help you in the future. Rome needs heroes, after all."

Heat rose to Varro's face. "I don't feel like a hero."

"That business with Fidelis, then?"

Varro leaned back in surprise. "You know of that? How many others know?"

"I'm on Galba's staff, remember? I only lost an arm, not my ears. Anyway, I don't know what you might have done. You and Curio are connected because of that stupid prank of yours. Falco's implicated just because it's well known the two of you are like brothers."

"He had nothing to do with it." The lie spilled from Varro's mouth easily, and it stunned him to silence. Tertius cocked his head and narrowed his eyes.

"Fidelis thinks you're lying and wants to find out why. You may believe Galba no longer cares since he's leaving. But last night he and Villius spoke. I was not present for it, of course. But Fidelis was summoned to meet with both. After leaving the consul's tent, he went right back to questioning Curio all night. So my guess is Villius will keep the investigation going. Which he should. Killing the consul's slave right under his nose is a threat if I've ever heard one. And the Punic War veterans are starting to make noise. It's probably one of them that did it. I can't see you doing something like that, or even guess why you would."

"Of course not, sir."

"I'm not your officer any more, Varro." Tertius laughed and the bandaged stump of his left arm wagged as if he were trying to wave. "Anyway, come find me when you return to Rome. I will always be glad to see you, and what is mine is yours as well."

"I told you to not worry for it."

"Everyone needs allies, father. Don't be too fast to dismiss one." Tertius extended his whole arm, and Varro braced it. They then stepped back, and Varro saluted his former optio a final time. Tertius returned it.

"Stay alive, Varro, and I'll see you in Rome."

He watched Tertius leave the way he had come then disappear around a clot of soldiers hunched over a raucous dice game.

When Varro turned back, he found Centurion Fidelis

watching him with his strong arms folded across his chest and a thin smile on his lips.

Varro stepped back in shock, but recovered himself and started back toward his men. He nodded to the centurion, who watched him pass like a chained dog waiting to be freed to savage his prey.

7

Two thousand men swarmed the parade grounds around headquarters. They dressed for battle, their bronze helmets creating a bobbing sea that flowed toward Consul Villius's tent. Their black helmet feathers appeared like seabirds resting on the golden waves. Varro stood at the far end, blinking in disbelief at what he had awakened to discover.

The morning light warmed the tunics of the Punic War veterans to a cream color. Their voices resonated with anger and their slogans joined into one sound that shook the camp. In the background, elephants trumpeted as if showing solidarity with these men.

"It's time to go home!"

This was the chant Varro pulled out from the thousands of voices calling to the consul's tent. He noted the hapless guards surrounding it, no more than a dozen men to face thousands. Did Consul Villius hide inside? Galba had been gone only a handful of days and already Villius had managed to push the veterans into open rebellion.

"It smells like trouble," Varro said. He thought he was speaking to the tessarius of the command group who had stood just behind him. Instead, Drusus's tired, rocky voice answered.

"It smells like a bunch of unwashed, sweaty men, is more like it."

Varro stood to attention at the centurion's arrival. Of course, like everyone else he would be drawn to the spectacle.

"What's going to happen, sir?" Varro followed Drusus's gaze across the road to the myriad of angry faces calling for relief.

"I suppose a few things could happen. None of them are worth guessing at, as they all end badly. You'll notice these boys are not dressed for dinner with grandmother. They're making sure we can't break them up without risking a fight among ourselves. That's not to say the new consul isn't stupid enough to try."

"But they're tired, sir. They've been at war for two campaigns. They were supposed to be home by now. They were promised."

Drusus gave him a strange smile. "You sympathize with them, do you?"

"Sir, I didn't mean I won't do my duty. It's just that they were promised something and now Galba sailed off without another word about it. They should've joined him on that ship, sir."

"True. Now keep your opinion to yourself. It's not like you're the consul's new favorite boy. Don't say more to get yourself involved with other trouble."

Varro tucked his head down. With the exchange of consuls, the entire camp was off balance. While officers such as himself and Drusus enforced regularity on the men, no one denied the strange air of Galba's absence and Villius's lack of visibility to his men. After his grant of rest and wine, he had made no more attempts to bond with the common men. He spent his days with tribunes and servants.

This had all been to Varro's relief. For he had not forgotten Fidelis's hungry look from three days before. Yet even he seemed to have vanished, probably reassigned a duty more meaningful to the new consul. If he expected the murdered slave was a threat of rebellion from the Punic War veterans, then now he had his confirmation. He had more than Varro to worry for.

At last, Consul Villius emerged from his tent. Varro and Drusus both leaned closer to hear what he said. He wore only his senatorial toga, not even appearing as one of the men. Varro found this insulting, and it was not lost on the veterans who howled as if he has shown his bare ass to them instead.

"What is this nonsense?" The consul tilted back his head as if daring anyone to step forward. "Return to your duties. Disperse!"

But the sea of angry soldiers rolled closer and Villius pulled back behind the unfortunate men charged with guarding him. This drew heckles from the veterans, calling him among other things a coward.

"That was a bad choice," Drusus said. "Disappointing. We're not getting far with this one in charge."

Varro had to agree. The consul shouted his own insults, but eventually retreated to the safety of his tent. The veterans let out gusty laughs, but no one pushed further. The guards at the entrance to the tent stood defiantly, but dared nothing more.

"It seems the veterans know how to conduct themselves," Varro said. "But would we have to disperse them if the consul orders it?"

"We would," Drusus said. "Though we wouldn't be too aggressive about it. Since we don't have that order yet, go get the men ready and we'll go for a march. I expect half the camp will have the same idea. Let's get our boys away from trouble before the tribune realizes he should order us to stay put in case we are needed."

He and Drusus gathered the rest of the command group from staring at the expanse of rebelling soldiers. They reluctantly followed Drusus down the path toward the rows of hastati tents.

At the end of the road, where it joined smaller tracks leading into the main camp, Centurion Fidelis stood with four other soldiers. He planted himself in the center, arms folded, heroic jaw tight around a dark smile. His abrupt eyebrows raised in recognition of Varro's arrival.

"Optio Varro," he said as they approached. The shouts of the rebelling veterans diminished his voice, but it was thick with pride. "I have been looking for you."

"Can't have been looking too hard," Centurion Drusus said. "He's been at the show with the rest of us. What do you want with my optio, Fidelis?"

The two centurions sized each other up. Varro backed into his fellows as he recoiled from the threat Fidelis offered standing in the road. In both size and experience, Varro judged the two men equally matched. Drusus would fight like a maddened bear, but Varro did not doubt Fidelis would be equally ferocious and probably cheat as well.

"I have orders from Consul Villius," Fidelis said. He held forth a papyrus sheet, which he presented to Drusus.

His head scanned side to side as he read, mouth forming unspoken words. At length, he thrust it back into the smirking Fidelis's chest.

"Looks like you'll be going with Centurion Fidelis." He did not meet Varro's face, and instead seemed to stare through his chest.

"Sir, what is this about?" Varro looked to Drusus, but Fidelis answered.

"You are to be held on suspicion of murdering the former consul's slave."

Varro blinked and his mouth hung open, yet no words in his own defense formed of the hollow gasp he exhaled. Before he could react, the four soldiers accompanying Fidelis surrounded him. They did not draw their weapons, but their hands hovered close to them.

"You have no evidence," Varro said as the four stern-faced men formed a box around him.

"The consul will decide that," Fidelis said. "He wishes a swift resolution to this outstanding matter. Your name has never been cleared of doubt. Now come with me."

Drusus at last met his eyes, giving Varro a pained and weary look. The others of the command group backed away from him as if proximity could transmit guilt. Fidelis extended his hand.

"Your weapons. Be swift about it."

Surrendering his sword and replacement pugio felt as if he were giving up his entire life. After all the blind hope of putting this horrible mistake in the past, he realized it would never be. The consul, be he Galba or Villius, could not be so blatantly challenged. Someone had to pay. In this case, Fidelis was correct in who should make the payment. Varro now shifted hope that he would be given a fair trial and that he could at least explain himself. Maybe Villius would be merciful and not want to execute anyone or else further stir up resentment against him.

Now stripped of weapons, he bowed his head and followed Fidelis. He could not look to Centurion Drusus, who stood stiff and silent in the corner of Varro's vision.

The roads were blessedly emptied of men. The spectacle at headquarters was either too much of a draw or else sent men into hiding. He did not speak and Fidelis and his guards offered no conversation. Fidelis led them as if on a victory parade through Rome. Without anyone to admire him, Varro concluded the centurion was admiring himself. He had the ego for it.

Their path eventually led them to the elephant pens where cages were set up nearby. The thick scents of elephant dung assailed Varro's nose. One of the guards groaned at the stench of it. In one of the black iron cages stood Falco and Curio. Their hands were white against the lattice of bars.

"You'll join your friends until the consul is ready to see you, which may be some time, given this morning's chaos."

Fidelis stood smirking beside the cage door. One of his guards opened the lock, while two others took Varro by each arm in a strong grip. They led him toward the cages.

"I don't know why you did it," Fidelis said. "But we'll learn it soon enough. Between the three of you, there has to be one who'll tell the truth."

The cage door swung open. Falco and Curio stepped back from it, and the two guards led Varro to the door. To his surprise, they did not treat him roughly. They released him inside, then slammed the iron gate shut to click the lock back into place. The iron bars rattled over his head as he stared sheepishly at Falco and Curio.

"I expect a fair trial," Varro said, turning back to Fidelis. The bars were tight enough that he only saw the outside world as small squares, like an ill-fitted mosaic.

"Trial?" Fidelis pressed against the iron bars. "I'm certain Falco's foot will fit the print. You and Curio are already implicated. What trial is needed? The consul wants a swift end to the matter. You'll go right to sentencing, and I think you know what that will be."

Falco roared and charged at the cage. He kicked the bars, his hobnailed soles screeching against them. But Fidelis just laughed.

"Prepare your final statements," he said. "And don't think to beg for mercy. Villius is not that kind of consul."

The centurion departed, leaving two men behind as guards.

Varro turned back into the cage. It was large enough to hold a dozen men and sat on the cold earth like an upturned box. Falco and Curio both stood with arms folded.

"You didn't fight back?" Falco's red face was tight with disgust.

"He had something in writing from the consul, and Centurion

Drusus released me. You would've had me fight both of them and the guards?"

"Well, you could've thrown a punch. Fidelis is going to have us killed anyway."

Curio shook his head and turned away. "But he can make it worse on us if he wants. Besides, you didn't fight either."

They exchanged stories of their arrests. Varro recounted his as if it was an event from another life. The slamming of the cage door had echoed with finality. He was now in a world where men waited for death. Falco and Curio were picked up together in the predawn when they were asleep. Fidelis had arrived at their tent, called them out, and taken them in. Falco spread his strong arms wide to show his gray tunic.

"Right out of my sleeping roll, just like this. Not even a minute to lace my sandals. He made us march barefoot and then threw us inside the cage."

"Such a thoughtful touch," Varro said. He turned back to the cage bars. The chanting of two thousand angry veterans filled the camp, but were distant now. The gray shapes of elephants wandering in their pit were also visible. But the stench of the beasts passed easily into the cage. Varro guessed he would acclimate to it, much as the men who rode them to battle must have.

"Do you have a plan?" Curio asked. This drew a snort from Falco.

"What plan? Are we going to flip over this fucking cage then fly out of the camp? Varro's smart, but he's not a god, and only a god will fetch us out of this mess."

"Drusus will help us."

The statement escaped Varro's mouth without his thinking. But upon hearing himself, he realized he was right.

"How so?" Falco now leaned with him against the cage, and Curio joined on the opposite side. Both looked eager for elaboration.

"I don't know how. But I think he knows we did something, and intends to help us. He knew I wasn't in my bed that night. But he never turned me in for it or even confronted me on it. I tried to explain more to him, but he didn't want to hear. He warned me that he'll stay out of it. But I have a feeling he won't, and I believe I am right."

Falco sighed and pressed his forehead to the bars.

"I hope you are right, Lily. We've escaped some tight spots, but never a fucking cage."

"I hate waiting for help to arrive," Varro said. "But I'm sure it will."

Conversation faded and each drifted away to their own thoughts. As the morning wore on, rain clouds crept into the sky. Falco walked in a circle with both palms upturned, feeling for rain. "Of course it's going to fucking rain. A nice blast of cold rain to wash all the rust and bird shit off these bars and onto our heads. Just wait."

"Shut up, Falco." Curio sat on the dirt, legs crossed and scratching nonsense into the dirt.

"You should've shut up before you devised that stupid plan to threaten the girl. You had to give Varro's name and use yourself as a distraction? What a fucking stupid mess."

"As stupid as the fools who went along with it." Curio erased whatever he was drawing in the dirt with angry scrubbing.

The shouting and voices of the veterans gathered at headquarters filled the brief silence. Varro expected Falco to leap at the smaller Curio, and his legs tensed expecting to intervene. Yet Falco finally laughed, rapping the back of head with his knuckles.

"You're right, of course. It's all my fault, really. I should've kept my pugio in its sheath. At the time I was thinking of choking her, but worried I might go too far." He gave a derisive laugh. "Imagine that? I still managed to go too far."

"We didn't want to hurt her," Varro said, leaning against the cold bars. "I wouldn't have let you choke her."

"Ah, then I could've blamed you for all this. How much better that would've been than knowing I got us all in this trouble?"

Varro was about to proclaim all of them shared equal blame. But Curio suddenly stood, staring ahead to the cage door. Both Varro and Falco followed his stare.

A figure filled the door, which broke the profile into a mosaic of flesh and white colors. The lock clicked open and the cage door swung in across the dirt.

The man who entered was not Centurion Drusus. He held himself straight like a leader and his eyes squinted at them as if he were staring into the sun. Dressed in a white tunic, he had no outward signs of rank. If he was a soldier, his graying black hair marked him as one of the triarii.

Lining up with Curio and Falco, Varro watched as the man smiled then swung the gate behind them so it would appear closed to a casual glance. He did not seem worried for anyone following him. So Varro assumed he was with the consul or Fidelis.

"At last we meet."

The man's voice was resonant, at odds with his lithe frame. But Varro's heart leaped at its sound. He had heard it somewhere before, though he could not place it. The man looked directly to Varro, ignoring the other two on either side.

"Do I know you, sir?"

"Not at all. Or at least you should not. But you use the correct term of respect. Perceptive of you. Now, who I am can wait a moment longer." The man now looked to Falco and Curio and offered a short nod. "For the three of you are coming with me."

"Going with you?" Falco folded his arms. "Is this some trick of the consul's to make us guilty of escaping? I mean, he has no other evidence that we did what he says we did. But if we run then he'll say that's proof enough to execute us."

Varro nodded at Falco's quick thinking. This might be the sort of ploy Fidelis would use to ensure they appeared as guilty as possible.

The man's smile deepened.

"Your suspicions are not unfounded. But I am here to help you, and the consul and Fidelis are not aware of my actions yet. Centurion Drusus alerted me to what happened."

"More words," Falco said, brushing his hand as if the man were a mosquito to chase off.

"Let me show you my credentials." The man reached into his tunic, fished around, then pulled out something he held forward on both palms.

Coiled on his wrinkled white palms were two lengths of braided gold chain each as thick as a man's thumb. Even under the dull gray sky, the chain sections gleamed.

The man's smile widened.

"You recognize this? It's the whole reason you're in this cage. Now, will you accompany me?"

Varro stepped forward.

"You lead the way, sir."

8

Stepping outside the iron cage felt strangely panicking to Varro, as if he had wandered into a public road without wearing any clothing. Even the breeze felt colder, though it might have been from the gathering clouds threatening rain. He stood aside from the gate, expecting to find the two guards Fidelis had set either unconscious or bound up. Instead, they had vanished. In the middle distance Varro saw the head of a war elephant with its ears up as if listening. Yet he saw no one else.

Falco and Curio both exited behind Varro. Falco wrapped his arms around his body as if he were naked, and Curio stared wide-eyed all around. Their older savior stepped out with a satisfied smile, then pulled the cage shut. The iron bars rattled as he ensured the door was tight.

"You've nothing to fear," the man said. He smoothed his plain white tunic as the breeze flipped a lock of his graying black hair upright. He patted it back into place, then gestured them to follow.

They took the same path away from the elephant pens as they had used to approach it. Varro was happy to leave the rank animal stench behind. No one challenged them, for no one was on their path. Across the rows of white tent roofs Varro saw the far edges of the gathered Punic War veterans. Their shouting had died down as the day progressed, but they remained encircling the consul's tent. Along with them were probably most of the army spectating. The unnamed man glanced the same way and chuckled.

"Galba should have warned him this was coming," he said. "But I suppose he was just as happy to leave the mess behind for Villius. It would not do to have his successor succeed where he failed."

"I'm sorry, sir, what do you mean by that?" Varro's curiosity overtook his fears. But Falco gave a low moan at the question.

"How bad would it be for Galba to learn upon reaching Rome that Villius had already brought Philip to battle and defeated him? What a tremendous loss of face for Galba. So it is far better that the army remains stalled while Philip prepares for battle on his terms. It will be a harder fight, one Villius might not easily win. Galba's reputation will be spared, at least by some."

Varro's mouth fell open. "But that means more of us will die trying defeat Philip. That can't be right?"

"Why can't it be?" The man continued to lead them along the path, turning now between tents toward the perimeter of camp. He did not look back as he strode ahead of them. "Are you shocked that senators would spend the lives of citizens to save their own reputations? If you are, then open your eyes, young Varro. Blots on a career are not washed away, but instead concealed with the blood of others."

"But Galba didn't do anything wrong. Philip escaped us, that's all." Varro looked back over his shoulder toward the rebelling veterans. Instead, he found Falco and Curio both staring at him as if he had lost his mind. He turned back. "There's no blame in that."

The man laughed, full and long, then shook his head.

"Galba's detractors will be sure to highlight his missed

opportunities. If Villius succeeds too quickly, even Galba's supporters might abandon him. This uprising by the veterans is perfect for him. And perfect for the three of you, I'll have you know."

Varro started to ask for an explanation, but the man stopped at the end of the track and pointed to a small tent. It was not a camping tent, as it was square and high-roofed. It seemed more like the tent where Galba had housed his slaves. No one stood outside and the flaps hung open.

"Inside where we can speak more freely." The man extended his arm.

All three of them paused and looked to each other. Curio shrugged and Falco frowned.

"If it's a different kind of prison, at least we might break out of cloth walls."

Their anonymous savior laughed at Falco's words and smiled as he swept them toward the entrance.

Once inside, Varro's eyes shifted from the flat glare of daylight to the darkness of the square tent. Yet in a moment, he recognized three packs and three racks of full gear.

"This is my gear," he said, turning in surprise to the man who now stood in the door.

Falco and Curio rushed forward, touching the racks of their armor and weapons as if to confirm they were not dreaming. But Varro scratched his head, wondering what trick this man was planning.

"It is everything you own," the man said. He followed them into the tent, but left the flaps open for light. "And I do mean everything."

He lowered his gaze at Varro and held out one hand and rubbed his ring finger with the other. His smile did not waver.

Somehow he knew about the rings he and Falco had stolen from King Philip. Whether he realized the original owner was unclear. But this man did not intend to steal that wealth from them, at least not yet.

"Now that we are here," Varro said. "May I know your name?"

"Of course you may. We do not often interact, but you'll know my rank if not my name. I am Gaius Sabellius, Tribune Second Legion."

Falco and Curio whirled around and joined Varro in standing to attention. While Varro knew the man must be of some rank, he could never have guessed from his plain appearance they had been rescued by a tribune.

Sabellius lowered his head as if embarrassed at the formality and waved them down. "Please, this is not army business now. We're all just citizens gathered for a common purpose. Please, be at ease."

The rigid formality faded slowly, both Falco and Curio waiting to see if Varro relaxed. When he did, the others followed. Varro rubbed the back of his neck.

"Sir, what cause have we gathered for? Is it connected to what happened to Galba's slave?"

"It is precisely that," Sabellius said. He spread his hands as if to gather them closer. "Galba was convinced his life had been threatened, and was even more certain that threat would pass on to Villius. Now he finds open rebellion facing him and Galba's suspicion feels much more like fact in this circumstance. I believe he intends to have the three of you flogged to death for your actions."

Falco stepped forward. "But it was an accident, and I was the one holding the blade. Stupid Varro was too scared to even hold his, so he dropped it there. Curio was just helping us get inside. Only I should face punishment, sir."

Sabellius held up both hands. "So noble of you, Falco. Such are the bonds of innocent friendship. But there will be no punishments. The killing of the slave was a mistake. You went to retrieve your stolen necklace but did not find it. Things became tense and in the confusion the girl was mistakenly killed. Is that not what happened?"

"Sir, that is exactly what happened," Varro said. "I didn't want to hurt her, much less kill her. I feel so guilty."

"But not guilty enough to die for it." Sabellius offered his disarming smile.

"It seems Fidelis would like it if I did."

"He likes to win. He's good at what he does, and is a friend of Galba's family. I don't believe he cares if you live or die, but only that he's declared victor in this matter. Villius, on the other hand, sees you as a threat to be removed. He will need convincing. That is where I will help you. I'm not without higher resources myself. I will make this problem fade away. No one cares about the life of a slave. But it will take time to accomplish."

Varro's back straightened up, for he realized nothing would be granted freely.

"Sir, while I appreciate this, I would like to know what you expect in return. You're not doing this out of any love for us. We have never met before."

"Varro, there is so much you do not understand." Sabellius clasped his hands behind his back and straightened his shoulders. Varro could see him as a tribune now even without his bronze breastplate and shining helmet. "Yes, there is always a price. But it is one that I think you can pay, given your reputations. But to say we have not met before is untrue. I have come to visit you many times while you stayed in the hospital. You were just never awake."

A scrap of memory flashed into his mind. He remembered after being struck by Gallio that someone had come to speak to the doctor about his condition. He could not recall anything but the voice which had been unfamiliar but commanding—like Sabellius's voice.

Sabellius's smile grew as he appeared to read Varro's recollection.

"So you might have been half-awake on my visits. My voice is familiar to you, then?"

"It is, sir. But why? Why check on me?"

"As Centurion Protus must have told you, there are different factions in this camp. Think of it as a patron and client relationship, only one away from the eyes of the public. When you sided with Protus against those who supported your father then you chose your client whether you realized it or not. These alliances shift, of course, as men die or move about—or as consuls rotate. While the patrons themselves never change. Though they are far away in Rome, their hands can touch their clients wherever they go, bestowing benefits in exchange for favors."

Varro looked to Falco, who stared in wonder at him as if this were the first he had heard of the story. But Varro had confessed all he knew of his father's criminal activities and how Protus told him he was under a sort of protection by a powerful figure. He had just never expected it to be a tribune.

"Sir, then you have been watching out for me?"

Sabellius nodded. "From a distance. And I am not the highest rank in this long chain. But there is no need for you to look higher than me, at least now. Also, you are not the most important link in our chain. But Protus believed you were a strong asset, along with Falco here. Drusus shares that assessment."

"Centurion Drusus is part of this?" Varro stared at Falco, who appeared equally astonished.

"He shared command of the maniple with Protus. How could he not be? But Drusus is not deeply involved. He is not the kind of man who needs to be. He likes to fight and win battles, and so that is the best use of his talents. For you, there may be other ways to help our patron."

"Sir, I still don't know why you of all people would protect me."

"I have not protected you, Varro. I've said I've watched you. You are part of my faction, so to speak, and as such I look out for junior members. Now it seems I've added Falco and Curio to the list of names to watch and call upon in the future."

Already short, Curio seemed to shrink even lower at the mention of his name.

"I'd rather not be part of anything mysterious, sir. But I can keep your secret."

Sabellius laughed, once more a rich and welcoming laugh that set Varro at ease. It was the laugh of a trustworthy man. He did not laugh out of derision, but out of what seemed genuine surprise for the innocence of the young men in his charge. This is what Varro wanted to believe, for the tribune seemed to hold their lives in his palm, much as he did the gold chain.

"There are no mysteries, young Curio. You will know what to do if I should call on you one day. And you will know when you should call upon me—just as Centurion Drusus knew to. And that brings me to our meeting today."

Varro swallowed hard, realizing the price for his life was about to be named. He looked to Falco and Curio, both who stared back with matching trepidation.

"You need to get out of this camp. Villius will be tied up with these rebelling veterans for a while. Galba was certain to leave agitators behind who are experts at keeping the flames of discontent alive. As long as Villius feels the threat of losing command of these men, he will not entertain any ideas of your freedom. Besides, Varro, you once told Galba the men might rebel. Galba did not forget that statement, which at the time he took as impertinence and an attempt to save yourself. In light of today's events, your statement on that day seems far more threatening. At least you seem more culpable to him. So, it is best you are beyond his sight or concern. Fortunately for you, I have a task perfectly suited to your abilities. I hope you will accept it."

"Of course, sir." Though Varro was grateful, he resented this being presented as a choice and twisted that resentment into his tone. "I would accept anything that spares my life."

"Anything? Even without hearing what it is? But I suppose I would do the same." Sabellius unfolded his arms from behind his back, then produced a bent papyrus scroll from within the folds of his tunic. He did not offer it yet, but tapped it lightly against his palm. "You were able to find the traitor Gallio among the Macedonians and bring back his head. That was a miraculous achievement, given you knew nothing of his whereabouts. In fact, it was such an achievement that many believe you had divine assistance. For how else could one sift a single specific stone from the ocean floor?"

"It was not so miraculous," Varro said, recalling the day of Gallio's death. "I think somehow he wanted us to catch him. I think he regretted what he did, and made it so we would find him and bring him to justice."

"If that is true, then he was a coward to the very end." Sabellius rapped the papyrus to his hand again and frowned. "But there is no denying your skill in bringing him back. So I am calling on the three of you now to create this miracle once more."

Varro tilted his head. "You need us to find someone, sir?"

"Precisely. A cavalryman was captured last winter during Galba's ill-fated clash with Philip. You should remember it well, as you spent a night in the marsh and survived it."

Falco chuckled. "Survived it, but I nearly coughed up my lungs for months after."

"You were luckier than most that day, and I needn't explain why. But our cavalryman in question was not killed. His body was not found and for a while we assumed he had been lost in the marsh. Yet when one of our men escaped from captivity by Philip's army, he revealed this man still lived as a captive. Without a doubt, this witness spoke with all the Roman captives and confirmed this man in particular."

"And you want us to rescue this cavalryman?" Varro gave a twisted smile. "Sir, at least I knew what Gallio looked like. I don't know one soul of the cavalry. I wouldn't know one if he stood with me."

"They all ride horses," Falco said, laughing at his own joke. But no one paid him attention.

Sabellius nodded patiently. "You will not be going alone. The witness will accompany you to point out your target once you locate where he has been taken."

"Are you sure this cavalryman hasn't been sold into slavery or killed?" The arguments came easily to Varro, as he had faced all these doubts while seeking Gallio.

"I do not think so. His name alone should inform you why I believe thus. He is called Marcellus Paullus."

Varro blinked. He looked to Falco and Curio, who stared vacantly. All three looked again to Sabellius whose face had reddened and the beginnings of a frown creased his brows.

"Paullus? You do not know the name?" He waited, eyes wide with expectation. "Oh my, all three countryside boys. Well, then perhaps you will know his more famous relation, Scipio Africanus?"

The three gasped together. Curio staggered back with his hand over his chest. "He's Scipio's son?"

Sabellius hid his eyes behind the hand holding the papyrus scroll. He shook his head as if crying silent tears.

"Not his son, no. But Paullus is his wife's family. Marcellus is not a blood relation, but through Scipio's wife he is connected. In any case, he is from a wealthy and powerful family. A family some say is among the most powerful in Rome. Undoubtedly Marcellus would have identified himself as a means of self-preservation against the fates you just described. Philip understands the structure of our army, and that our cavalrymen represent the elite of our city. So a ransom demand was expected, but never arrived after Philip hastily split his forces and fled. As luck would have it, our witness used the confusion to make his escape and confirmed Marcellus went with the northern group."

"Sir, if I may," Varro said. "With such an important person at stake, why send the three of us? Couldn't the most powerful family of Rome afford to hire someone better? Or else just send a ransom offer directly to Philip?"

"Philip went south and his general went north to face the Dardanian invasion. Sending a ransom over such long distances through enemy territory would never work without a negotiated arrangement. So a large escorting force would have to travel with the ransom, drawing opportunity attacks from the Macedonians. No, it would never succeed. Besides, once Marcellus is located he will simply have to be escorted back. I doubt such a wealthy hostage is in chains, but rather simply under guard. And as for sending the three of you, the selection of this team has been left to my discretion. I have recommended you three based on your achievement in finding Gallio. You will not let me down."

Varro nodded, looking to Falco and Curio who followed along.

"This papyrus shows the likely locations for Philip's army. It is a map of sorts that should aid you in reaching Marcellus. Also on it is proof of your official capacity in this matter. Along the way you may need to prove your identities and influence locals. Having proof the Roman army is behind you will help in this."

Sabellius extended the scroll, which Varro accepted. His worries must have read as hesitation to the tribune, for he inhaled sharply.

"Come now, Varro. Besides restoring your reputation and life, I will keep all your gold safe for your return. And the Paullus family may even be moved to reward you further. But if that is not enough, then let me appeal to your humanity. Power and status aside, you are reuniting an only child with bereaved parents who had thought their son dead and lost forever. Surely you can see the goodness in your sacrifices to bring him to safety."

Varro looked at the rolled scroll in his hand. The papyrus was rough and warm, and creased from being carried against Sabellius's body. It felt heavier than it should. But Varro considered the tribune's words, realizing this mission might serve as his penance for having killed the unnamed slave girl.

"I swear to do all I can to deliver Marcellus Paullus to his family."

Sabellius smiled and looked to Falco and Curio, who made the same oath.

"Excellent. You may rest today in this tent. You will leave before dawn."

9

Varro yawned in the predawn gloom as he stood outside the tent Sabellius had provided for rest. While Falco and Curio had snored throughout the night, Varro's sleep had been fitful and incomplete. Now he waited alone in the chill of a springtime twilight with his gray wool cloak wrapped over his shoulders. He stood on his toes and scanned across the camp. Glowing orange campfires marked where the Punic War veterans had stood all night. They were quiet now, along with the rest of the camp. Even in rebellion, the veterans maintained strict noise discipline in the night. Varro admired how training defeated outrage.

He had already strapped on his gear, leaving his helmet resting by his feet. His scutum shield was in its leather bag, ready to be slung over his back during the march. He had studied the map during the night, leaning close to a clay lamp and tracing the spidery lines. It was small and drawn to indicate waypoints along the path. If they followed the roads Philip's army had taken, they would make good time. But it seemed the army's path led off the road. Varro feared becoming lost at that point, and so his dreams had all been nightmares of wandering dark woods filled with menace.

More important than the map was the declaration by Tribune Sabellius written and signed at the bottom of the papyrus. It invested Varro and the others with the authority of the tribune, allowing him to demand the rights and respect owed to a representative of Rome. He doubted holding up the papyrus would do much against enemy soldiers. But it might be handy in some situation he could not foresee.

Now Falco yawned from inside the tent, and he growled at Curio to awaken. Varro had thought to allow them more rest, as Sabellius had not arrived yet. The journey ahead would be long, perhaps a week following the roads or maybe two if forced off the road. During that time, no one would have a good night of sleep.

"Is he here yet?" Falco asked from the inside. Varro confirmed they were alone, and Falco stepped outside in his tunic. His hair was disheveled and covered his eyes. "I'm thinking this whole thing is going to much harder than Sabellius says it will."

"Of course," Varro agreed, searching the blue darkness for signs of the tribune. "He's made a lot of assumptions seem like facts. This Marcellus Paullus might be dead. Maybe we just won't find him. What will we do then? We could claim he is dead. How would Sabellius know if we lied to him?"

Falco shivered. "We're not lying to him. He knows too much about us. A man like that will discover if we lied and then we'll both be floating down the Tiber one body part at a time. I can't believe Gallio is dead but still making trouble for us."

Varro chuckled. "I hadn't thought of it that way. We got ourselves into this mess when we killed that girl. Gallio had nothing to do with it."

"It was an accident." Falco squatted on his heels and picked up Varro's helmet. He brushed the black feathers. "You should probably remove these when we travel."

"Maybe it was an accident." He grabbed his helmet from Falco and placed it on the ground again. "But I held her firm and so ensured her death. I know she was just a slave without a name and that she threatened to kill me one day. But I will be guilty for the rest of my life unless I do something to atone for it."

"How are you going to do that? Let me guess. You're going to whine about it until your lips fall off?"

"No, this mission is my atonement. It is going to be harder than Sabellius is making it seem. But I have a chance to save a life now. If I can reunite this Marcellus Paullus—an only son—with his family, then I will have done good in the eyes of the gods. I will dedicate that success to the slave I helped kill."

Falco brushed his hair from his dark eyes and stared at Varro.

"I know it's a stretch," he said, turning back to watch the road ahead. "But what else can I do? I can't find her family and help them."

"Especially since you killed her family," Falco said under his breath.

"Shut up! I need to know I'm doing something good, something to atone for the evil I've done in the name of greed. I lost my pugio for this. It was blessed at the temple of Mars, and now it has left me. If that is not a sign of the gods' disfavor, then what is?"

"That's a fair point," Falco said. "I wonder how the gods will disfavor me? I drove the blade into her throat. What will I lose?"

"Ah, don't worry for it. You did not swear a vow of peace before the gods as I did."

Falco gave a slow nod, then slipped back into the tent to prepare with Curio.

Varro listened to the pair mumble and bump about the interior. He drew his wool cloak closed at his neck and peered into the receding darkness. A faint white stain already formed at the east as thin tendrils poking above the camp walls. He did not search long before four shapes emerged at the far end of the road. They could be an early morning work team. But Varro knew it was Tribune Sabellius, though who accompanied him remained to be seen.

The group rounded a tent and following behind was a mule laden with packs. The tallest of the men led it as it plodded along the track. Varro announced to the others the tribune had arrived, drawing a gasp and creating a flurry of noise. Curio ducked out of the tent flap first, with Falco close behind. His hair remained a mess, but he stood at attention to greet the tribune.

"Ready as planned," Sabellius said as he closed the distance. He smiled warmly, like an old uncle coming to visit the farm. The men behind him were less pleased, each remaining as impassive shadows in the faint light. The tribune's clean white tunic seemed to blaze in comparison.

Varro saluted as did the others. Behind the tribune, he thought one of the men seemed to smirk at their formality. But Sabellius himself accepted the required respect. That smirk, if it had been one, irritated Varro.

"You've studied the map as I suggested?"

"Yes, sir." Varro looked to Curio on his right. "But none of us claim to understand it clearly. We've no experience with such things."

Sabellius smiled and the man who Varro suspected of smirking seemed to shake his head.

"I did not expect that of you, young Varro. You of course read my letter, which is far more important. Do you have any questions?"

"None, sir." Varro wanted to ask a hundred questions about this mission. But he suspected Sabellius knew less than he pretended to know. Both understood he and the others were assigned a mission with a high chance of failure. Just as both understood there could be no return if they failed. He and the others would be better off dying in service than returning to face Villius empty-handed.

"Excellent, but I expect you must have some questions you are too embarrassed to ask. I've anticipated what some of these must be. First, let me introduce the team to you."

"Team, sir? I thought it was me, Falco, and Curio?"

"As you've said, you don't have all the experience needed to make a long trip through enemy lands. And while this mission is best accomplished by a small force, there is comfort in numbers. So I've doubled your size. Here are three men to accompany you."

The tribune extended his arm to the man at his right, who stepped forward so Varro could see him clearer in the low light. He had sandy hair and a serious expression, as if he had never learned to laugh. He was perhaps a handful of years older than Varro.

"This is Marcus Gala. He has recently escaped capture by the Macedonians and spoke with Marcellus Paullus. He will help you identify him."

Gala inclined his head. Varro wondered if the gravity of his expression was due to his experiences as a captive. Such a harrowing experience should change a man, he believed.

"Next, is Primus Casca." The tribune shift to indicate broad-shouldered man with deep lines dropping from his hook nose. He did not step forward, but the tribune's shift in position allowed more light to strike Casca's face.

"You know his brother," Sabellius said. "Secundus Casca is in your century."

Varro looked again at Primus, the older brother of a man under Varro's charge. If he shared a family resemblance with his brother, it did nothing to help Varro identify him. The only clue he had was Casca seemed unenthusiastic to meet him. Yet since becoming an optio, Varro had discovered many men disliked him for that reason alone.

The tribune continued. "Casca is a practiced guide and scout. You will depend upon his knowledge for survival, so treat him well. Now, here is the last man of your team. He is a bit older than all of you, also with much experience in scouting. But he is also fluent in Greek, and will help you negotiate with the locals and perhaps even the odd Macedonian solider."

This was the tall man who had sneered and shook his head at Varro while behind the tribune's back. Now under the tribune's gaze, he stood to attention as a model soldier. He took a measured step forward as if presenting himself for review, which seemed to please Sabellius who smiled appreciatively. He had bulging eyes like two grapes and short black hair that had gown long enough to begin curling at the edges. He was at least ten years older than Varro.

"He is Julianus Piso. I was eager to assign this role to him, as it suits his skills perfectly."

Sabellius clapped his hands together with a gentle puff of air. He at last indicated the mule.

"And your fourth member. A mule to carry your tent and other gear. I've managed three days of rations and acetum wine to mix with the water you will need to find along the way. You should have everything you need."

Varro thanked the tribune, who folded his arms and admired his work. The sun was fast rising, now a brighter stripe on the eastern horizon. If they waited much longer, the camp would awaken for the morning.

"As this is still a military undertaking," Sabellius said. "There must be an officer in charge. As Marcus Varro is an optio, he shall lead the team. You will obey his commands as you would mine. Make no mistake that this operation must succeed."

The three men straightened up to acknowledge Sabellius's order. Varro suddenly realized these three men must also have some debt or problem hanging over them. All six of them had done something to need Sabellius's aid and now they must repay the debt. He wondered what sort of problems he might inherit by associating with them. Of course, they might wonder the same about him.

"Make haste along the main road north," Sabellius said. "Dawn is near and men will be out to forage, or at least that was planned. With soldiers in open revolt, it may have changed. Take no chances. I have arranged everything for your absences. Your officers will understand and be ready to accept you on returning. The consul will as well, eventually. Your only concern is to find Marcellus Paullus and deliver him home with all haste. You will not only have my gratitude, but that of the consul as well. Villius will want to award your accomplishment no matter what his mood is today. I will ensure he will greet you all as brothers. I guarantee it. That is how I will support you while you undertake the dangerous work ahead."

The tribune indicated they should prepare to leave. Varro and the others loaded their meager possessions on the mule. He knew Falco worried for their gold chain and kingly rings in Sabellius's possession. But they could not carry these in the field or else risk their loss. Still, as they strapped their packs onto the patient mule, they shared a long stare.

"He better have the rest of our belongings when we return," Falco whispered.

Varro smirked, feeling smug for having guessed his friend's thoughts. "All we can do is trust him."

They parted with the tribune, who raised his hand in salute as they followed the road to the northern gate. They passed the guards there with neither challenge nor password offered. Sabellius must have arranged this as well, for the guards swung open the wooden gates and allowed them to pass.

The first step outside the confines of the camp felt to Varro as if he were leaping from a cliff. Whether anyone else felt the same panic as he did, they did not show it. Each looked to his footing in the poor visibility of unlit paths. Yet it felt like a fall to Varro, as his stomach lurched and his hands went cold. He was the officer in charge, with half the contubernium older and more experienced than himself. Outside the camp, he was the final authority.

Any mistakes were his to own. Any who died would have died for his commands. Any challenges to his authority were for him alone to address.

He did not realize any of this until his first step on the road leading north from the camp. The burden of command did not sit easily with him. He thought of the smirking Piso with all his experience. Then he considered Casca and his brother already under his command. Did Casca learn to dislike him from his brother? Who was he and what had Varro done to him? Finally, serious Gala. What if Varro got him captured by the Macedonian's once more? Gala must be worried for the same thing, and so could not smile expecting a swift return to the danger he had just escaped.

Such thoughts clamored for his attention as he headed north along the track. They proceeded in a mixed pack with no order. The mule being laden with so much weight lagged behind with Gala leading it. Yet once the sun broke into a gray and unfriendly sky, they had already marched for several miles. They pressed on another hour in silence, with Varro leading the disorganized group.

"Optio Varro, how about a rest?" Piso, the tallest and oldest of them, had already stopped. Casca did as well, pulling off his helmet and then sitting himself in the grass.

"All right, let's rest," Varro said. His face burned with shame for having not called the pace himself.

"Do we need a rest?" Falco asked in a hushed voice. "Don't these men march like we do? I could go until afternoon without a break. We're on a fucking road."

"They've already sat down," Varro said. "Let's go with it for now."

Falco and Curio shared a glance, but Varro did not want to indulge in the sting of his first failure. He approached Piso, who joined Casca in sitting by the roadside. Gala led the mule off the road to tend to it.

His shadow fell across the two men seated in the grass. He did not have a vine cane, but thought of what Tertius or even the malevolent Optio Latro would say in such a situation. Yet his mind blanked. He could not stand over these men without reason, so he opened his mouth and hoped to sound like an officer in charge.

"Rest your feet well. We're going to march without stop until late afternoon. I'll be setting the pace from here out, Piso. So you won't need to remind me of when breaks are necessary."

The older man squinted up at him in the flat glare. Casca lowered his head as if to hide his smirk.

"Yes, sir," Piso said.

Varro nodded. "Casca, did you find that statement humorous? Is there something you want to say?"

"Nothing at all, sir. I agree with you, sir."

The three of them blinked at each other in silence. Though Varro was certain a smirk would bloom on both their faces once he turned aside. At last, Piso rubbed the backs of his legs and spoke.

"Sir, if I may make a suggestion?"

Varro raised his brow, feeling like Tertius would do the same.

"We can maintain a fast pace, sir. We're trained for it. But the mule needs her rest more often. She's used to long but slower marches. We wouldn't want her to go lame."

"Aren't they supposed to be hardy?" Varro looked at the mule. Gala massaged and patted her neck. She gave a blank stare and flicked her ears. "She's a Roman soldier as well. She'll be up to the task."

Piso seemed about to rebut that claim, but Varro held up his hand.

"I'll see to the animal. Don't waste your rest educating me on mules."

He left them to return to Falco and Curio, who also sat in the roadside shade. They were surrounded by trees with fresh spring leaves and green grass stretching higher. Insects buzzed among the fresh blades and birds chirped overhead. While the sky was flat and gray, it would not rain, making for good marching weather.

Varro sat in silence with his friends and realized he could not create this kind of division. He already regretted handling Piso and Casca as he had. It probably made him appear more insecure than anything else. He stuffed back a sigh and determined to not repeat that mistake.

"I probably shouldn't spend all my time with you two," Varro said. "I need to make us a contubernium rather than two teams."

"Give yourself a break," Falco said as he picked grass and flicked it into the air. "You've been in charge for a few hours. You'll get to where you need to be. Me and Curio will support you."

"I suppose I will," Curio said, rubbing his face. "If it suits me."

Falco blinked in surprise, but Varro laughed. It caught on and all three shared a chuckle, which drew curious looks from the others. At last, Varro stood and called them to resume.

"Let's not bumble along in a disorganized crowd. We'll go two abreast until we reach our first checkpoint. We'll find water there. Is that right, Casca?"

"Yes, sir. We should find streams ahead. We will need time to scout a camp location and to forage."

"Understood," Varro said with a crisp nod. "We'll have the benefit of the road for a few days, but we'll have to veer off to follow the Macedonians' route. At that time, I want you to scout ahead for trouble. We should be safe on this road for now. All the enemies are either north or far south of here."

So they drew up a line with Varro and Falco in the lead and Gala guiding the mule at the rear.

Varro then marched them up the road feeling firmer in his role.

And leading them into an ambush.

10

Varro was thinking of water as he closed in on the bend ahead. Trees blazing with springtime green lined both sides of the road, which was well worn and rutted. For hours they had met no one along its length, which was just beginning to feel odd. Close to the Roman camp, he had expected locals to stay away. This far out, people should be on the road. Yet he kept the pace and approached the bend.

The midday sun threw sharp shadows across the dun-colored road. The hazy clouds had broken apart to increase both light and heat. A trickle of sweat rolled from beneath Varro's helmet, past the side of his ear, and into the collar of his tunic. The straps of his bronze pectoral dug into his shoulder and the shield on his back fought his progress. He would soon allow a rest, but the expected streams were just ahead.

"We should head left into the trees here," Casca said from behind.

Varro was grateful for the direction, since he did not know how to translate Sabellius's map onto the actual landscape. He steered the column left toward the trees.

Javelins from both sides of the road sailed out of the green haze between the trees.

A thin white shaft clattered at his feet, digging up clods of earth a thumb's breadth from his toes. Curio shouted in pain just behind him.

"Ambush!" he shouted. His scutum was still in its traveling bag and useless to him. Instead, he drew his gladius and pointed at the trees. "They can't hit us under the trees. Forward!"

The mule let out a horrible, prolonged scream. It was not like a horse, but deeper and rougher. Though it was a mere beast, it sounded full of frustration and sadness. Yet Varro did not even turn to it.

With Falco at his side, he rushed toward the trees where men were already charging out to meet them. Varro was reminded of the Illyrian bandits that had also ambushed him from the forest. These men looked much the same, wearing padded shirts and hiding behind small round shields. The foe ahead was all wide eyes and flashing bronze sword as he leaped to strike.

Without the benefit of his shield, Varro felt naked against the attack. They met at the edge of the woods. Despite his advantage, the enemy acted too cautiously and focused on Varro's gladius. He cried out in victory as his shield knocked Varro's stab aside.

But true to his training, Varro stepped in and punched the man on the side of his head. The blow sent sparks of pain running through his knuckles, but his enemy blew spit and blood from his mouth and toppled backward. Varro stepped again and stabbed him in the gut which stretched out before him. The enemy wailed as the blade punctured flesh then tore out, expelling scarlet blood like a split cask. Varro did not watch for his death.

Others were attacking.

Falco and Curio had followed close to him and each traded blows with an enemy. Without shields ready, both were disadvantaged. Yet both seemed to hold their own, though Curio's face was covered in blood that flowed from the top of his head.

In the respite, Varro unslung his shield and pulled it from the bag. Yet the enemies from the other side of the road now sprinted across to join the fight.

He could not count the enemy. That they outnumbered his small force was obvious.

In the time it took for Varro to equip his shield, Falco had finished his man and aided Curio with his. Piso and Casca were both preparing their shields. Gala was out of sight.

Varro rushed into the open, hoping to draw the attacks away from the others already engaged. Four men were in the road, dressed in dark, padded tunics and carrying shields that now appeared as toys against Varro's scutum.

"Right here, vermin! I'm your prize!"

Two broke off to face him while the rest charged past, swords raised and crying out for blood.

Bracing behind his shield, Varro knew he could not hold two men for long. One offered him weak, prodding strikes as he sought to dance around Varro's shield. The other man hammered at him as if he were mining for silver ore. The hammering fool did not understand combat, so Varro whirled to face the one trying to flank him.

He led with his sword and got a lucky cut that sliced the enemy's sword hand along the knuckles. It was deep enough for him to fumble the blade and drop it. Varro immediately stepped over it, then slammed his sword pommel into the enemy's face. He crashed away.

But the other enemy swept down on Varro faster than he expected. The wild blow clipped against the back of his helmet. His chin strap bit into this throat as the helmet shifted back, but remained on his head. Counting his luck, he slammed his shield into the overextended brute. As he collapsed with a painful bellow, Varro again turned back to the other man only to find he had fled.

He pounded the head of the prone enemy at his feet with the iron edge of his shield. Surveying the road, he found the ambushers had vanished. Most had died under the trees, but at least one bloodied corpse extended his bare legs into the road. Piso and Casca knelt beside the mule, but paid it no mind. Varro feared the worst. He stabbed the man at his feet through his kidney. He made no sound, perhaps dead already from the blow to his head. But he would not risk the fool rising and attacking once more.

Curio sat at the edge of the road while Falco fussed over his head, combing through his hair with bloodied fingers. He met Varro's eyes, then frowned and shook his head as if to confirm Curio's wounds were not serious. So he ran past them to join Piso and Casca.

The mule had taken four javelins, three on one side and a fourth on the side it collapsed on. This javelin had actually pushed through the mule's neck and popped out the other side. Their tent and packs were scattered in the road in an ever-widening pool of wine-dark mule blood. Beside the animal, Gala hissed in pain.

"How bad is it?" Varro asked as he leaned in.

Piso was wrapping Gala's calf with a brown cloth. Strips of it were piled beside him and sopping with blood.

"A javelin cut his calf, sir. It's deep. I'm not sure this will close the wound." Piso did not look up, but tightened the wrapping while Gala groaned.

"I'm sorry, sir. I didn't see them." Gala's serious face had paled and his brows shaped into an upside-down V.

"Don't apologize," Varro said. Seeing he was only in the way, he shifted to kneel beside Gala, who propped up on his elbows. "It was my job to ensure our safety. I failed you, and I'm sorry for it."

"Don't apologize." Piso snapped the statement as a harsher echo of Varro's own words. "You're our leader. Don't be sorry. Be a commander."

Again Piso did not look up from his work, but sat back on his heels and blew a puff of air into his cheeks as he studied the wound.

Casca, on the other hand, looked up under his brow at Varro.

"You never had a problem with command while in camp, Optio Varro. Why start now?"

Varro stood and glared at Casca, who dropped his gaze and returned to idly patting Gala's good leg as if he were a dog to be comforted.

"All right then, Casca. You are the scout and guide. You are responsible for scouting the enemy and you led us right into them. Should I enact some sort of punishment for you?"

"Those weren't my orders, sir."

"Then they're your orders now. And stand up when I address you. Stand!"

Primus Casca was an imposing man. His shoulders were square and broad, built up from the hard training of the Roman soldier. The deep lines around his hook nose deepened with the first quivering signs of a sneer. Despite his stature, Varro was not intimidated.

"I don't know what your problem is with me. But I'll hear it now before we go too far down this road. We've got to depend on each other until this is all done."

Casca stared at him, his eyes darting around Varro's face as if looking for an opening. But he seemed to conclude there was no gap to exploit and he stared past him.

"Sir, you had my brother march all morning around the perimeter of the camp. He just asked a question, sir. Now his feet are covered in blisters from it."

"Blisters, you say. What a fucking tragedy." Varro did not

need to imitate any of his old officers. The rage bubbled up naturally to him. "Now that you mention it, I know exactly who your brother is. And he did not ask a simple question, Casca. He complained about an order that applied to every man in the century. He dug at me to undermine my authority before the others. Much like you do. I suppose you're on this little trip with me because you've made a mess of something that Sabellius had to clean up for you. Trouble must run in your family. But trouble with me needs to end now."

"I'm sorry, sir. I forget myself." Casca's shoulders dropped and he lowered his eyes.

Expecting worse, Varro stood with his mouth open and a curse half-formed. The apology disarmed him.

"Well, see that you don't forget again. Now check the area and be sure the ones that got away aren't returning with friends. We're going to need that water more than ever now."

The blood drying on Varro's hands already felt tight and scaly. Casca saluted then headed toward the trees.

"The bleeding is not stopping," Piso said. "And he can't march on a sliced calf. The mule is dead."

"Thank you for reciting our doom," Varro said. "Now you're the experienced one. So tell me what needs to be done here."

"Send him back to camp," Piso said. "He's useless."

Gala groaned and shook his head. "I can't go back unless it's with Marcellus Paullus."

"We'll carry you close enough," Piso said. "Maybe get a local farmer to take you in a cart. They're always looking to get in good with us."

"Impossible. You can't find Paullus without me. I'm the only one who has met him."

"That's a fair point," Varro said. "You should describe him to us in case anything else happens to you along the way."

Gala turned his head aside. Piso tied up the bandages then stood beside Varro.

"He can't go with us, sir. He'll only slow us down."

"I can walk." Gala scrabbled to rise, patting the dry road around himself as if seeking a support. He struggled, castling on his good leg then using his shield to lever himself up. To his credit, he did manage to stand.

"Blood is already flowing through that bandage," Piso said. Varro saw it was true. The upper laces of his sandal were already pooling up blood. "You can't walk another ten feet."

"I don't have a choice," Gala said.

"We'll have to find a place for you to rest," Varro said. "Piso is right. You can't come with us. That wound is going to take weeks to heal and we don't have that time to waste. We'll leave you behind and pick you up on the way back."

Piso shrugged at this, and Varro thought it made sense, as Gala clearly could no longer keep pace with them.

"Where will you leave me? I'll end up a slave or worse if you leave me alone. I just escaped from the Macedonians. I don't want to go back there."

"Then go back to camp," Piso said. "We're close enough still."

Gala lowered his head and Varro sighed in frustration.

"None of us can go back without Marcellus Paullus. And Gala's right. Leaving him alone is just like killing him. We'll have to find a place to rest where there's water, game, and safety. After a week, his cut might be healed enough to resume the march. If it's not, then Gala will have to keep pace as he can."

"Thank you, sir!" For the first time, Gala's serious face broke into smile. Yet somehow it looked strained on his face, as if he only imitated something he had seen others do.

"Sir, a whole week camping within a day's march of camp? That's ridiculous."

"I didn't say we'd camp here. I said somewhere safe, which this place is clearly not. And while I'm grateful for your opinion, consider how you express it to me. Understood?"

Piso's bulging eyes widened, then his face grew dark. "Yes, sir."

"Do you know how to stitch a wound? I've been shown, but I've never done it." Piso nodded. "Then when we get to the water, you'll guide me in stitching Gala."

"Sir? I think my leg isn't bleeding anymore. Really. The bandages are working."

Yet Varro did not remain to listen to complaints from either man. He had to learn what happened to Curio and wait for Casca's report.

"How did he get his scalp cut wearing a helmet?" Varro stood over Curio, the gash in his head like a red furrow in a field of barley. Falco was wiping his hands on a cloth and rolled his eyes. Curio did not answer.

"Curio, I've asked how you got your head cut. You wore your helmet in battle."

"I had it off for the march," he said. "Looped it around my neck. The damn javelin just scratched me. It's nothing serious but bleeds a lot."

"He's lucky the bastards didn't know how to throw," Falco said. "Or that javelin would've went through his ear and out the other side."

"No doubt to less injury," Varro said. "Curio, I realize we were marching with shields stored. But you keep that helmet on while we're marching. You can take it off during breaks and when you sleep. We're still Roman soldiers out here."

"I'll remember."

Varro sighed and waited, hoping Curio would use the proper address. But his pride had been stung and his mood grew strange when it did. If alone, Varro could forgive it. But with Piso and Gala both watching he could not ignore it.

"What did you say, Curio?"

"I said I'll remember to wear my helmet. How can I forget it with the top of my head split?"

"Stand up, Curio." When he cocked his head in answer, Varro tried to beg him with his eyes to obey. But Curio seemed to misunderstand and looked to the others.

Varro seized him by his tunic and hauled him upright. He was bigger and stronger than Curio, and the smaller man flew up with a surprised shout. He shook Curio to attention.

"Address me as sir, and look at me when we are speaking. Do you understand?"

"Yes, sir," Curio nodded hard, as if he had just awakened from a dream.

They stood back from each other just as Casca returned to report a clear path to the stream.

"All right, we've got to divide up the gear from the mule and get the beast off the road. Leave the enemies where they fell as a warning to their friends. Falco, Curio, have a look over the bodies. See if you can figure out who they were."

They recovered all they could from the mule. The gods had favored them when the mule fell on her side that held the tent and poles. Rations and other more fragile gear were on its back and opposite side. The tent was stained with her blood now, but it was better than losing their rations.

Gala stumbled and fell three times during their efforts. He rebuffed any offers to help him stand. But he did not fool Varro or anyone else. His serious face was beaded with sweat even though they worked in the shade of a cool spring day. The clouds regathered, further easing any stress from heat. Yet Gala appeared as if he had marched up a mountain in full gear.

They followed Casca along a winding path through sparse trees toward the stream. Falco and Curio had recovered a handful of silver Macedonian coins, but nothing that identified their ambushers. They were either bandits or deserters, for they were not Philip's troops. Why they had attacked a heavier armed force remained unanswered. Varro realized he would never have answers to questions like this. All that mattered was Gala had been too injured to continue.

They cleaned up at the stream, ate hard bread with the wine they mixed with stream water, and rested. No one spoke except for short exchanges. Everyone knew Gala was a problem with no easy solution except to abandon him. Piso and Casca seemed agreeable to the idea. Curio and Falco would support Varro. He hated having to make the choice.

"Casca, where is our next checkpoint along the route?"

"Sir, the map is not so specific. In fact, it loses details past this point. I only know there are mountains along the route, and where a pass is shown. There is a river that this stream joins, and I would expect Philip's men stayed close to it on their march north. But where we camp ahead, I cannot say until we get there."

Varro rubbed the back of his neck and groaned. "We can't stay here, in case those ambushers bring others. They might have just been lying in wait for anyone to pass by, but they could've also known we were coming."

"That seems unlikely," Falco said. "Er, unlikely, sir."

"Our mule must've looked like a fat target to them," Varro said. "Anyway, we have to press on. Which means a few things. For one, we march with shields ready from here on. Second, Gala will describe Marcellus Paullus to us. We can't have just one man holding that key bit of knowledge."

Gala shook his head, but Falco growled at him.

"It's the optio's orders. Plus, it's not like we won't be able to figure out who the wealthy hostages are without you. So just make it easier."

"Piso, you'll help me stitch Gala's wound."

"Sir, I don't need to be stitched."

"I'll guide you, sir," Piso said, smirking at Gala. "But you wouldn't need stitches if you just went back to camp."

"Enough of that," Varro said. "Gala, it's the only way I can keep you on this mission. Which brings me to my next point. I've been thinking about this. We're all assigned to this mission for our own reasons. I'm not going to ask you why you got stuck with this task. I know you all owe Sabellius, or you need his help. This task is his price. We're going to make him a hero to the Paullus family, and he'll take care of us in return. So none of us can go back until this job is done."

He looked around the men seated in a semicircle beneath the trees. Dull light filtered down on them and birds called above. The stream behind flowed in a gentle gurgle. No one denied what he said. Falco and Curio looked to their sandals. Varro wondered what Gala had done to be so eager to please Sabellius. Of all of them, he seemed the innocent survivor who had the unfortunate luck to report having seen Marcellus Paullus. But his fear of returning empty-handed meant he too had a story.

"Since we are all committed to this, I believe each one of us will push on no matter what happens. You're not going to desert the army. You could've done that by now, and stolen the mule too. So like me, you want to remain a proud Roman soldier until your last breath. Today I was reminded that last breath could come at any time. For this mission to succeed, we need to maintain our order and discipline."

He watched the effect of his words, and felt a growing pride at the attention and acceptance he read in each of the men. For once, he felt like a real leader as the words came unbidden to him. These were words everyone needed to hear.

"As part of that order, there must be another in command if I should fall or otherwise be unable to continue. There can be no bickering among you about who is best to lead after me."

Falco leaned forward now, his smile growing. His eyes gleamed beneath his heavy brow.

But Varro swallowed hard and continued.

"Therefore, I name Julianus Piso my successor. He is experienced and can lead you after me."

His face radiated heat. He thought Piso was likely the better experienced leader overall. For his part, Piso merely inclined his head.

Falco leaned back and lost his smile. Both Casca and Gala slid their gazes to him, but neither spoke. Curio seemed to have not heard, continuing to stare sulkily at his feet.

At last, Varro stood. "Let's take care of Gala's leg now. Then we need to begin the march again."

Casca and Curio wandered off toward the stream. Falco remained seated, looking at Varro with narrowed eyes and tight lips.

Varro turned to Piso, and directed him to Gala.

Not even a full day in command, he thought, and I've made enemies of all my friends.

11

Varro washed his bloody hands in the cold stream. Red streamers flowed off his fingers and curled away on the running water. He stared at his own reflection, all fuzzy colors of bronze helmet and patches of flesh not lost in shadows. Gala's screams were still echoing through his head. He had not expected skin to be so difficult to pierce. He had used an antler needle and gut thread, thoughtfully packed along with bandages and splints by Tribune Sabellius. They had wasted half their bandages already. But at least Gala's wound was sealed and would heal faster for it.

He scrubbed the blood from the creases of his knuckles. Piso had been a competent but impatient guide. Varro had to learn to stitch men if he was going to be a leader. Every recruit was taught the basics, but for the battles Varro had fought there were always others to handle the wounded. On this mission, everyone looked to him.

He blew out a long sigh while splashing cold water on his face, then removing his helmet to cup it over his head. The others had left him alone while waiting for Gala to recover from his ordeal enough to walk. With all the gear to shoulder, no one could carry him. Casca had been fashioning a crutch while Varro did the stitching. Once that was completed, they would start out.

Hobnails crunched on dead leaves beside him. He saw Falco's reflection in the stream.

"The water is cold. It feels good."

Falco crouched beside him, removed his helmet, then doused his head. He shook his hair out, flecking Varro with cold points along his arm and shoulder. They both sat in silence until Falco replaced his helmet.

"I think the crutch is ready, sir. We should leave while there's daylight enough to get away from this place."

"You think I made a mistake?" Varro looked to Falco, who still remained looking into the stream. "It should've been you instead of Piso?"

"Or Curio. It didn't have to be me. But what do you know about Piso or these others? They're on this mission because they've fucked up like we have. At least you know why Curio and I are here. Just because Piso acts like he knows everything, doesn't make him a better choice. You've only met the guy this morning. What if he's done something really bad? He wasn't Sabellius's choice for leader, was he?"

"I've made my decision. If you don't like it, then don't let me die."

Falco snorted. "I'll probably have to keep Piso from pushing you off a cliff so he can take over."

"Please do. Now, let's get the others together. Gala will slow us down and I want to reach a place where we can rest in safety tonight."

"Running ahead without knowing where we're going," Falco said as he stood. "That's how this whole mission is shaping up."

"Keep that to yourself," Varro said, slapping Falco's arm with the back of his wrist. "It's a secret."

They gathered up the packs, tools, and posts that had been the mule's concern. With all the weight Varro was accustomed to, the extra gear did not burden him. They kept their shields ready, various colors of black, red, green, and white held in hand. Each bore the scars of battle, from long gashes to divots in the wood. They all leaned into the march with Varro at the fore. Gala hobbled along with the aid of his crutch. He shouldered the same load as anyone else, though his hair was matted with sweat from the intense stress and pain of getting his stitches.

By nightfall they reached a campsite off the main road where they set stakes and created a defensive ditch. It seemed foolish around such a small group. But none of them thought twice about it. They laughed about the pathetic size of their defenses. Yet the angry, sharp stakes and the ditch would keep away humans and large animals alike.

They travelled like this for three more days, following the road at a pace far slower than Varro wanted. Gala delayed them, but his stitches held. As Falco had noted, they were rushing ahead with no firm destination. Each day was like a forced marched with even less purpose than a drill. Yet they had still not reached the point where Sabellius indicated the northern branch of Philip's army would have passed off the roads and into mountainous territory. That would be the true test of Gala's condition. He could not imagine him navigating rocky inclines with a crutch.

Now the day was late and the mountains that had been lost behind trees or folds in the land now rose up as a blue wall against the northern horizon. They had been traveling ever uphill, following a road that would lead to a walled town they must avoid. Traffic had at last increased, with groups of travelers and their carts heading south along the road. Due to Casca's scouting ahead at intervals they thus far had avoided contact with others. But now they had to concern themselves also with traffic catching up from behind as local farmers headed into town.

They paused at the roadside. Each of them let their packs haul them backward into the tall green grass. Fields spread out on both sides of the road, and trees were too far back to be useful for ambush. They drank the wine they mixed earlier in the day. Varro felt the breeze cooling his sweat-slicked flesh.

"We must move off the road," he said. "A bit earlier than I wanted, but we can't risk someone reporting six Romans alone in the open. And one with a crutch. What do you say, Gala? Can you manage off the road?"

"The road's not much more even than the fields, sir. I'll be fine. I swear it."

"Then we'll be relying on you, Casca. Our supplies are running out, too. We might find a farm where we can resupply. There's only so much time for foraging in a day, and it's not good out here."

"There should be plenty of farms this close to a major town. I'll find us one."

Varro checked his packs. Like the others, he carried two pila, both light and heavy. These were the hardest to carry on his back, for they constantly slipped out of the bindings he tied. Usually they were carried to battle in the shield hand. He wondered what he would use them for on this mission, being that once thrown they would be useless. But having more weapons was better than not enough.

They struck out again, and Gala was good to his word in ambling along over the ground. No one complained, but Varro knew the injured man must feel the unspoken pressure of slowing their pace. Once they reached the farm, Varro planned to seek shelter there for a week to let Gala rest up before heading into the mountains. The others might complain, but if the farmers accepted them then he would enforce the delay.

The farmhouse seemed much like a Roman one to Varro, at least from the distance where Casca showed it. He and the others looked down from a sharp rise where trees dotted the ridge. Neatly cut stumps led down the slope. No one was outside. The house was low and square with a terra-cotta tile roof. Smoke floated above it, white against the darkening sky of thick clouds. Varro's mouth watered at the hint of spices. The others reacted to it as well. Falco patted his stomach.

"Maybe a juicy strip of meat for tonight's dinner. What do you think, Optio?"

"If they'll oblige us, of course. We're not here to start trouble, though. We're days deep into Macedonian territory. We're not going to be overly welcomed."

"People don't care about what their king is doing," Falco said, waving both hands to gather the weak scents to his nose and inhale them. "We'll be fine."

"Piso, you'll speak for us," Varro said. "Let's approach, carefully but not hostile."

They picked a path downslope, shields up but swords sheathed. Gala went ahead, since Varro thought his condition might make them appear less threatening. As he slipped and struggled to maintain his footing, he appeared pathetic in Varro's estimation. Hopefully the farmers would feel the same.

A dog began to bark, not a playful bark but throaty barks of warning. The wooden door shook before it opened, and a pale face hung out a moment before slamming the door again. The dog continued barking.

"Raise your sword hands," Varro said. "Piso, tell them we're here in peace."

Piso shouted something across the distance as they approached. The dog's barking grew wilder and more vicious as they approached. They reached level ground which was a maze of stumps and rocks leading to the wood fence encircling the yard. At the same time, the door opened and four men rushed out with spears and round shields. One held a dog on a chain, rather than carry a shield. The dark brown hound stood on its back legs as it pulled to be released.

"We mean no harm," Varro said, smiling and sword hand up. Piso translated.

Of the four men, two were older with iron-colored hair. One was about Varro's age and another younger still, and clearly not a man. But all were armed and frowning.

"Did you tell them we mean no harm?"

"Of course, sir." Piso barely disguised his impatience.

"Well, tell them again. They don't seem to believe us."

Piso repeated the statement, or so Varro hoped. Angry words flowed back from the farmers and the dog continued to jump and pull against his handler, one of the older men.

"They want to know what we're doing here, sir."

"We're traveling on a diplomatic mission. We only seek a place to rest and perhaps trade. We have silver to compensate you."

Varro knew offering coin was not as good as offering something of immediate value. Piso's translation drew confused looks from the farmers.

"I hope he really can speak the language." Falco whispered in Varro's ear, but Piso flinched as if he overheard.

"You have a barn," Varro said. He pointed across the field to a low stone building with a straw roof. Wide doors hung open into darkness. "We will pay you to stay there, and pay for food as well. You've nothing to fear from us."

Once Piso's translation ended, the man with the dog alone answered. Varro guessed he might be the oldest male among the farmers. He pulled the leaping dog to his side, and patted his shoulders to calm him. He frowned at Varro when he finished speaking, pointing with his bearded chin toward the mountains.

"He doesn't trust us," Piso said. "He wants us to leave."

"Ask him how many drachmae he wants for us to stay a week."

Piso raised both brows over his bulging eyes. "A week, sir? I thought we just needed a night?"

"Gala's wound needs time to heal before we climb into the mountains. His crutch will be useless there."

"He won't be healed in a week, sir."

"I'm aware. Just ask them."

Piso sighed, which in a real army unit would merit discipline. But Varro had greater concerns now. The translation resulted in a new exchange between Piso and the farmers. They then conferred with each other, and a woman hidden behind the cracked farmhouse door added her voice.

"They're arguing about how much to ask for," Piso said. "I got them to see things our way."

"Good job," Varro said. "I just hope I can pay."

He had a pouch of coins of his own. For all Sabellius's thoughtful preparations, he had not supplied them with money. Or else one of the others stole it, he thought.

After a few rounds where the door opened farther and the woman's voice grew louder, the man restraining the dog made what seemed an offer to Piso. Yet he spoke longer than it should take to name a price.

"They want three drachmae in advance. We can remain in the barn and they will share one meal a night with us, not including tonight."

"I agree with that," Varro said. He only realized how tense his neck had been when it released upon hearing this good news.

"But they still don't trust us. We have too many weapons. They want us to surrender them."

Piso's grapelike eyes fixed Varro as if in warning not to agree. This angered him more than the outrageous demand.

"You tell them a Roman solider does not disarm himself ever. And you tell them we have an injured man who needs rest. We simply want to remain in the barn and bother no one. But our swords are our own."

"Gladly, sir."

Piso's translation sounded harsh to Varro's ears. He hoped this did not cost the negotiation. The dog growled but remained steady under his master's command. The old man mumbled something to the rest, and eventually answered.

"He agrees, sir. But he wants another drachmae for it."

"Another coin will make him feel safer? Strange folk, but I'll pay."

Varro stepped forward, setting his shield down and shaking the coins into his palm. The young man among the farmers accepted the coins with a greedy smile. Varro did not like that look, but this was an ideal location for rest. So he tried not to think more on it and instead focused on setting up in the barn.

"The wonderful scent of goat," Casca said as they entered the dark barn. "I suppose they'll be herded in here with us tonight."

"As long as they don't shit on me, I'll be fine," Falco said.

They spread out in the barn, which was more spacious than their tent. Despite the rank odors and stale air, Varro was glad to have space between himself and the others. Each man dropped a pack where they intended to sleep. Without a fire, they ate the last of their cold rations of salted pork, cheese, olives, and wine. Varro would especially miss the olives once they had to rely on foraged food and game. Maybe the farmers would sell them more.

He established an order of watches for the night, with a plan for the week. They had been hard on the march for a week already and had mountains still to cross. From there, they had to reach the battle lines where Philip's army clashed with the Dardanian invaders. No one knew how long that would take. Finding an army at war should not be difficult, though he recalled how long it took for Philip to find the Romans in his own territory. He had to prepare for a long search.

The week passed with each day duller than the last. They repaired their sandals, cleaned and sharpened weapons, reinforced shields, but soon ran out of chores. They hunted small game and foraged where they could. A good catch of rabbits caused a debate with the farmers on what was owed to them. They claimed game caught on their land was their property. Varro settled the debate by handing over two of the five caught.

As Gala rested his leg, and the men grew idle, Varro had hoped to learn more of their backgrounds. But no one was willing to share stories. He thought to break this tension by sharing his own, but both Falco and Curio prevented him from revealing their crime. So he fell to silence.

After a week together hiding in the confines of the barn, it seemed their bonds were no closer than the day they had met.

The morning of their departure, Varro met the women of the farmstead for the first time. They had hidden the soldiers in their barn, not even allowing their goats or other animals to use it. The mother was squat and homely, but smiled easily and appeared to be a gentle person. Varro liked her immediately. Her husband, who had held the dog that still only tolerated them, was likewise friendly and had delivered the promised meals each night. He now came out with his young daughter to see them off. She was unlike the others, with long and full golden hair and red lips. She might have been thirteen or fourteen, a prime age for marriage. Varro thought she was pretty and would make a fine wife. The others reacted as well, surprised that such a beautiful girl could have been under their noses the entire week.

As they departed for the foothills, the family saw them off. Piso translated their well-wishes and Varro's gratitude. Once they had distanced from the farm, all the men speculated on the beautiful girl.

"She just looks pretty because we haven't seen a girl up close in so long," Falco said.

"I wonder if she cooked any of the food they sold us?" Curio asked wistfully.

"What does it matter?" Piso asked. "We had to pay for it, didn't we? It's not like she made it because she loved you."

"I paid for it." Varro slapped his coin pouch. "And I can't pay for much more. So the rest of you will have to open your pouches next time."

They were now traveling into the foothills. Long grass brushed at their knees as they marched. Gala was still loping and slow, but no longer needed his crutch. The wound had joined into a violently red line. Removing the stitches was weeks away, and Varro did not look forward to it.

They continued heading into the foothills. Casca scouted ahead at intervals while they rested, then he would rest before moving out once more. It allowed for a careful but steady pace that Gala could match.

By late afternoon, when the clouds once again mustered for rain that refused to fall, Casca sprinted back over the rise where Varro and the others reclined in the shade at the bottom of the fold. He stumbled to a halt amidst the others, directly before Varro.

"A dozen riders," he said breathlessly. "Spears, shields all. At the gallop right for us."

Varro sat up from resting on his pack. Casca leaned on his legs, blowing hard as he recovered.

"Did they see you?"

When Casca shook his head, Varro crawled up to the edge and scanned the expanse of green grass. Waves rolled across the fields with the wind. A dozen black figures on horseback raised a brown cloud that slanted hard behind them.

"They're coming right for us," Falco said. He had crawled up on his right side.

"We're not getting away from them." Varro rubbed his face,

hoping he would discover they vanished when he finished. But the horsemen still charged ahead.

"Doesn't seem like it," Falco said with flat finality. He slapped a heavy hand onto Varro's shoulder. "Well, sir, what are your orders?"

12

As Varro slid back down the grass slope, cold grass blades stroked his cheeks. He imagined the thundering hooves vibrating through the earth under his body. But the riders were still too far away, at least so he believed. Falco slid down with him, until both could stand at a crouch to rejoin the others at the trough in the steep folds of the land. They huddled in shadows that had been flattened with the dull sunlight of the late afternoon. Four sets of wide eyes seemed to glow beneath bronze helmets as the men looked to him.

"Casca, did they spot you?"

He shrugged. His hook nose broke out from the shadows filling his face. It was a bright triangle that drew Varro's attention.

"It's possible, sir. Though I kept low to the grass and removed my helmet. I eventually had to run at a crouch. My profile might've been obscured by the trees and hills leading up into the mountains. No matter since they're headed directly for us."

Varro growled and looked back over his shoulder.

"We can't outrun them even if we abandoned all our gear." He looked to Gala, who certainly could not run, and all the blood had drained from his cheeks. "What are cavalrymen doing out here? They should be with Philip's army."

"I don't know what they're doing," Casca said. "But they seem to know we're here, sir."

"The farmers reported us," Piso said. "Isn't it obvious? As soon as we traveled far enough to not disturb their farm, they sold us. You can't trust the enemy to be kind."

While Varro disagreed with this, as the farmers could've betrayed them at a more opportune time, he did not argue. He shoved his finger under his chin strap and stretched it to relieve the itch around his neck.

"We fight. There's no other choice." He looked to the others, expecting protest. Their eyes were wide and brows furrowed. Even grape-eyed Piso seemed to have lost his color. But no one protested.

"Piso, Falco, Casca, you three in front with shields up and heavy pila set. The rest of us will be behind with shields overhead. Horses won't charge into that. If we're to be cut down, we'll make them pay."

They assumed the most pathetic testudo formation Varro could imagine. Six men could either form a fighting ring or turtle up. He felt more hopeful breaking the charge with a wall of shields, and they could reform into a circle if needed.

He raised his shield, standing behind Falco, and settled it over his.

No one spoke. No one breathed. Gala alone shook, only because he favored his injured leg.

The thundering of hooves was clear now. The ground shook and gruff voices called to one another.

Falco crouched lower, setting his pilum into the hard earth. Varro pressed against his, arms holding the shield steady so that they were encased in shadow with only the gaps in their shields.

The first horse appeared above the ridge.

Varro clenched his teeth.

But the horse galloped along its length at incredible speed. Neither beast nor rider looked to the sorry block of Romans huddled in the shadowed dip below.

More horses followed the first. Each was muscular and sleek, black, brown, and gray coats gleaming with sweat. Their hoofbeats pounded against Varro's eardrums. The throaty calls of their spear-carrying riders chilled his blood. But the magnificent display of raw power blasted along the ridge and past them, sending clods of earth and dust spinning away behind them.

Through the narrow gap in shields, Varro watched their rear legs beating the earth as they vanished as swiftly as they came.

"By all the gods in Olympus," he said. "What was that about?"

He retracted his shield, and the rest stood up to watch the riders fly along the rise into the distance.

"It's a steep drop," Casca said. "Maybe they did not want to charge into a ditch and risk breaking a horse's leg."

"They could've dismounted and still had advantage," Varro said. "It's as if they didn't see us. But how could that be?"

While they stood in a shadowed depression, he expected their bright shields and the gleam of bronze armor to betray them.

"They are moving fast," Falco said. "Maybe they just didn't have time to see us."

"If that's true, then they'll be returning again." Varro spun around and looked to the mountains. "We need to get up there to be safe."

"Sir, the pass is still several miles away." Casca pointed vaguely to the east. "These are high and rocky hills. We'll make slow progress."

Varro hefted his pack and looked to the others.

"And we'll make no progress if a dozen cavalrymen trample us into the ground. There must be some passage through the mountain that will hide us while we head to the pass. It will be guarded in any case. Have you thought of that much?"

Casca lowered his head to indicate he hadn't. Even Piso put his hand to the back of his head and looked away.

"So there is the difficulty," Varro said. "One way or the other, we need to gain the pass by first climbing into the mountains. Philip's men will have a sizable rear guard. This patrol, or whatever it was, has warned us that we're not too far off from danger. We need to get into the mountains and find our own way through. That's why you're with us, Casca."

Varro smiled without humor. Casca grimaced. Yet all of them shouldered their packs and hurried up the slope and toward the mountains.

They moved slowly with heads tucked into their shoulders and searching all around, expecting the mounted men to return. Yet they had vanished. Varro wondered if they had even been real and not ghosts of long-dead soldiers doomed to forever haunt these fields. Who could say what happened in this place long ago? The thought made him shiver.

Drizzle began to dust across their marching column. Falco groaned and cursed. "The sky has been begging to rain for a week and now it's going to start once we travel again?"

"When the gods gift a boon," Curio said. "They wrap it in misfortune. That's what my father often said."

"You had a father?" Falco mimicked touching his cheeks in surprise. "Really? I thought you sprang from the earth. First time I've heard of family from you."

"Keep it down," Varro said, anticipating Curio's anger. "You don't know what's near."

"Maybe Curio's father," Falco muttered.

A ripple of laughter ran along the column. Even Varro smiled.

Their initial climb into the mountains went smoothly. Casca had found a shallow grade with few trees or stones to impede them. They were hidden from the plains, relieving fears of the riders catching them again before reaching the mountains. Yet soon their easy path ended in walls of jagged brown rock. The misfortune that had wrapped the boon of the easy approach, Varro thought with a wry smile.

Casca led them, often doubling back to report no way forward. These mountains were steep and rocky. Torturously shaped trees and rough, dull green bushes twisted their roots into the brown sand. The drizzle continued, accumulating on Varro's helmet and rolling onto his face. The shoulders of his tunic had absorbed enough to feel wet.

"We're going to have to find a place for the night," he said. "Let's focus on that while we have sunlight."

Higher up the mountain seemed to offer no hope, and returning down the slope would expose them to view from the plain. So they cut lengthwise, climbing gradually higher until Casca reported the discovery of a suitable location.

"It's just ahead, with a good flat ledge and surrounding walls. It might've been a campsite before. It can hold us."

Varro smiled but it died as Casca did not join him.

"But there's a short climb, sir. I can make it without my pack. I'm not sure how everyone else will do."

Resisting any urge to look at Gala, Varro waved Casca ahead. "We can hoist the gear up along with anyone who can't make it alone. We're a team, right?"

"Yes, sir," Casca answered in a tone suggesting they were anything but a team.

He led all of them to the base of the ledge. Varro looked up, the cold drizzle falling from a sky of black clouds. The ledge itself was twice his own height, but could be reached by standing on rocks. Casca set his pack down and demonstrated the climb.

"You make it look easy," Gala said. His serious face creased with worry.

"Then you come up first," Casca said, crouching at the edge of the ledge. "I'll grab you and the others can help you up."

"But how will I get down again?"

"We'll throw you off," Casca said with a laugh. But serious-minded Gala simply looked to his injured calf.

"Enough of that," Varro said. "I'll help steady you on the rock and Casca will haul you up. We'll get this gear up next. Come on, now."

The process went smoother than Casca had made it seem it would. With assistance, Gala had no issues reaching the ledge. The rest then handed up their packs before making the climbs themselves. Varro dusted his palms against his thighs as he surveyed their home for the night.

The ledge was set into two walls of brown stone. A third wall was beyond a short gap large enough to fit one person in it. No danger could approach them from that side, leaving only the climbing side open. While the stone would not easily accept a tent and stakes, they would have shelter from rock overhands higher up. Even the drizzle began to slow.

"Not a bad spot," Falco said. "But what if I have to shit in the middle of the night? Can I use your helmet, Curio?"

"Use your own. It's normally filled with shit anyway."

Falco gave a playful shove to Curio and the others laughed. Casca, who always enjoyed a good insult, stood at the narrow gap between the ledge and the rock wall.

"Just piss into this gap, it's deep enough."

He leaned forward to look down.

Then vanished.

Varro blinked trying to understand what he had seen. It seemed Casca had stepped into the rock wall across the gap. Nor was he alone in the surprise. Gala and Falco both straightened up and stared at the same spot. Piso stared with his mouth open. Only Curio had his back turned, and was searching his pack when he realized everyone else was dumbfounded. He looked over his shoulder.

"What happened?"

"Casca vanished," Gala said, his voice quivering. "Spirits swept him away."

"Gods," Varro said, rushing forward. "He fell off the ledge."

He dared not stand on that ledge, but he clearly saw where the rock had broken and sent Casca plunging silently into the gap.

"It happened so fast," Falco said in astonishment. "I thought he vanished."

They crept forward, but Varro barred them with his arm. "It's not safe. Let me look over."

"Why?" Falco asked. "So that Piso can become the leader sooner? Curio's the lightest. Let him look. Ah, I mean, I suggest Curio, sir."

Curio did not complain, but gingerly stepped to the edge and leaned forward yet extended a leg as if to leap back.

"He's there, stuck halfway down." Curio cupped his mouth and called Casca's name. No answer came.

"He died?" Piso's bulging eyes widened as he pointed into the gap. "Just like that?"

Varro growled and rubbed his face. He wished he could have been anywhere else now. If Piso was leader, he could just do whatever he was told. But he shook his head and pulled Curio back by the hem of his tunic.

"He probably hit his head and is knocked out. But who knows? In any case, we're not leaving him trapped between the rocks."

"But he might be dead," Piso said. "And how are we getting him out?"

"I'll remind you a last time before I throw you in after Casca. You address me as your leader." He pulled Piso around to face him. The older man scowled, but Varro did not care. "If you were trapped in those rocks, you'd think differently, wouldn't you? So we're going to get him out, even if he is dead."

He shoved Piso back and dismissed him from his thoughts. Carefully shifting to the ledge, he looked over into its shadows. Night was fast approaching and the dark clouds did not aid visibility. Yet Casca's head and wide shoulders were clear in the shadows. The gap narrowed halfway down where both walls bulged out, and Casca was wedged in between. His helmet was gone and his head hung to the side. No signs of blood, but then Varro could not see clearly.

"I'll get him out of there," he said. "I expect it'll be easier to hoist him back to the ledge. Do we have rope?"

"We have a coil of rope," Gala said, limping to his pack. "It's not all that long, but its strong twine."

"I'll go down to fit the rope around him," Varro said. "Then the rest of you haul him back up."

Varro stripped down to his tunic, setting his gear with his pack. He only kept his pugio in case he should need it as a tool. Falco stuck close to him, leaning in to whisper.

"What if he's dead? Then who's going to lead us through the mountains?"

"I will," Varro said. He had no idea why he spoke with such confidence, but only knew it was necessary. Falco stepped back with a frown.

"Since when did you learn to navigate mountains?"

"Since it became necessary, that's when. Now, I'm going down into that gap."

"Shouldn't Curio do it? He's smaller."

"He'll fit into the crack better but will he be tall enough? Either you or I should do it. I don't trust Piso to make a fair assessment of Casca's condition."

Falco narrowed his eyes and smirked. "Yet he's your second."

Varro clambered down off the ledge. This was rougher than

climbing up, since he had a short drop to the rock that if poorly done could roll his ankle or worse. But he made it, then circled around the ledge in shadow. The drizzle had slowed, but it was like cold sweat gathering on his skin. The oncoming night ushered in cool air that was worse in the darkness of the crevice.

He slipped into it easily enough. It was wider at both the base and the top than in the middle, as Casca had disastrously discovered. He discovered Casca's helmet, which was now dented from the landing among the rocks at the bottom. Something fled at his arrival, a small animal whose claws scratched on stone. The sudden noise gave him pause, imagining something worse than a squirrel or whatever vermin made a home in the mountain foothills.

Looking up, he saw Casca's dangling feet. His hobnails caught the vestiges of light reaching into the crevice. Behind him the sky showed as a violent crack of light gray. As Varro stared up, no drizzle reached him this far down. Yet something wet struck his cheek beneath his left eye. He flinched back, touching it with his finger. It was thick blood.

"How does he look?" Falco called down, his voice echoing off the brown stone walls.

"He's bleeding," Varro called back. "But I'm not convinced he's dead. He's too high to reach, but I might find a way yet. Start lowering the rope."

He essayed what seemed two promising footholds. In the first case, the rock wall flaked off and sent him sliding to the bottom. The sound of it drew calls from the others above, which he answered. The second foothold allowed him to climb higher but still out of reach. He dropped back down. The rope was now lowered, dangling beside Casca as if teasing him.

"There's space enough for me to get up beside him," Varro said. "But I can't climb higher."

"Can you pile up some rocks?" Falco asked.

Varro heard Piso's derisive laughter and it drew his lip into a snarl.

"Not that high." Varro stood at the bottom, both hands on his hips. The rock walls were so close together the he struggled to turn around.

Then it occurred to him that if he could reach the narrowed gap, he could brace himself against the back wall. The idea might have been plain to anyone with more experience. But to him it was a revelation.

"I think I know what to do," he called up.

Returning to what he had considered an unpromising section of wall, he now climbed back up. The wall gently bulged out, and this had defeated Varro last time. But now he set his feet against the barest ledges. The hobnails on his soles aided in the grip. He reached across the narrowed gap and found he could brace himself on that wall. He jumped himself up, crawling up the wall with his feet while his back pressed to the rear wall. The cold and rough stone supported his back, and he was able to bring himself into the narrow gap. From there he drew level to Casca's waist. With some searching, Varro found a way through the gap to draw up enough to reach his torso.

"I can do it! Hold on, I'm going to tie him."

Casca was pinched between two rocks at the chest, having fallen into the narrowest point between the two stone walls. His bronze pectoral had been driven up under his chin. Blood ran from the corner of his mouth. His eyes were closed and surrounded by dark circles. His limbs hung limp and his head lolled.

Varro pushed with his legs against the back wall, and when he felt safe enough, he tied Casca under both arms. He tested the rope, then shouted up.

"He's ready. Just be careful you don't hurt him more."

Falco made a sarcastic reply Varro could not here. He helped dislodge Casca after the first few pulls did not succeed. Yet soon he was slowly rising over Varro's head. He smiled and wiped the grit and cold sweat out of his eyes. Casca rose higher and higher, until he was at the edge.

Then Varro fell.

He landed hard on his hip, sending bright and searing pain through his side and down his left leg. The world went white. But he had not fallen too far.

"Are you all right?" Falco called down.

Varro checked himself. "I think so. Just slipped a distance."

His hand did not come away with blood. So he stood up, wincing as he did. He had actually landed on Casca's helmet, which he picked up. His hip would hurt for a while, but he had not broken bones.

"How's Casca?" He looked back up expectantly. But no one answered. Perhaps they had not heard him or just were busy tending Casca.

He slid out from the crevice, back into the gathering twilight. Mounting the ledge was now harder for his exertions in the crevice. His arms quivered with the effort of scrabbling back onto the ledge.

Four men stood over Casca, who remained tied under arm, a long coil of rope trailing out from beneath him. From their wilted postures, Varro recognized the bad news.

He rushed to Casca's side. He appeared as Varro had seen him before. But now under the brighter sky with the thin veil of drizzle coating him, the waxy pallor of death was unmistakable.

"Must have crushed his guts," Falco said. "Poor bastard didn't even make a sound."

Varro touched Casca's neck for a pulse and found none.

He lowered his head in mourning for the first man to die under his leadership.

13

The next morning Varro awakened to the sound of distant thunder. His eyes flicked open into what he had first mistaken as night. Yet a vague light suffused the ledge where they had camped, telling him morning had arrived. He sat up beneath the makeshift tent shielding them. His hip throbbed from falling the day before. But his eyes shifted to the covered body laid out by the ledge. Far better to have suffered a bruised hip than Casca's fate.

The other four men were wrapped in their blankets. Curio left no more than a tuft of hair showing. Piso and Gala both snored. Falco stirred at Varro's side, angrily pulling his blanket over his face.

Let them sleep, he thought. There is a whole day of fighting the mountains ahead.

He crawled out from beneath the lean-to they had erected. Surprisingly the posts had stood the night wedged into cracks and supported with rocks. Constructing shelter might have been a task for Casca, but they had managed on their own. Varro admired the work, but felt the pull of the corpse behind him. At last he turned, then approached the covered body.

Crouching beside it, he set his hands on the cold cloth pinned down with rocks. The gusts of wind set the edges of it flapping. Of all the deaths Varro had witnessed since joining the legion, Casca's was the most shocking. Death swept him away in an instant, with no warning and no chance for a final word.

"Don't let it bother you."

Falco squatted beside him, still wrapped in his blanket against the wind. His eyes were puffy with sleep.

"But he died under my command."

"He fell off a ledge. It's not like you ordered him to do it. All men die. Nothing special in it, really. Don't take this accident on yourself. Save the grief for when you really have to order a man to do something that'll get him killed."

"I suppose you're right." Varro patted the cold fabric. "But I still feel badly."

They stared at the shrouded corpse in silence, only the crisp wind blowing grit over the stone made any sound. The air smelled of the earthy promise of rain.

"Is this worth it? I mean, who is Marcellus Paullus, after all? Why is his life more valuable than ours? It doesn't seem fair." Varro stood up, wincing at the pain in his hip as he did. "Whatever wrong Casca did to get assigned this task, it couldn't have been as bad as what we did. But he died for it, and I am fine. It seems our fates should be reversed."

"She was a slave, Varro. Besides, isn't rescuing Marcellus Paullus your atonement? Won't you feel better when he is safe from the dangers of war?"

"I suppose I will. I can't think of what else to do for that poor girl. I'm lucky her ghost does not haunt me." Varro scratched his head and stared up into the increasing glare of the new day. "A storm is coming. We need to make progress before it halts us."

"What about Casca?" Falco pulled his blanket tight against the wind, and he nodded at the corpse.

"I've recovered the map and Sabellius's letter. We'll divide his pack and gear. Then we'll cover him with stones. We can't dig deep enough in this earth to bury him. I wish we could do more."

"And yesterday you were telling me you could lead us through the mountains?"

"I did say that, and I intend to do so. We'll have to trust to our luck once again. The pass is east of here, and we'll just have to try to gain it directly. Maybe we'll sneak in under the cover of night. Maybe this storm will blind the enemy to our presence. But we must go forward, through these mountains and north. The Macedonians are up there somewhere, shoving their pikes at the Dardanians. I only hope Paullus is still with them. Or Casca died for nothing."

Varro awakened the others. They were sluggish and slow, and Varro had to dig into his memories of Tertius and Latro to find the correct curses to motivate them. Before they set out, they gathered rocks to the ledge and covered Casca's corpse. Varro figured he should rest close to where he died and that animals would be less likely to disturb him on the ledge. They propped his helmet where his head lay beneath the rock.

No one challenged Varro's leadership even though he knew no more than anyone else about the mountains. Gala hobbled along with his injured leg. Piso remained darkly silent. Perhaps he and Casca were closer than Varro understood. Yet no one in this group outside of Curio and Falco appeared to have any affinity for each other. More than anything, the increasing grumble of distant thunder and the blowing wind stifled everyone's mood for talk. They plodded on in silence, a thin line of men crossing against the unforgiving mountains in their path.

Midafternoon darkness drew upon them with the blanket of low and thick clouds. Every head turned skyward as Varro picked an increasingly crooked and arduous path across the mountains. The smell of rain could have choked him. But he lowered his head and pressed on.

When the wind began to buffet them against the boulders and ridges along their path, Varro knew they had to find shelter.

"This is going to be a storm to remember," he said. The wind now gusted in bursts strong enough to shove his feet back and dissipate his voice. He tried to laugh about it, but no one else joined him.

Ever-serious Gala covered his eyes against the wind.

"Sir, storms like these can kill a man in the open. What if Jupiter should see us and hit us with a lightning bolt?"

"You're not that lucky," Falco said. "Jupiter doesn't care about you. But Favonius might just blow the wind hard enough to push you off a mountain."

Falco laughed but the joke was too close to Casca's real death for anyone to join him. Varro wished Casca were here now. He had to lead them out of harm's way but had no practical experience, just bits of folk wisdom like everyone else.

"We shouldn't camp on the foothills," Varro said. "If there is much rain, and it seems there will be, we could be flooded. Plus we are in the open for the wind gods to do what they will with us. We should climb higher and look for shelter against the weather."

"Should've done that a while ago, sir." Piso marched at the middle of the column. His voice was thin behind the roaring gusts, but aggravated Varro nonetheless.

"Gods blast you, Piso. I've told you to offer your opinions. If you think we're in danger, then say something. You know, we're all on this mission together. Don't act like my failure won't have anything to do with you. Because if I lead us off a fucking cliff, we're all falling together."

While Piso mumbled an apology, Varro hid his heated face from the others by studying a path up into the rocks. It seemed a rough climb, but one they best start before the clouds unleashed torrents upon them.

With the added weight of Casca's share in their already full packs, each man pulled himself into the rocky path. Varro had ordered them to secure their shields in their travel bags. Both hands were needed to navigate the narrow confines of the twisting path.

Fat drops of rain struck Varro's helmet, chiming like a bell on his head. The hollow echoes repeated for everyone's helmets. He hoped the worst of the rain would hold off while they climbed. Yet once he had led them deeper into the winding paths and rocky passages of the foothills, the storm arrived.

A blast of lightning as brilliant as the sun announced the storm. A deafening peal of thunder followed on it, shaking the ground and causing Varro to fall flat. Rain pelted him like stones from a sling, popping against his bronze armor. When he recovered, he looked across his shoulder and expected the others to be smirking at him. But all of them had thrown themselves down as he had.

"I take back what I said," Falco shouted over the wind and the pelting rain. "Maybe Jupiter has noticed us."

"We need to keep climbing," Varro said. "I think there is a place ahead where we can get beneath a ledge."

Though it was only late afternoon, the sky had darkened as if twilight had arrived. It felt unnatural and oppressive, as if the black clouds above were pressing Varro ahead. Yet through this rain and wind, he was certain a lengthwise crack higher in a rock wall ahead offered shelter. There seemed a natural path to reach it as well.

Clumps of pines and tall bushes filled the path ahead, all leaning with the wind and turning their leaves silver. The rain sheeted on them, blinding Varro and causing him to slip on loose mud and stone. Gala fell and cursed, but Curio helped him stand again. Varro continued forward, mad to reach the slope that would gain them that precious crevice in the rocks.

He shouted encouragement and waited for the others to catch up. From this vantage, he could see a much wider area where they might stand upright. It seemed the gods would grant him another favor. For the angle of the rain did not seem to reach under the rock.

"We'll have space for a fire," he said, smiling. The others shared his smile at the expectation of shelter.

He had taken too long to seek a place, he decided. He hated that Piso was right, and it confirmed for him that he might be the better leader after all. As he waited for the others to plod and slip their muddy paths through blasts of wind and rain, he resolved to plan ahead. After he passed this storm, his next order would be to collect fresh rainwater, then see about catching small game. Once they got into the pass, they would have to move as swiftly as possible to avoid an encounter with enemies. Then beyond the mountains, he would only have to ask locals where the battles were taking place. It was a simple plan, but thus far he had not thought beyond the next campsite.

Falco was the first to gather to him. Water flooded down his helmet into his face. He noticed Falco had removed the helmet feathers. In another circumstance he might say something about it. But not now with gusting wind blowing stinging rain into their faces. Gala arrived with Curio holding him up. A splash of red showed at Gala's leg. Piso was the last to join.

"It's up this ramp," Varro said. "I saw a ledge with a high roof and wide shelf. It will be a perfect spot to wait out this storm."

He started up the natural ramp. Water washed over his feet and wind gusts pushed him against the wall to his right. But he pressed ahead until reaching the corner where the path turned into the ledge. He paused to check everyone behind him. Falco struggled under his heavy pack. Piso loomed behind with Gala and Curio struggling together at the rear.

Varro rounded the corner and entered the safety of the covered ledge. He sighed with relief as the rain cut off. The gusting winds still blew through the ledge, whistling in the narrowed space. But as he had guessed, he could stand and the ledge provided ample space for all of them. Judging from the mud and debris here, he guessed others had used this place for a campsite before.

"See? A perfect site," Varro said, spreading his arms to indicate the breadth of the area. "The ledge is deep and the roof high. I must say, I've done well to find this place."

"Congratulate yourself after the storm," Falco said, stepping past him to admire their temporary home. "But it's dry enough. Wide but not too deep, though. If the wind changes direction we'll still get wet."

"Don't be so jealous of me," Varro said, slapping Falco's back as he stepped past.

He stood at the corner to meet the others as if he were welcoming them to his new house. Piso ducked in, rainwater sloshing off his feet. Curio and Gala arrived next, and Varro ushered both into the shelter of the ledge.

"It's dark back here," Falco said. He now crouched to look into the narrowing recess at the rear of the ledge. All was shadow, but one point appeared darker than the rest.

"Do you smell something?" Curio asked, pausing at the edge of the ramp. He released Gala to hop on his own into the interior.

"Nothing," Varro said, sniffing. "Just the mud and cold air."

Curio shook his head. "No, something rank. Like—"

"A bear!"

Falco screamed in terror as he leaped away from the rear of the shelf. A throaty, deep roar boomed from the darkness that plucked the bones of Varro's spine with terror.

In the next instant, a black shape stumbled out of the shadows into their midst.

Piso whirled around, having been staring out over the ledge.

The black shape rose up, unfolding into the unmistakable outlines of a bear. Its snout revealed glistening yellow fangs. Its thick paws raised overhead, wicked black claws extended. A flash of lightning lit the beast in jagged, silver slashes.

With a single swat, the bear sent Piso flying off the ledge with a horrified scream. It remained on its hind legs, its head touching the stone ceiling. It let out another ghastly roar and turned to Varro.

He dropped his pack and pulled out his heavy pilum. Curio and Gala wrestled with their packs for the same purpose.

In that instant, the bear charged at them.

Gala vanished into the mighty beast's arms. He screamed and struggled, but in the time Varro took to ready his pilum, Gala was already a bloody pile at the bear's feet.

Yet rather than charge Varro, the bear roared again and flailed around at Falco.

A heavy pilum hung out of the bear's back, and red blood streaked down its gleaming coat to splatter on the stone. Falco vanished behind its upright bulk.

"Kill it!" Varro shouted as he charged forward, using his pilum like a spear. Curio followed at his side.

They both struck the beast in the back. Varro felt the iron tip slip beneath the monstrous creature's shoulder blade. A pilum was designed for a single throw, and to bend on impact to deny the enemy a chance to throw it back. So the shaft bent as Varro leaned into it, and he released it to draw his gladius. To fight so close to the bear would be his death. But he had no other weapon.

Curio too had found his mark, and rather than back away he shoved harder on his pilum. It squelched into the bear's flesh, pushing out blood and drawing a murderous cry from it.

The bear swept around at the new threat, forgetting Falco.

Its massive paw collided with Curio's shoulder and sent him crashing against the wall to bounce off and land beneath the bear.

Varro saw its fangs flash and paws rise. The bear was going to demolish Curio.

He ducked under the impending blow and punched up with his gladius. The short blade, sharpened to split a blade of grass in a single stroke, tore through the bear's rough hide. It plunged between ribs and deep into flesh.

Yet the monster continued to fall upon both Varro and Curio.

The rank, bloody fur crushed Varro against Curio, who groaned with the impact. The mass of the beast radiated foul heat. He saw nothing but black fur. He heard nothing but the grumblings from the bear's chest. He felt nothing but its weight and the steaming flow of blood rushing over him.

Something pawed at his leg. He felt the beast shudder, then roar again. This close it sounded louder than thunder. But he heard its gurgling wheezes as it died, along with the muffled shouts of Falco's victory. He could not believe he had survived, and hoped Curio had.

"Are you alive?"

The answer was indistinct from beneath him, but he felt Curio move. Varro twisted his face to keep the black fur out of his nose and mouth. He tried to shove against its weight, but had no success until Falco joined from above. Together, they levered the beast aside.

The air was instantly colder on Varro's face, but ruined with the odor of blood and entrails.

Falco's heavy brow was drawn down as he hovered over him.

"You're alive! You saved my life, you little bastard."

"I did?" Varro accepted Falco's outstretched arm. "But what of Curio?"

He peeled away and flopped beside the black bear. Now that it was slain, three pila and at least Varro's gladius buried in its body, it seemed to have shrunk in size. Steaming blood pooled beneath Varro, causing him to flinch away.

Falco was already turning over Curio.

"I'm alive," he said, though weak and coughing. "But I think my arm is broken."

"I'll accept that," Falco said as he examined Curio's body. "Let's hope that's all you suffered. It bounced you off the rock wall like a child's leather ball. How about you, Optio?"

Varro blinked, touching his face and running his hands over both arms.

"Not even a scratch, I think."

The wind whistled across the ledge, brining rain to fleck cold and hard against Varro's exposed flesh. He stared at the scene before him as if it were not his own eyes seeing it. Numbness clung to him like a sodden cloak.

Falco inventoried Curio's wounds as he lay flat beside the black lump of a dead bear. Lightning flashed to light up the sheets of rain beyond the ledge where Piso had been knocked away. Gala lay slumped where he had fallen. No one had to examine his wounds. His head was twisted at an unnatural angle, flesh all turned ugly blue, and his guts hung out of his stomach.

Falco seemed satisfied Curio had nothing worse than a broken arm. He offered to hoist him up, then discovered another wound.

Curio screamed and collapsed against Falco, holding his left leg.

"Gods! I think it's broken too. No, I can't stand on it! Put me down."

At last Varro recovered his wits. His rubbed the hideous stench of bear from his nose, then joined Falco who had rolled back Curio's tunic to study his left thigh.

"I don't see any lumps," he said. "Not even a bruise."

"I know what I feel," Curio said. "It's broken. My whole left side is ruined, arm and leg."

"Do you think Piso survived?" Varro asked as he shifted to look toward the edge. He had to look past the corpse of the bear that had done them so much evil.

"It's a fair drop," Falco said. "And the bear hit him at the throat. I don't think so."

"Still, maybe he's still alive. I can't let him stay out in the rain if he is."

Falco gave a slow nod as if indulging a child's story. But Varro picked up his light pilum and stepped back out into the rain.

The ramp down was like a stream now with the rainwater rushing down it. As he had expected, the bottom of the ramp was flooded up to his ankles. He stepped carefully into the clearing where rain pounded the rocky earth with the fury of the gods.

When he did not find Piso below the ridge, he guessed he might have crawled away into a corner. But the punishing rain made searching the area impossible. Besides, Piso could not have crawled far and was nowhere within reach of where he should have landed.

"Is he alive?"

Falco's voice was weak against the noise of the storm as he called down from the ledge above.

When Varro looked up to answer, he at last discovered Piso.

He had crashed into one of the pine trees dotting the floor of the area. He hung upside down in its branches like a discarded toy. A steady stream of blood mixed with the rainwater flowed off of him. Varro could not stare long, for most of Piso's face was torn away.

"Looks like you're second in command now, Falco."

14

Varro sat clutching his knees to his chin, staring out across the ledge at the glare of a new day. He inhaled the smell of rain, preferring it to the horrid odors of death permeating the space under the ledge. Once the wind had stopped during the night, scents of blood and entrails had become overwhelming. He followed the water dripping across the bright gap. Beyond the ledge birds sang and runoff dripped through branches below. Falco was awake behind him, shuffling through their gear.

The storm had sealed them into this space. After discovering Piso in the tree, Varro had to flee back to the ledge from the fury of the storm. It did seem as if Jupiter would spear him with a lightning bolt had he remained outside. Along with Falco and Curio, he huddled in the death-shrouded ledge all night.

Curio awakened with a groan. Varro continued to stare at the brightening sky. A hawk skimmed and circled above the treetops level with the ledge. The bird seemed to enjoy the simple pleasure of gliding on the air, and Varro envied its freedom.

"My leg is throbbing," Curio said.

"Well, I braced it as best as I could," Falco said. Even without looking, Varro could see the frown on his friend's face.

"I didn't say it wasn't braced properly," Curio said with strained patience. "It's just painful. Like everything. My whole body is in pain. I think the bear broke everything. I can't move."

"You feel like that waking up after a hard blow like the one you took." Falco dragged something heavy that scraped over the gritty stone floor. "Maybe sit up and get some food. Warm up and some of the soreness will go away."

"I just said I can't move."

Their argument faded away as Varro considered all that had befallen them. This was squarely his fault. If Casca been alive to guide them, he would have recognized the signs of a bear's lair. There were scratches on the stone floor, bones of animals strewn about, and an unmistakable animal spoor. Casca would have checked for caves or other dangers before guiding anyone to this place. But Varro himself had blindly stumbled into the bear, frightening it as badly as it had frightened them, but to devastating results.

"Er, Optio, I'm talking to you."

Varro shook out of his thoughts, realizing that Falco stood beside him. When Varro simply stared up, Falco rolled his head on his shoulders then sat beside him.

"I've divided the packs best I can. We don't need half this stuff anymore. Rations are good now, though Piso lost his over the ledge. Anyway, Curio is patched up for now."

"Thank you. I just, I guess, I just…"

"Don't blame yourself again. I was the fool who looked into that cave. It smelled like an animal. I should've known better than to try to look inside. I'm the guilty one."

Varro did not have an answer for it. Instead, he watched the hawk spiral down until it skimmed the tops of the pines below.

"Curio's banged up bad," Falco said, leaning in and lowering his voice. "I set his arm. I can see that break. But I don't know what's going on with his leg. Worse yet he's bruised all over. He might be a lot worse than he seems. It was one fucking swipe, but the bear just wrecked him. If you hadn't got him with your sword, Curio would be dead. Me too probably."

"And me shortly after. But we all got the bear. It took three pila and two lucky sword strikes to bring it down. This wasn't any single person's victory."

"It's a sorry waste to leave all the fur and meat to rot. We might take some bear meat for tonight, but that's it."

They sat in silence. Varro now tuned his ears to Curio's movements, wincing with every groan he made. Falco looked over his shoulder.

"It's over, Varro. We'll be lucky to make it back to camp. But Curio's not getting better in a hurry and we can't live here forever. Probably can't live here another day. How much game and forage is there around here? Is there even water nearby? So we've got to go back."

"We're not going back." He spoke softly, watching the hawk wheel once more toward the ever-brightening sky. "Not until Marcellus Paullus is with us."

Falco snorted and lowered his head. "Forget about that. It's just the two of us now. Curio is a liability. You want to carry him along while we break Paullus out of captivity? We're not legendary heroes. We're two fools from the countryside. There's only so much we can do."

"You'll note some of the things Sabellius did not tell us before we left." Varro at last turned to Falco, a bitter smile on his face. "He did not instruct us to return after a certain number of us died. He didn't say it because it doesn't need saying. Returning in failure is to return to our deaths."

"He's not going to kill us because we failed to bring back Paullus."

"But he's not going to help us if Consul Villius decides to. Or if Centurion Fidelis decides to handle us. You think Villius will not name us deserters upon returning? Falco, you're more practical than that. Where have we been in others' eyes? They'll say we deserted and that we were recaptured."

"Then let's make it so."

Varro leaned back, unsure of what he had just heard.

"Let's desert," Falco said. "We can't reach Paullus and we can't go back. So let's do what Gallio did. Let's join the enemy. They'll take us and probably won't kill us for it."

"That's not funny, Falco. Don't repeat such garbage."

"It's not a joke." Falco shifted to face Varro. He narrowed his eyes and curled his lip. "We are dead in either circumstance, going back or moving ahead. So let's act for ourselves, preserve our own lives. Right now, we're not soldiers anymore."

"We are Roman citizens," Falco said through gritted teeth. "And it is an honor to serve in the legions. We are soldiers, and I am your optio. So you will not speak of desertion again. Do you understand?"

Falco laughed. "Optio? Of what, me? Oh, and half-dead Curio?"

His shout echoed around the rock confines of the ledge.

"I'm not dead." Curio's voice was small, perhaps frightened.

"Well, we'll all be dead if Optio Varro has his way." Falco stood up and kicked a rock off the ledge. "He won't go back without Paullus. Well, I'm not going to be part of that stupidity. We might as well fetch him out of Pluto's hands. We probably have a better chance than trying to find him in the north."

Varro stood now, but rather than match Falco's rage he sought calm. He raised both hands for peace.

"It is a hard mission. Curio is badly wounded. But there's still half of us left, and I dare say the best half."

"Come on." Falco turned his head aside. "Don't try to talk like a fucking politician. It doesn't suit you."

"All right. But what I said is true. Half of us are alive and we are capable men. We found Gallio and brought him back when no one thought we could."

"The man who knows what Paullus looks like is dead. The man who can lead us through the wilderness is dead. The man who can talk to anyone in this fucking country is dead. Are you seeing the trend?"

Falco had pounded the word "dead" hard enough to test Varro's resolve to remain calm. But he bit his lip and nodded in silence until he felt able to reply.

"We have challenges ahead. But we have as many behind us. I know you want to tell me that ahead lies death. Maybe it does. We can't know for sure, can we? You cannot look into the future and tell me our deaths are waiting in the north, can you?"

"Balls, Varro! It doesn't take a prophet to see what's coming."

"It does take a prophet, and you're not one." Varro stepped closer and dared to put his hand on Falco's shoulder. "So we don't know what is ahead. But we are certain death waits behind us. We cannot go back, as that is to choose death. But to go forward is to choose life."

"That's ridiculous." He shoved Varro's hand from his shoulder.

"It's to choose a chance at life," Varro said, louder than he wanted. "A chance is all we have. So we must take it. Your choice will lead to death, either in our camp or Philip's camp when we try to desert. You might recall some reasons why that would be."

He did not want to state aloud their encounter with King Philip in the marsh last winter and the theft of his rings. Even with death so close, he did not want Curio to know about it.

Falco seemed about to protest, but then lowered his eyes.

"Philip is in the south. But I get what you mean."

"All right, then go with me. I can't do it alone. All three of us will have to finish this."

"I can't move," Curio said. "Are you really going to carry me?"

"Yes," Varro said. Falco and Curio both looked up with brows raised. "We'll carry you back to the farmhouse where we rested Gala's leg."

"They sent horsemen after us," Curio said. "They'll kill us if we go back."

"No, I don't believe it. Those horsemen could've been riding for any reason. If that family wanted to turn us over to the enemy, they'd have done it in the night. Half the time Piso was on guard duty I discovered he had fallen asleep. We were vulnerable the whole night long, but they never molested us. They were good to their word. I believe we can trust them."

He searched their expressions, finding a mix of hope and fear in both. Rather than press them, each had to agree to the plan on his own. Division on any point would lead to disaster given their small numbers. So he held his breath. Curio was the first to relent, lying back and balling the fist of his one good arm.

"It feels like such a risk. But there is no other realistic choice. I'll join you."

"I was hoping you'd disagree," Falco said, folding his arms. "But now I'm outvoted anyway."

"You can suggest something else," Varro said, trying to sound open when he really wanted to close the debate.

Falco waved his hands. "It's just one shitty choice out of more shitty choices. I'll go along. But I'm warning you, Curio. You sided with the optio on this one. If the farmers attack, you'll deal with it."

"Don't worry, Falco. I'll protect you." Curio raised his one good arm as if holding his gladius. They all laughed as his arm wavered with the effort to hold it out.

Though the laughter fell away as Varro's eyes turned to Gala's covered corpse. The stitched leg poked out from beneath the gray cloak set over him. Despite all the violence, the stitches held even though blood had leaked from the wound.

"We'll have to give him a proper burial."

Falco lowered his head. "I hope this pays for whatever crime he did to end up with us. Poor bastard. He was nice enough, and I was starting to like him."

"And we'll have to get Piso down from the tree," Varro said. "He can't hang upside down for birds to peck at his eyes."

"His eyes were like two grapes. Birds will love them. He was an ass, and we don't have time to get him down."

Varro frowned. "You can't be serious. He's a fellow soldier. He's not to be left hanging upside down like a criminal."

"Fine, I'll agree to that. But he's high up in that tree. Getting him down will be a struggle."

"He just needs to be dislodged. It's not like we have to worry about a graceful landing." Varro rubbed his face. "Let's get some food in us and then handle these tasks. We have to move fast across the plains or else risk those horsemen finding us again."

They ate a simple meal of bread and wine. Falco spent the time speculating on how they could harvest the bear. Yet this needed time, tools, and skills they did not possess. The corpse would remain here for scavengers to find and devour.

After breakfast, Varro and Falco began their dour work. They had considered moving Gala's corpse from the ledge to bury him in the mud, but his body threatened to tear if moved. They would leave him where he fell. The burial took longer than Varro expected. They spent an hour collecting enough rocks to cover the body.

Both dripped with sweat while Curio, now propped against the wall, watched with a solemn expression. After offering a few words to commemorate a man who was still essentially a stranger to them, Varro wiped the sweat from his brow with the back of his hand.

"Now to work on Piso."

"Forget him," Falco said. "We've spent enough time. He's in the tree safe from wolves. We'll just say a prayer beneath him before moving on. It's not like we can dig a hole deep enough to spare him from scavengers anyway. Let's be practical."

"You might be fine leaving him like that. But I was his leader. I do not need his ghost following me around because I left him hanging in a tree for ravens to eat his eyes."

They moved their packs and gear off the ledge, then fetched Curio down. The odor of death still clung to them, but being in the fresh air was a relief. Curio moaned with every jolt but tried to hide his pain. The bear had rattled every bone in his small body. Varro counted him fortunate to have survived.

Now they set him on a dry stone and stretched out his broken leg on a log to keep it out of the mud. Varro stood beneath the tree where Piso's blood had darkened the muddy puddles around the pine tree's roots. He looked up to the stark white flesh caught in the limbs. The sunlight thankfully shadowed his face.

"I'll climb up and dislodge him. You can start digging a hole."

"You really are warming up to this officer role," Falco said with false humor. "Make me dig in the wet mud while you climb the tree. Yes, sir."

"All right, I thought climbing might be riskier. But since you seem to think it's the easy work, then you get him down."

Falco snorted a laugh. "It's just knocking him out of the tree. I'll take that work."

Varro took the shovel from their gear and began digging in the clearing. Falco stripped off his armor and sword, hung them on a branch, then pulled into the limbs of the pine.

The mud was easy to dig but he soon struck rock. All the while

Falco whistled cheerfully as he climbed into the tree. With each new limb he mounted, water and needles showered down.

"I'm almost there," Falco called down. "How's the hole coming along, Optio?"

"Fine," he shouted back. But he paused to watch mud sliding into the hole and undo all his labor. He gave a suffering look to Curio, who smiled in sympathy. He pushed the shovel in again.

"All right, I've reached Piso. Oh gods, he's impaled."

"Don't give me the details," Varro shouted back as he tried to lever out a stone. "Just get him down."

"Well, I can't see how," Falco shouted back. His voice was muted across the distance. Varro's shovel rang out against the rock. "Ah, I think I see a way. All I have to do is this."

Then wood cracked and Falco screamed.

Whirling around, he saw Falco smashing through the limbs and branches of the pine tree. He crashed into the muddy earth with a wet thump and a shriek of pain.

Varro threw down his shovel and raced to his side.

Falco lay on his back, eyes shut tight and teeth clenched. He was covered in twigs and pine needles, his face red with scratches and cuts. Blood covered his left side, but it was from Piso who had landed beside him. His corpse was balled up, head tucked under his body so that his backside faced the sky. A branch had punched through his torso just below his pectoral. It stuck out his back. But the blood there was dry. Fresh blood now flowed out from beneath him.

"My fucking foot!" Falco shouted, holding his head against the agony. "I don't want to look at it."

Varro knelt beside him. "Don't look. It'll hurt worse if you look."

"Oh shit, it hurts! Is it still attached?"

Falco's left foot was turned ninety degrees from where it should point. It also bulged out on one side of his sandal, as if the entire foot had been dislodged from the ankle and was connected only by flesh.

"Is he all right?" Curio's voice was small and distant. It faded against Falco's moaning.

"You'll be fine," Varro said. He shifted so that he blocked Falco's view.

"Is it broken? It's on fire, Varro!"

"I think it's dislocated."

"What? Are you sure?"

He was not sure of its actual condition. But the foot was certainly wrenched out of position. He now sat atop Falco's legs, gingerly taking the red and swollen foot into his hands. Falco screamed.

"What are you doing?"

"I want to see if there's anything stuck in it. Just hold on."

This was not delicate work, and something he had no direct experience with. But he understood to leave the foot out of joint would lead to worse damage.

He grabbed the foot with the speed of attack and wrenched it into place.

Falco bucked and screamed. But Varro heard bone click and the foot shifted into alignment.

"What the fuck did you do to me? I'm going to kill you! I swear it."

"I put your foot back. You'll be kind enough to thank me for it before killing me."

"I'll kill you twice, you little shit! Gods but that hurts."

He set Falco's foot down, then examined the rest of his body. He found nothing worse than scrapes and minor cuts. Falco looked aside with tears in his eyes, until Varro sat back and proclaimed him otherwise uninjured.

"Was Piso worth it?" Falco asked through his gritted teeth. "Now he's a bloody wreck. How are you even going to bury him?"

"Let's get you out of the mud. You can stand, just not on that foot."

They wrested together until Falco stood once more. He leaned on Varro's shoulder, hissing in pain as he hopped to where Curio sat leaning forward.

"Falco had an accident," Varro said.

"A bit of an understatement," Falco roared back. "Look at my fucking foot, Curio. When it's healed I'm going to kick it straight up Optio Varro's ass."

Varro left him seated on the rock beside Curio. He then collected branches and stones and covered Piso where he had fallen. He had no strength or will to dig a hole. Once he had covered the bleeding corpse, which he avoided looking at too closely, he offered his apology.

"Please forgive this. I can only do so much alone. Be at rest, Piso."

He then returned to Falco, whose face was puffy red and streaked with tears. The pain must have been intense to do this, Varro thought. He endured Falco's glare as he walked past him to climb back onto the ledge. Once there, he found Gala's crutch where they had discarded it. He carried it back down to Falco.

"We'll brace your ankle and you can use Gala's crutch," he said. "We've got a long journey ahead, and it just got longer."

Falco accepted the crutch, closed his eyes, and thumped it against his head.

"Those farmers feel a thousand miles away now. What are we going to do, Varro?"

But when Falco opened his eyes, Varro had no answer for him. He simply extended his arm to offer him help up.

15

Varro set Curio behind a large rock and bushes just on the side of the ridge that blocked view to the farmhouse. Falco dripped sweat and cursed as he hopped over to the rock, dropping against it.

"Wait here and I'll see what we're up against."

Beyond the ridge the farmer's dog barked and growled. Varro could imagine her straining against her chain and the old farmer holding her back. He hoped she did not smell him from this far away.

"That dog," Falco said, barely catching his breath. "I thought she'd accepted us before we left."

"Maybe she's barking for another reason. I'm going to find out. Give Curio some wine while I'm gone."

This was the second day after their disaster at the ledge. A whole day of marching got them halfway. They endured a fearful night camped in the open with no fire. The gods had allowed them to continue this day without harassment. They had marched all day at the fastest pace Falco could manage, which was better than Gala's had been but not as fast as they wanted. Carrying Curio on his back had left Varro shaking and weak.

They had to abandon all their gear except shields and weapons and a basic kit for water and rations, which would deplete after today. As Varro now crawled to the top of the ridge, he realized everything rested on this gamble. If the farmers rejected them, or attacked, he could not predict the outcome. In their condition, they would all likely die.

The cool grass stroked his face as he elbowed his way to the top of the ridge. He feared to see the farmers running for him with their wild dog leading the way. Yet looking down, he found the farmhouse with the front door open and a yellow glow spilling out of it. The wife, daughter, and husband were standing outside chatting with two other men. The husband held his dog, which jumped and growled at the visitors, who also had a small dog on a chain.

Varro smiled. The dog was excited for another dog and not his scent. He watched as these two visitors engaged in what seemed friendly conversation. He guessed they were leaving with the onset of twilight, and was gratified to see them wave then turn away. The farmers turned back into their house. The door closed and the yellow hearth light cut off, leaving the square farmhouse in a pool of thin blue shadow.

He scrabbled back, then returned to the others to report.

"The farmers seem in good humor. The dog wasn't barking at us. We're not much of a threat despite all our weapons. Let's go knock on their door."

"I hope you're right," Falco said. "And they didn't sell us to our enemies."

"We'll know as soon as they open the door," Varro said. "Besides, we're a mess. Look at your foot. Look at Curio. He clearly needs help and we can pay for it."

"Or be robbed," Falco added.

"Ever hopeful Falco." Varro shook his head and roused Curio, who had started to nod off. His broken bones had been set, but over the last day he had become quiet and sleepy as if sick. Varro feared the bear had delivered a worse wound than broken bones.

Getting Curio onto his back required Falco to help. Now he had the rock to brace against. But more than once they had all fallen into a pile trying to shove Curio into position. While this did not worsen any broken bones, Curio shrieked in horrified pain each time. Fortunately, this time he slipped on without issue. Falco gathered three shields and two packs, then tucked his crutch underarm. The sorry group navigated the slope down, avoiding the numerous stumps along their path.

The barking dog had alerted the farmers to Varro long before reaching the door. Though her bark was less vicious than their first meeting, she was not pleased at their sudden appearance. The door opened a crack, but the angle was poor. A yellow line of light blinked before the door opened with the farmer and his leashed dog.

Varro could not raise his hand, for he had to keep Curio stable on his back. Falco waved, but the farmer and his dog did not shift.

"Don't stop," Varro said. "Just keep moving. He can see we aren't a threat."

The dog stood up on hind legs while her master restrained her. She barked and growled and her tail wagged furiously. The old farmer held his ground, but as Varro neared, his shadowed expression turned to surprise.

They halted beyond the range of the dog, whom the farmer had pulled closer. She jumped and whined, but no longer barked. The farmer looked from Varro to Falco, then to Curio. He blinked and called back into the farmhouse.

"I'm sorry to bother you again," Varro said. "I don't think you can understand me. But you can see we are in desperate need of aid. You helped us before. I believe you will again. Please tell me I'm not wrong."

The wife and beautiful young daughter appeared, but the other older man and the son did not. They were all amazed to see them. The wife stepped forward, brow creased with worry as she looked to Curio whose head rested on Varro's shoulder. She asked him questions, evidently looking for Piso to translate.

Varro shook his head. He pointed to himself and the others, hoping to communicate they were all that's left.

"Can't they see how beat up we are?" Falco asked through a false smile. "Either set the dog on us or let us in."

"Have some patience," Varro said, also trying to hold up a friendly face.

But he was relieved to find that the wife seemed to authorize their return. She gestured them inside the farmhouse.

"I'm so hungry," Curio moaned.

"It smells like good food in there," Falco added.

"Just mind yourselves and we might have a chance." Varro bowed his head as he entered.

The farmhouse was unlike Varro's in every way. This was simpler and darker, but was filled with warmth and savory scents. A fire glowed in a stone hearth. The other two men were not present.

After they settled their packs and stretched out on benches beside a plain wooden table, they went about the struggles of communication. It took many gestures and guesses to piece together the stories from both sides. During this time, they were fed and provided sour wine. Varro was grateful for it all. Curio got special attention from the young girl, who seemed to fret over his feverish condition.

It seemed the horsemen had come to their farm and took away their able-bodied men, leaving only the old farmer behind. Varro believed that while the farmers might not know exactly what happened, they were clear the others had died. Curio's and Falco's conditions were evident. They seemed to be welcomed to stay, though the farmer held out his palm as if he wanted more coin. Varro dumped everything he had onto the table, a small pile of silver coins. The wife scooped them up without a second thought.

Falco and Curio would get the beds of the missing men, while Varro could content himself sleeping on the floor. That night he slept better than he had in months.

And he would sleep well for months to come. For Falco and Curio both needed at least until the summer to heal their wounds. While Varro had feared the return of the mounted men, it seemed their recruitment effort was over. From what he could glean from gestures and expressions, the farmers seemed to believe their young men were off to war and no one would come looking again.

Varro offered to work on the farm, and Falco would pitch in as able. Curio, however, had remained too ill in the first month of his care to do much. The young girl seemed infatuated with him, but her father guarded her carefully as Curio's condition improved under the care of the two women. The husband was a genial and hard-working man. Varro admired the type. He taught him useful words in Greek, enough to facilitate the work he trusted to him.

By midsummer, Varro's and Falco's torsos were tanned from labor under the sun. As time progressed his healing, Falco went on short but vigorous marches with Varro in what he termed aimless circles. But they needed to recondition. They practiced with sword and shield in the evening, while Curio pretended to be too sick each night to join them. As he grew stronger by the day, he lost his excuses to join marches and drills. Varro was merciless to him, knowing Curio had to catch up months of inaction.

The farmers seemed to have accustomed themselves to the three Romans living with them. During the busy months of early summer, a few visitors arrived to send them all hiding in the barn. Varro was convinced one neighbor knew something strange was going on and visited too often. Yet they were never discovered as far as he could tell. The farmers smiled happily and enjoyed having strong backs to aid them in their labors. Not to mention Varro had paid them handsomely to cover their troubles. It was likely more silver than they could make at market in a year.

Yet the day to leave arrived too soon. The farmers also knew it and their moods had grown subdued. They had stayed on to let Curio grow stronger, but the urgency of their mission only intensified with each day. By now Marcellus Paullus might indeed be dead or sold off to a place where he would never be found again. Yet this did not excuse them from their duty to find him.

Varro tried to show the farmers Sabellius's letter, hoping that it explained their official need to continue on in their mission. But the farmer could not read. Instead, he had focused on the crude map. Varro showed them the mountain pass and tried to communicate it was their destination. This seemed to mean nothing to the farmer, who simply nodded and returned to his work.

By late morning, they had gathered at the barn where Varro wanted to coil rope and arrange tools in good order before leaving. Over the course of months, he had reacquainted himself with the simple farming life and come to think of these duties as his own responsibilities. Falco and Curio both checked their packs and gear. Both men were pensive and quiet.

"It's high summer," Falco said. "I wonder if Villius settled the veterans by now?"

"According to what Sabellius said, he's probably still dealing with them." Varro fed rope through his hands, the friction heating his palms. "Hopefully it didn't get out of hand. I'd hate to think of what could happen."

The sun was bright in a clear blue sky. The grass swished with the breeze and the farmer's dog barked in the distance. Varro paused, wondering at the angry note to her barking. But he saw or heard nothing from the farmhouse.

"Marcellus is dead by now," Falco said. "Or not where Gala said he went. It has been too long."

"You can't be sure of that," Curio said. "Besides, what are we supposed to do? I didn't heal up a broken leg and arm just to have them broken again by my own countrymen."

"Thank you," Varro said, frowning at Falco. "We go forward."

"Yes, sir." Falco dug in their pack and tightened the straps. He too looked toward the barking dog, but likewise saw nothing alarming. "Well, I'll tell you one thing that better be there when we get back to camp. That fucking gold necklace. If Sabellius tries to keep it, I'll gut him where he stands and damn the consequences."

"I promise to help you do it," Varro said. "But that won't be the case. We are going to find Marcellus. If he went north last winter, then he's still there since the Macedonians have not come south again. We're going to reunite him with his parents. That could be worth more than a gold necklace, given how powerful that family is. Even if he's dead, we can at least bring them the peace of learning his fate."

Falco chuckled and shook his head. "Well, you make me feel noble. But I wouldn't be after him if Centurion Fidelis hadn't caught me. And what is that dog barking at? She doesn't sound happy."

Now all three stood up and faced the farmhouse. It sat in the bright summer morning, a pleasant curl of white smoke above it and birds lining its tiled rooftop. No human shouts joined with the dog's barking. Yet she was agitated.

"We'd better go investigate." Varro set down the rope. He adjusted his gladius harness, but chose to leave their shields against the barn wall.

The barking was louder and more intense as they closed in on the farmhouse. But there was no shout of alarm. Still, Varro drew them to the house corner then leaned past it to view the front of the house.

The farmer held his dog on her chain as she barked and growled at a line of five covered carts with oxen and drivers. One man with a ball of curly gray hair and wearing a Roman-style white tunic spoke to the farmer. His arms were folded but his face was full of smiles. They spoke easily to each other, despite the dog wanting to attack the men waiting on the carts.

"It's a caravan," Varro said, ducking back behind the wall. "But they are friendly."

Yet before either Falco or Curio could react, he heard the farmer calling for them. They looked to each other in silence, but as the call repeated, they all rounded the corner.

The farmer seemed aware of their presence behind his house. He laughed and beckoned them closer. The man with the ball of gray hair smiled, keeping his arms folded.

"You are the Romans, then?"

All three of them staggered back at hearing Latin, albeit with a heavy accent. The visitor nodded at their surprise.

"I trade with all people. So I must know these words, yes? Come closer. You are friends to my cousin. So I will be your friend too."

Varro led their small group to join with the farmer and his cousin. Up close the man's skin was like leather and creased heavily at the brow and around his nose. He had a squint from a lifetime of staring into the sun, but his yellow-toothed smile was genuine.

"I am Dimos. Which one of you is Curio?"

Curio looked astonished to be named. The man called Dimos laughed and looked him over.

"You are healed now, yes? This is good."

"It is good," Curio said. Oddly, his face turned red and he tried to hide by lowering his head.

"Nikolas says you three are rich men, but not rich any more. He has your coins now, yes?"

"That is the truth," Varro said. "But we were glad to pay him. We would've died without his help."

Dimos spoke to his cousin, who listened and laughed at the end of the translation. He replied and slapped Varro on the shoulder as he continued in Greek.

"You have a letter to go north," Dimos said. "You are Romans. Enemies, yes? But you go north where our sons fight. Do you go there to kill our sons?"

"We are on a diplomatic mission," Varro said. "I have a letter from my tribune to explain it. We don't want to kill your sons."

"But maybe our sons want to kill you," Dimos's smile disappeared into his wooly beard. He extended a thin, wrinkled hand. "May I read the letter? Maybe I can help you."

Varro produced the letter, now bent and torn from jumbling around his pack. But Dimos squinted at it, holding the papyrus at different distances as his brows rose and fell with the effort.

"Eyes not so good anymore. But I see this letter and this drawing." He carefully refolded the papyrus and handed it back to Varro. "You want to go north. So, Nikolas asked me to take you with us. We go north to trade. Good trading in war. You can be guards for me. War brings bandits too."

"Of course we can," Varro said, his heart racing. "We will guard anything you want. You can take us through the pass to the Macedonian camp?"

Dimos nodded.

Varro looked to Falco and Curio who were as dumbfounded as he was.

"We are ready to leave," he said to Dimos. "You only need to give our orders."

So they arranged their assignments, made introductions to their traveling companions, and stowed their packs into a cart.

Within the hour, they were prepared to depart. They once more gathered outside the farmhouse, now with Dimos to translate their gratitude and thanks. Dimos nodded and waved, mimicking a pat to a coin pouch. He was glad for their help and their coin. But Varro guessed he would have aided them even if they had no money to pay.

Before they left, the daughter rushed up to Curio. She shoved a pressed yellow flower into his hand, then fled back into the house. Both father and mother laughed as Curio held the flower in both hands as if he did not know what it was.

"Looks like you're the one for the women," Falco said. "Me and Varro are the ugly but competent type."

"Speak for yourself," Varro said. "I don't have a brow that could put shade over all of Rome."

So they departed with Dimos, marching alongside the plodding oxen. They kept their swords and armor ready, but shields remained in the cart. After an hour had passed, Falco whistled.

"I didn't even know the farmer's name was Nikolas. But he knew our names. Why do you suppose some people are so nice?"

"Because not everyone is a beast like you," Varro said.

"Yes, but we're their enemies, right? Dimos spoke truth. If their sons meet us, maybe we'll kill each other. So I wouldn't help out someone who might kill my own son. Yet he did."

"He had his reasons. The coins certainly helped," Varro said. "But some people are good by nature and disposed to aid anyone who needs it. So it must be with Nikolas."

Falco shrugged. "Well, he took all our coin. Not that we need it now. But that's not really being good by nature. I think he was glad for the money and just got to liking the free labor."

"True," Varro agreed. "But maybe he was kind for another reason."

He looked to Curio, who marched along in silence holding the pressed yellow flower in both hands.

Falco leaned in and whispered.

"I think he wishes he stayed on with that girl. He might be thinking twice about the mission. You better be kind to him, or he might just run back to Nikolas and his beautiful daughter."

Varro gave a weak smile, and marched north with Dimos to find Marcellus Paullus, no matter if he was alive or dead.

16

The Macedonians had encamped at the edge of mountainous terrain where the Dardanians fortified themselves. As the caravan rolled the final distance to the camp, Varro counted columns of gray smoke rising from hundreds of campfires. The walled enclosure sat atop a hill, and seemed a near duplicate of the camp King Philip had built so close to Consul Galba last winter. The smoky stink of the camp flowed downwind over Varro and the others.

They had walked four days, and their feet were sore and faces stiff with dust. Dimos's caravan moved slowly but relentlessly. From sunrise to sunset, the wheels of his carts turned. The pass was narrow and rough, and the carts hard to manage. But stubborn oxen driven by even more stubborn men had vanquished that challenge to emerge on the other side. One more day of travel across rough plains and they reached their current position. Varro and the others' guard duty had been nonexistent. The pass north was devoid of any threat worse than a mountain goat. Varro shared a pained grin with Falco and Curio at the ease of their passage.

"No worse than a crowded alley in Rome," Falco had muttered. "And probably less dangerous."

Now Dimos's wagons rolled to a stop, and he leaped down from his cart to gather Varro and the others.

"Well, my Roman friends, here is the camp. You have your tribune's words. Do you wish to present yourselves?"

Varro's expression must have betrayed his shock at the question, for Dimos's smile bloomed in his wooly beard.

"So, not diplomacy. You do come to kill our sons? I should bring you as prisoners for a reward, yes?"

Falco reached for his sword, but Varro stayed his hand. Dimos's grin never faltered, nor did he look at Falco. The dozens of other men in the caravan would easily cut them down if violence began.

"He's teasing us," Varro said. "Be at ease."

Dimos laughed, his puff of white hair wagging as if it would slip off his scalp.

"But you are not here on peace," he said, then wagged his finger at Varro. "You lied."

"I am here to find one of our own," he said, squaring up to Dimos's chiding finger. "We will not harm anyone who does not stand in our way. But we will fight if we must."

Dimos's eyes narrowed and he retracted his finger. His suspicious smile never left him.

"Very well," he said. "My cousin has a generous heart. Not me. But you paid him and were fair. He likes you, and I believe him. Besides, you worked hard for me too. But I cannot be found with Roman soldiers. So we are done here. Go your own ways, and may the gods be with you. If I am asked about you, I will not lie. But I will not speak freely, either."

Varro looked down the long stretch of five wagons. Each was filled with amphorae, crates, and sacks of all manner of goods an army would need. Dimos would sell all of this for a tremendous profit, and buy new items from the soldiers to trade elsewhere. The drivers at the front of each cart sat watching him. The oxen gazed lazily to the sides, flicking their tails and shaking their heads. He then looked skyward, to high clouds blushed orange with the end of the day approaching.

"Very well, Dimos," Varro said. "I am grateful for what you've done."

Falco snapped the back of his knuckles against his shoulders. He ignored this, knowing Falco was worried about entering the camp without Dimos's aid. But he had formed a plan.

Dimos smirked at Falco's dismay, then inclined his head.

"Not friends, but not enemies," he said. "Let us remain so until we can meet again in better times. Gather your packs and shields, and we will part now."

They had walked at the lead of the caravan. This close to the Macedonian camp, no one walked in escort of the carts besides Varro, Falco, and Curio. There was no threat of attack here except from the Macedonians themselves. So they hauled out their packs and shields, then lined up to the side to let Dimos pass.

He mounted the driver's bench, then waved down before goading the oxen forward. The cart wheels squealed and groaned as the line of carts began to plod ahead.

"How are we getting inside without help?" Falco stood lined up with him, ostensibly watching the slow departure but growling at Varro through a clenched smile.

"They'll help," Varro said. "They're a lazy lot. Haven't you been watching them these days?"

"What does that mean?" Falco faced him and folded his arms. But Curio answered.

"We jump into the back of the last cart," he said. "They won't check even if they hear something. They'll roll into camp, and we'll duck out before anyone knows we're there."

Varro smiled at Falco, then waved at the third cart to crunch along the path leading to camp.

"You don't think they'll notice?"

"They won't," Varro said. "For one, they're relaxed so close to their destination. And these carts make so much noise, they won't hear us jumping in. Now, it's almost time for supper. So they're not going to open their wares tonight. They'll be fed and share news, and tomorrow they'll do business. We've got plenty of time once we're inside."

"The shields are going be hard," Falco said.

When the final cart rolled past, they stood and waited for anyone turned back. But no one did. They jogged to catch up to the rear cart. It was piled high with crates covered with stained white tarps tied to the cart rails. Curio ran first, easily leaping onto the rear of the cart then pulling himself over. Even his cumbersome shield slid over with him. Varro and Falco kept pace, both crouched down should someone stand up in the driver's seat. But soon they were all crowded together under the cover of the tarp.

While there was space, there was no comfort. Their shields fit to either side, pressing them together like the shells of a clam. Their bodies were jammed against each other, with Varro in the middle. As the cart rolled ahead, every rut and rock sent shudders through them. By the time they halted outside the gates, Varro's face was numb from the constant vibrations.

He heard friendly exchanges and excited calls from within the camp.

He also heard them opening the carts to check the goods.

A fire erupted in his gut. Of course, he would do the same to ensure against exactly what he was attempting. In the dark under the tarp, with their breaths hot and humid in the tiny space, they looked to each other.

All they could do was huddle down and fight discovery.

It seemed a lifetime, yet the Macedonians were proceeding

swiftly down the caravan. Their voices drew nearer. Varro pressed to the smooth planks of the cart bed, wishing he could vanish through the wood.

The tarp flipped aside, then light and fresh air flowed in.

The Macedonians were talking spiritedly with the drivers. Varro kept his head down as they prodded and bumped at the front of the cart.

Then the tarp flipped back, the darkness and stale air returned, and the cart rolled ahead with a jerk. The Macedonians were still chattering alongside the cart as they entered the camp. Varro held his breath until it rolled to a stop. The wagon shuddered and shook as the oxen were unyoked and led away. They remained pressed to the floor as the cart drivers tightened loosened ropes. Varro could see their shadows between the gaps in the cart sides. The drivers laughed with each other and did a cursory check of the cart perimeter before leaving.

Varro remained still. His knees and back ached but he dared nothing. The sounds of camp life filtered into him. He had been so long from his own camp that these familiar sounds made him nostalgic for the life of a simple recruit. Officers shouted orders; men shouted obedience. Animals drew carts and workers scurried between locations. The stench of soldiers long-gathered in one place was over-awing even beneath the tarp. This was something Varro could not tolerate about other races. They were in no way as clean as a Roman, but then nor were any of them as civilized. Yet these Macedonians dared to call the Romans barbarians.

He let these thoughts occupy his mind and assuage his need to burst out of the cart. But soon Falco and Curio both were stirring, doubtlessly as eager to unfold their tortured limbs as he was.

"Let me peek outside," he whispered.

Sitting up on his knees sounded like hammers pounding boards. But the noise was amplified in this restricted space and

Varro knew no one outside would hear it. Still, it gave him pause before lifting the edge of the tarp with his finger.

He levered up a gap to let the fading light of the day into the cart. His eyes needed to adjust, but he saw the carts arranged in a semicircle so that his rear cart now faced the front where Dimos had been. Two of Dimos's men sat on the lead cart, talking and swinging their legs from its edge. Varro pulled back inside.

"We can't get out this way. Curio, get to the front and tell us if we can escape that way."

Turning around and forcing his way through the narrow edges of the cart, Curio confirmed the front was clear for their exit.

They slipped from hiding to land outside of the carts' semicircle, facing the camp wall. A purple night sky forced the last light of the day below the western horizon. The camp itself shed orange light from campfires to infuse the sky with a golden haze.

"Enemies on every side. Makes my blood cold," Falco said. He pointed to the cart. "Our shields?"

Varro shook his head. He had removed his helmet while in the cart and had it tucked under arm. He slapped it to make a hollow metallic ring.

"If our armor doesn't give us away, those shields would. Once we get Paullus, or at least find where he's kept, we'll sneak back here and retrieve the shields."

"Right," Falco said with a smile. "We can probably be done in an hour. After all, there's only eight or nine thousand soldiers here. We can peek into all those tents in that time."

"Now's not the time to complain," Varro said, drawing both Falco and Curio closer. "Look, I've had all summer to think on this. We don't even know if Paullus is here."

"Or what he looks like." Falco added, patting Varro's back as they huddled together.

"That doesn't matter," Varro said. "If he's here, he'll be obvious. Paullus is a high-value hostage that an officer would've ransomed for a fortune had he the time to do it before Philip sent these fools here. In fact, Paullus must be worth quite a bit, and so you know the commander of this force will be the one to keep him in the meantime. He's not going to let some junior rank grab all that potential ransom. Just like us and our gold chain."

Curio sighed. "I wonder if he has had as much bad luck as us. But luck always favors the evil, doesn't it?"

"No matter, we're going to change his luck and snatch his prize," Varro said. "The way I see this, Paullus will be treated well even though he's a prisoner. We just go to headquarters and find the nice tents with a few guards outside. Paullus will be inside one of them, I'm sure. We don't have to peek inside nine thousand tents."

Curio frowned as if to deny the plan, but Falco shook his head at him. "That's the way of the rich. They take care of their own even if they're not the same people. But take us prisoners, well, they'll give us the whips and cages. Paullus will be like the commander's guest, I expect."

"I expect as well," Varro said. "If he's not near the commander, then he's not here. No one else would have possession of such a valuable prize."

"All right," Falco said, looking over his shoulder. "We better do something other than stand in the open. And how are we getting him out? You don't mean to go through the gates. We'll never escape this place without being seen."

"Sabellius gave us everything we need to get Paullus away from the Macedonians. He just didn't explain it to us."

"But you figured it out?" Falco raised his brow. "What are we going to do next, fly?"

"It's not that hard to figure out. He gave us a good length of strong rope. That's all we need." Varro pointed at the crude wooden walls surrounding them. "When we go to sleep, we bar our doors and windows so that not even the strongest man in

Rome can enter easily. But mosquitoes torment us all night. We're mosquitoes to this wall, which is meant to ward off armies and war elephants. Not little bugs like us. If I stand on your shoulders, I can reach the top, tie off this rope, then we can scale the sides and be gone before anyone knows."

"With all our gear on our backs?" Falco scratched his head.

"I haven't been idle all summer. My back is as strong as ever. You and Curio might need a hand, but we can do it."

Varro crept to the cart, then reached in to find their packs. He pulled these closer and pulled out the start of the rope. He set it on the rails to be easy to grab even without light.

"It's dark enough now that if we act natural and stay distant enough, we won't be noticed even with our sword harnesses. But it's still early enough to be out without question. So we don't have time to waste. Headquarters must be at the center of camp like ours."

"You still have the feathers in your helmet," Falco said. "Put that on and you might as well scream your name."

"I thought about it," Varro said. "But I also want Paullus to know we're with the army he left behind."

"He'll know it because you'll speak to him in flawless Latin, you fool."

"I'm still your optio. Watch yourself."

"And you watch those feathers," Falco said, pointing at the helmet. "Now lead the way, sir."

The safety of their secluded position behind the carts had emboldened Varro. Yet now that he took his first steps into the camp, he felt a strange mixture of fear and excitement. They did not have purposefully designed roads as the Romans did. Their paths were worn from the natural walkways between areas of the camp. They were inside the southern gate where a wide area had been set aside for carts and pack animals. He guessed the oxen drinking at a trough were Dimos's. Empty crates and barrels were piled up in random places. Soldiers or workers, Varro could not be sure which, stood chatting in pairs around the open space. If anyone saw them, no one reacted.

The main camp seemed a haphazard sprawl of dirty and faded tents. Just like the poor Roman soldier, these Macedonians squatted around their fires and cleaned up after their dinners. Many sang strangely melodious songs, others laughed, some cursed, and some tents were already dark. Perhaps the soldiers of these tents had worked a long day and only wanted their sleep.

They walked swiftly but not as if running. Varro's heart raced as he realized he could be seized at any moment. Yet he passed men who did not look at him, each absorbed with his own thoughts. When these men came close, within the distance of a tent, Varro felt as though the feathers on his helmet must be sticking out a mile before him. Yet he kept it underarm, as did the others. Even without feathers their helmets were distinct from the Macedonian style. Their pectorals might be unusual, but their scutum shields would have been obviously out of place.

They did not speak, not daring anyone to overhear a stray phrase of Latin in a camp of Macedonians. These men looked much like Romans up close. Varro had never seen them at ease, and while he would not come close to one, as he progressed through the camp, he felt more comfortable.

Of course he expected to be challenged as he neared the camp center. Yet soldiers did not encamp here, and neither did it seem officers. These Macedonians followed a different hierarchy, Varro decided, which might make his task easier. Without soldiers right up at the commander's tent, he only had guards to concern him.

He crossed a wide path that seemed to demarcate the transition to a noble space. Across the dirt path etched into the grass, numerous tall and clean tents stood in neat order. A bonfire burned at the center of the open space. Guards stood outside some of these tents, dressed in mail coats with round shields and spears in hand. They did not seem vigilant, but neither were they distracted. Here were bored men about their work, feeling no threat deep inside the camp.

With an outstretched arm, Varro halted their progress. Looking back for the first time, he saw both Curio and Falco with eyes wide enough to reflect the bonfire. They looked terrified.

"Don't give us away," he said, whispering as calmly as he could. "This is the place. So let's find a spot to watch. Paullus must be nearby."

Here was Curio's chance to lead, as subterfuge seemed more his art. He slipped ahead and Varro followed with Falco trailing. They walked swiftly until Curio bent low. Varro and Falco imitated him until they arrived behind the end of a long row of tents. It had the best view of the center space, and was close to the grandest tent.

"This feels familiar," Falco whispered.

Varro smiled, feeling the same way. All their troubles began with them hiding behind a tent at headquarters. He prayed his bad fortune would not repeat.

They hunkered down. Without speaking, Varro angled Falco to watch one direction behind them and Curio the other. This way no one could stumble upon them without notice. Varro alone would look for signs of Paullus.

Few men came or went from this place. The commander's tent glowed from the inside, but no shadows passed along the cloth walls. Perhaps he was away, but Varro could not think where at this hour. Guards left their stations, some relieved by others and some seemingly abandoned. The fire burned lower. He would have to call off their vigil if no signs were discovered, for they would need to escape before dawn. When the camp was asleep, he might try to investigate a tent if one seemed promising. He had to see how things developed.

Yet the gods were on his side this night.

A man ambled up the path that led toward the center bonfire. Two soldiers accompanied him, grim-faced with spears and shields and gray chain shirts. The man in the middle wore a Roman-style toga. While Greeks also wore them, this man could not appear more Roman than if he were carved in marble and standing on a plinth at the Senate.

"Here he is." Varro's whisper brought Falco and Curio to his side. They peered over his shoulder, each leaning out as far as they dared.

"How do you know?" Falco's whisper was hoarse beside his ear.

"Just look at him. Plus he's under guard. I'm going to get closer."

He felt Falco's fingers brush his shoulder as he failed to prevent his leaving. But Varro was certain he had found Paullus. So he slipped along the rear of the tents, darting from one dark canvas wall to the next until he lined up with the three men.

As he considered his next move, the two armed guards stopped and saluted the man in the Roman toga. He raised his hand in acknowledgement, just like a Roman orator, and waved these men off. He seemed ready to turn into the tent Varro hid behind.

The two guards walked back the way they had come, while the Roman watched them go. He then turned to enter the tent.

Varro slipped on his helmet and stepped out of the shadow.

"Marcellus Paullus," he said as loudly as he dared. "We have come to save you."

The Roman leaped back as if he had barely avoided falling into a pit. His eyes shined with the glow of the bonfire. He looked about, then leaned forward to peer into the shadows between tents. He stared at Varro.

Then frowned.

17

"Don't worry," Varro whispered while stepping closer to allow Paullus a clearer view. "We're here to bring you home. We're on a special mission from Tribune Sabellius."

Paullus's toga shined golden in the bonfire light. Hard-lined shadows flowed along the stiff, clean material. His regal face remained folded into a frown. He was a handful of years older than Varro, perhaps no more than twenty. Yet he seemed to carry the weight of a much older man. He held still, only his eyes catching the gleam of firelight as he searched Varro up and down.

"Your guards are leaving." Varro nodded beyond Paullus's shoulder, where the two mail-clad spearmen now crossed into the dirt track that separated what seemed like headquarters from the main camp. "Just step back here with me, and we'll be off."

"And who are you?"

The question, asked with a note of irritation, caused Varro to pause. But he straightened his shoulders and answered.

"Optio Marcus Varro. I'm here with Caius Falco and Camillus

Curio. We're escorting you home. Come, we have a way out prepared. You'll be among friends soon enough."

Paullus shook his head, putting his finger to his nose as if blocking a foul odor.

"Optio Varro, you've come far for no purpose. I'm not leaving."

"I'm sorry. I don't understand."

"Then let me make it clear." Paullus stepped closer, rounding the corner of the tent. He was about Varro's height, lean and royal, and smelled of fresh linen. "I no longer have any allegiance to Rome. I belong here now."

"What is he saying?" Falco arrived behind him, his rough voice shocking Varro from the horror of what he had just heard.

Curio answered for him. "I think he declared himself a deserter."

Paullus clicked his tongue at the two new arrivals, but he did not seem alarmed.

"Look, I appreciate what it must have taken to come so far to find me. But I have a new life here." He extended his hand toward the tent that cast shadows over them. "You may call me a deserter or whatever you like. I care not one bit."

"But you're a prisoner," Varro said. "What kind of new life is that?"

Paullus's hard, senatorial frown melted. He closed his eyes and smiled, shaking his head gently as if recalling some pleasant memory.

"Yes, I am a prisoner. A prisoner of the heart. Do you know love, Optio Varro? The real love of a beautiful woman?" He held up his palm and turned his head aside. "Of course you don't, or you would not wear such an astounded expression. None of you do. So how can I explain this to ones with no conception of the heights of happiness I have reached here? It would be wasted breath."

"Well, we're wasting a lot of fucking time." Falco stepped

forward as if to grab Paullus. But the toga-wearing fool slipped back, his sandals scratching the dirt as he did.

"Watch yourselves," he said. "I am an officer and with a word can summon this camp to my aid."

Falco did not seem to believe, but Varro caught him by the arm. He pulled him aside then tilted his head at Paullus.

"An officer? A Roman officer in a Macedonian army? That is not possible."

"But it is," Paullus said. "At first I was a captive, but once my name became known, I was made a guest of General Athenagoras. And that is when I met his daughter."

"His daughter?" Falco folded his arms. "What is she doing with the army?"

"Visiting," he said with a bright smile. "Or at least she had accompanied messengers to her father when we arrived here. That is when we met, only months ago but it feels like a lifetime. We were madly in love from that instant. There could be no separating us. Athenagoras recognized it as well. So what began as an indulgence of his daughter's will, soon became true admiration for my skills on horseback. We have been hard pressed with the Dardanians, as you must know. It only took one battle, a trial I imagine Athenagoras set for me, to prove I must lead men and show them how to fight."

"You mean betray what the Roman army taught you to the enemy?" Falco unfolded his arms. "We've heard enough of this shit. Let's get him."

"A final warning to former brothers-in-arms." Paullus raised his hand high and smiled. "You are surrounded by men who would love to see you flayed alive. I will allow you to return to Tribune Sabellius. Send him my regrets. But I have chosen a new life."

"What about your family?" Varro struggled to find something convincing to this fool. Yet his question elicited a sneer.

"What about my family? You speak of prisons. There can be none worse than the prison I was made to live in as a member of the great Paullus family. I had no choice, no freedom, and no love. But I have all of that here. Now go, or else be caught. I will not aid you if you are."

Varro saw the resolve in Paullus's face. The stern, senatorial cast returned and he seemed as immutable as the marble statue he resembled. He would not be convinced.

He would have to be caught.

"I cannot return without you," Varro said.

"Then join me. You would be welcomed. Prove yourself to Athenagoras and he might reward you as he did me."

"He'll give me your woman, then?" Falco reached for his gladius. "We're not leaving without you, or at least part of you. Summon help, if you dare. I'll have your head off faster than they can arrive. And we'll be gone faster still."

Paullus gave Falco a mocking pout.

"A regretful choice. Goodbye, my former companions."

Despite his voluminous toga and relaxed stance, Paullus struck with lightning speed. His fist landed under Falco's jaw, snapping his head back and crumpling him to the dirt.

He then backed out into the full light of the bonfire and cried for guards.

Falco had been knocked out at Varro's feet. He reached for his sword out of instinct, but in the next moment guards from the surrounding tents rushed forward.

"Run, Curio!"

With a grunt, he hefted Falco off the ground. Holding him felt like a shifting sack of grain as he moaned back into consciousness.

"What happened?"

Varro dragged him into the darkness. But he could not escape the guards, who were already converging on Paullus. Even as Falco regained his footing and shook off the blow, he was still lagging. Curio had already vanished.

He heard Paullus speaking in a loud voice in what sounded like mangled Latin. His Greek must have been confusing, or else he allowed Varro a chance to flee, for the guards he summoned surrounded him as he tried to explain himself. None of them appeared to comprehend him.

"Get your legs under yourself," Varro muttered. "We've got to run."

"That prick! I didn't see that coming."

But Varro simply growled for Falco to move ahead. They stumbled toward the dirt path that was now painted blue with moonlight. After a dozen strides, Falco was on his own again.

"Over here!" The hiss came from their left, and Curio hid in the shadow of a large rock. In a Roman camp, the surveying team would have pulled that up before the first tent spike was set. Yet Varro was grateful for Macedonian laziness, and fell in behind the rock.

"What are we hiding from?" Falco asked, rubbing his jaw. But Curio pointed across the rock.

"A patrol," he said. "You would've stumbled right into their path."

Varro hunkered down behind the wide rock. It seemed ridiculously small for three men, but he soon discovered a cart parked beside it where Curio crouched. They pushed into its shadow as Varro heard the voices of the guards approaching.

His feet itched to run. Behind them the headquarters guards were alerted, though so far Paullus had not sent them in pursuit. Now the camp seemed somehow on edge, as if Paullus's lonely shout had roused all eight thousand Macedonians. It was a foolish thought, but it would not take thousands of enemies to take him prisoner.

They crouched down, with Falco sliding over to Curio and

leaving Varro to cleave to the cold rock. He pressed his face to it, once again wishing to vanish from sight. The bronze of his cheek plates dug into his skin as he clung. The voices were deep and clear, just two men on their rounds. They were not yet alert to danger. As long as Varro and the others remained still and shadowed, the Macedonians would pass.

He closed his eyes like he had as child, believing if he could not see then he could not be seen. But the voices paused in front of the rock.

Another voice had called them to a halt. Distant, but drawing closer, the new voice sounded excited and breathless.

He opened his eyes, staring at Falco and Curio pressed into the shadow of the cart and rock. A silver stripe of light fell across Falco's eyes, defeating his heavy brows to reveal a wide-eyed stare. Curio clung to him as if he were sheltering against his body from a violent storm. Were their situation not so dire, Varro would have laughed.

Instead, he held his breath.

The new voice flowed in a rush. Though Varro understood none of it, he assumed this was one of the headquarters guards informing the others of the danger in their camp. The two patrolling guards interjected with surprised expressions, and Varro could hear their feet shifting on the ground as they likely searched around after being warned of Romans.

Varro pressed harder, his fingers digging into the rock. He prayed they would pass him by. But instead he realized that all three had gone silent.

He waited for them to resume, but when they did not, he instead looked to Falco.

His eyes were wide enough to seem ready to pop from their sockets. He shifted them above Varro's head and mouthed the word "feathers."

The black feathers Varro had left in his helmet protruded over the top of the rock. In an instant, Varro realized he had given away their hiding place and the Macedonians' silence was their creeping up on him.

With a snarl he drew his pugio, knowing even the gladius would be too long for such close work. He whipped around to face the edge of the rock. His instincts were not wrong, for a mailed guard hugged the rock as he too had drawn his long dagger.

Varro surprised him, crashing forward to shove the attacker back. The hard links of the mail coat pressed into Varro's shoulder as he drove the Macedonian back. The guard cried out, and in the same instant Falco and Curio sprang from their hiding places. But Varro only heard their feet on the dirt and their growled curses. He pushed atop his opponent, one of the headquarters guards.

His pugio rammed into the guard's mail-armored side.

Then snapped.

The weapon was the dull and old pugio Curio had replaced for him. Varro had forgotten he no longer carried his beloved blade, blessed at the temple of Mars and gifted to him. This was junk lifted from a scrap pile and it left him with a hilt in his hand and a dull blade in the dust.

The Macedonian did not waste time. He kicked Varro in the crotch, sending lightning bolts of agony into his stomach and dropping him to the side. He landed atop the shattered pugio, feeling its cold hardness mocking him.

A stream of curses flowed, and the guard recovered with his own blade held flashing overhead. He was a shape of moon-brightened bronze and iron with yellow teeth gnashed and gleaming in his shadowed face.

But Varro used the pugio hilt to strengthen his own fist and punch hard into the Macedonian's face. Pain spread across his knuckles as they dragged through the enemy's teeth. But spittle and blood showered down on Varro, and the Macedonian's strike turned aside.

With both feet, Varro launched the Macedonian backward again. His mail scraped against the dirt path and he let out a winded shout as he thumped flat.

Varro leaped to his feet, lighter and more agile with only a bronze pectoral, helmet, and single bronze greave to weigh him down. He drew his gladius with practiced ease, but the enemy did not immediately rise, being pinned under the weight of his own armor. Instead he turned behind.

Falco was lying over the rock, holding a Macedonian spear with both hands and struggling to shift its point away from his stomach as the enemy leaned into it. Curio and the other guard were out of sight.

In two strides Varro collided with Falco's enemy. He briefly saw a gladius shining in the dirt as he tackled the guard to the ground. They wrestled until Varro realized his heavy helmet was as good a weapon as any. The wide-eyed Macedonian had lost his own, and so Varro butted his helmet into his face. It struck with a hollow thud, shifting backward on Varro's head.

This slacked the enemy's strength, and Varro was able to straddle him. But Falco had recovered and now held the guard's own spear.

He drove it at the guard, who had one unpinned arm to attempt to ward it off. But instead the arm snapped back to his throat as Falco drove the shining bronze spearhead through his neck into the dirt behind. A hot fan of blood erupted onto Varro's arms and face.

The headquarters guard recovered now, and called for help. Varro jumped off the corpse and saw he was backing away with spear lowered against their attack.

Falco snatched his gladius off the ground and a blood-streaked Curio stood up from behind the rock.

"I don't know where the cart is," Varro said. The realization made him dizzy. He had anticipated sneaking back through the camp, not running blindly through it.

"I do," Curio said as he dashed across the dirt track.

Varro and Falco followed, but the mail-clad guard marked them and trailed behind, calling for others to join his hunt.

Curio was like a gray rabbit, ever vanishing into dark paths between grimy tents. This was a warren of common soldiers in their haphazard organization of living quarters. The tents were all dark and flaps drawn. Curio zigzagged among them and Varro and Falco huffed after him. Farther behind was their dogged pursuer shouting as he labored under his heavy mail shirt.

"I can't keep up with the little bastard." Falco managed the words through his gasping.

They had trained for long and steady marches but not sprints like this. Varro already felt his thighs growing tight and hot. But fear of his life kept him limber.

"Keep going," he said, cutting hard to the left to keep Curio in sight. "We'll get away."

But their pursuer's shouting had finally had an effect. As Varro sprinted into a turn between tents, he found a Macedonian emerging from the flap to check on the noise. His eyes were half-open and his hair a twisted mess. As soon as he realized Varro was running for him, he ducked back inside with a shout.

He and Falco thumped past this tent, but left the Macedonians shouting and swearing among themselves.

"Where did he go?" Varro paused, and Falco crashed breathlessly into him.

"I was following you. Where's the little shit?"

But Curio had vanished. They stood between tents, and four possible paths led away from their position.

"Curio?" Varro shouted, knowing he would awaken others but not caring.

"He left us here?" Falco's words fought his labored breathing, but his shock was evident.

Varro repeated the call, but instead he only heard the Macedonians behind him piling out of their tents.

A tent flap next to him snapped open and an angry voice called out a question from the darkness.

"This way." Varro picked a path that seemed likely. He tried to see above the maze of tents, but could not find the camp walls which would help him navigate. How Curio knew the path in such a bleak and confused setting seemed as magic to Varro.

With every stride forward, Varro hoped Curio would resolve out of the darkness. But only more dirty tents emerged ahead.

Behind, the angry voices grew louder.

Every pause to check for a glimpse of the camp walls allowed the enemy time to catch up.

"Run, you fool," Falco pushed him as he stood on his toes to see over the tents. "They're almost on us."

"I think we went deeper into camp."

But Falco shoved him ahead, and now both were running. The enemies in pursuit drew closer, but their numbers did not seem to increase.

Then a horn sounded.

"It took them long enough," Falco said. He laughed, sounding breathless and frustrated.

Moans and curses were muffled through the tents surrounding them in this intersection of paths. Varro kept his gladius ready in a sweaty grip. But Falco leaned on his knees.

"It's over," he said. "We're not getting out. Might as well save ourselves the struggle."

But Varro rose on his toes again, and now saw the tops of the camp walls.

"No, I know where to go now. I can see the walls from here. We must've come to higher ground. Hurry."

He stepped forward and the tent next to him opened. A thick-muscled Macedonian emerged, his face torn in rage at his interrupted sleep. He looked to Varro, saw his feathered helmet, then charged with a roar.

The Macedonian was as fearsome as the bear that had attacked them in the mountains. Varro felt just as small and helpless beneath the lurching bulk of the giant enemy. But his gladius was ready.

He plunged it into the enemy's guts and staggered back under his falling weight. He was naked but for his loincloth, and with no armor or shield to stop the sharp blade it dragged along his stomach and spilled his guts.

Even in defeat, the mighty enemy's weight collapsed Varro to the dirt. The groaning Macedonian lay over both his legs. From the black tent opening, he saw other darker shapes gathering in confusion.

"Keep going, Falco."

"I'm not leaving you. I'm not Curio."

Falco bent to lever the body away, but the other enemies were now in the tent opening. The first man out stood dazed at the scene.

"Go straight," Varro said, struggling to worm out from the huge corpse bleeding over his legs. "Find the wall, trace it back to the carts. You know what to do."

"I can't leave you."

"It's my fucking order! I'm your optio!"

Varro fell back, surrendering to the weight of the body. As he did, in upside-down vision he saw the other pursuers reaching the intersection of tents.

When the nearest Macedonian realized what had happened, he struck out for Falco with a knife, but his companions were gathering spears. Falco sprang back and retreated to the edge of the intersection of tents.

He gave a pained looked to Varro.

"Go!"

And then he turned to flee where Varro pointed.

He slumped back, his fight over. Some of the Macedonians chased after Falco. But most surrounded him.

Spearheads touched every exposed patch of skin. Their bright cold tips threatened death for the slightest motion. The slain Macedonian giant lay facedown over his legs, the stench of his entrails bringing tears to Varro's eyes.

The faces surrounding him were grim and angry, glistening with sweat and radiating hatred.

"You were right, Falco. I should've taken those feathers out."

18

Varro did not sleep his first night in the cage. It was much like the one Centurion Fidelis had placed him in before leaving on this ill-fated mission. The bars were black iron and thick with rust where they intersected to form a lattice. The dirt under his legs was cold and made him feel wet. He had been stripped down to his tunic and thrown inside. Dried blood tightened and flaked on his legs. The dried flecks of blood on his cheeks felt thick. Despite the violence of his capture, he was uninjured but for a frighteningly deep bruise on his left thigh.

The sun rose over the camp into a pale sky of thin clouds. Black dots of birds fluttered in pairs over the expanse of worn tents comprising the Macedonian camp. Varro smelled the cooking fires, and also smelled rot. Other cages beside his were empty, but down the row he saw a pale lump on the ground. Flies swarmed everywhere, but they seemed concentrated in that direction.

"Be joining you soon," he said.

No one had come to torment him, or to even look at him. He watched the camp rouse from sleep. He was far from the center of it or where he had been captured. Yet he was close to the walls, which now seemed impossibly high and distant between the iron squares of his cage. Still, he waited for Marcellus Paullus to come gloat.

But no one arrived.

He waited all day. Soldiers crossed in front of him, never close enough to reach. Some glanced at him, while most were absorbed in their own worries. By late afternoon, the absence of attention began to calcify into a hard pit of worry in his stomach. He pressed to the bars and began to search for signs of attention. Yet the Macedonian camp thrummed along as if Varro had never run rampant through it, killing their fellows and sowing chaos. Shouldn't the commander of this camp at least want to learn why?

Yet by the end of the day, a group came with a man stripped to the waist. His pale flesh was scored with bloody cuts and welts, the outcome of a flogging. Varro was relieved it was not Curio or Falco. He hung limp between two soldiers while a younger man followed with two pails balanced on a rod over his shoulders. They threw the unfortunate victim into a cage at the far end. The iron gate clanged and rattled, and the lock clicked shut.

They then slid down to Varro's cage. The excitement of finally receiving attention at the end of the day died when he saw the flattened and scarred noses of the surly men.

"Are you here to take me to Athenagoras?"

The answer came with the young boy hurling a bucket of water into Varro's face. He fell back from its force. The water was slick and oily, but nonetheless refreshing. One of the men laughed as Varro blew the water out of his nose. The younger man flung in crusts of bread that landed in the fresh mud.

Then they moved down the row to where the flies gathered. Varro rushed back to the bars, pressing against its roughness and calling out to them. But they ignored him, instead covering their noses and swearing. One opened the cage and began shouting at the younger man, who seemed assigned to clearing out the remains of whoever had been left to rot.

Realizing he would receive nothing more from them, he turned back to the bread and water. The ground was greedily drinking the water meant for him. He desperately cupped it out of the ground, cursing himself for wasting it. He managed two dirty handfuls before he could manage no more. The bread crusts were dry and hard. But he ate.

Finally the sun set. He called out to the prisoner at the far end, but he only wept and cursed at the moon. When Varro could take no more, he slept.

This process repeated for two more days. The guards with broken noses would deliver bread and water. But now they allowed him to drink from a ladle extended through the bars of the cage. The younger guard would ram it into Varro's teeth at times, eliciting guffaws from his companions. But Varro drank and ate what he could. For they left him on the edge of thirst and hunger each day.

Each night he sat at the back of the cage, leaning against it and wondering if Curio and Falco had escaped. They must have, or else they would be imprisoned beside him. He took comfort knowing his capture had probably allowed them both to flee. By now, they must be arguing what to do. Falco would be insisting on a rescue plan while Curio probably argued to give up. After all, he had a beautiful farm girl that had gifted him a flower. He kept it close, even if he thought no one else had noticed.

Why not return to her? Varro thought. And Falco, there are eight thousand enemies between us. Just go home and finish your time in the army. Forget about me. Give my share of the gold to my mother. She'll need it.

Such thoughts repeated in his head as he drifted off. Sleep would weave in and out, so that he never knew wakefulness from dreams.

But he certainly dreamed.

On the second and third nights of his imprisonment he dreamed of the slave girl he had killed. She had been the whole reason for him to be here. He would be free had he not been greedy for a gold necklace that now felt sadly valueless for all the death that followed it. The unnamed slave girl, Consul Galba's lover and servant, had died at his hand. Now her ghost haunted his dreams.

She seemed delighted at his fate. Each night under the moonlight she stood before his cage, staring at him and smiling. There was something lascivious in her look, as if she wanted to devour him. Varro expected she was hungry for his soul to leave his body, that she might snatch him away and have an eternity of vengeance upon him.

The ghost would vanish with daylight. But Varro knew he would join her soon enough. She had seemed real, so that even upon waking, the impression of having been visited lingered throughout the day. Besides the cruel men who delivered him scummy water and stale bread, it seemed he would have no other visitors.

Until new men arrived.

On the gray and windy morning of his fourth day in the cage, soldiers in dull mail shirts arrived. Seven of them with round shields and spears parked on their shoulders surrounded his cage. One man would have been enough, for Varro's arms quivered with weakness and his throat burned with thirst. He'd have sooner attacked them for their wineskins than to escape. Yet still, even in his dirty and weakened state, he managed to stand up. He was a Roman solider and citizen. He would not cower on his knees before the enemy.

One soldier fetched him out of the cage, offering a perfunctory smile that seemed out of place for the situation. Yet he clasped

Varro by the arm and led him from the cage. The door slammed behind him and shook the bars.

They surrounded him and led him back to the center of the camp. He realized he must at last be taken before Athenagoras for questioning. As he stumbled along with his escort, threading between tents where dark-faced men gave him flat looks, he smiled. He had been softened up, so that even an offer of water would be enough to get him to betray his friends. He had to admire the Macedonians' finesse. For in a Roman camp, captives would simply be flogged until they expelled all their secrets, then summarily executed.

Headquarters appeared different in the flat daylight. The rock he had hidden behind no longer had a cart beside it. Though Varro noted the dark bloodstains of the slain enemy remained. Looking at it now, it was not a hiding place suitable even for a child. Perhaps the gods had not wholly abandoned him, at least not that night. The center bonfire was now a pile of blackened wood in a pit surrounded with rocks. He could not determine which tent was Paullus's. They all seemed similar, except the largest tent at the top of the circle that formed the command area.

This is where Varro's escorts herded him. Two guards in mail shirts stood outside this tent, and their hostility was evident. Both narrowed their eyes and frowned. Yet they stood aside as Varro was ushered into the tent.

Inside was expansive and dark. The overcast day did not contribute much light despite the opened flap. Bronze lamps burned at points around the spacious interior. Posts held up the ceiling high overhead. Rooms had been constructed by hanging fabric. A shadow moved behind one where an orange globe of light shined.

But his eyes fell upon the men gathered in the center of this makeshift audience chamber.

A central figure dominated the space. A tall and muscular man with friendly eyes and curled hair that hooked over his brows sat on a trestle chair. His black beard was trimmed into a tight wedge. A white scar marred his angular right cheek, and at least a dozen smaller scars crisscrossed his hands folded at his lap.

Two men in mail shirts and bronze helmets flanked him. They were clearly his bodyguards, each one thick-necked with the expression of a wild boar. An older man with strangely shaded gray hair and a long face stood left of the seated man. It seemed as if his fringe of thick black hair had been dipped in gray paint, creating a stark contrast with the top of his head. Varro had never seen the like.

But most galling was Marcellus Paullus standing to the left side of the seated man. His two guards flanked him. He still wore his Roman toga and smug expression, and raised his brows as if greeting an old friend.

Varro felt like spitting.

"Optio Marcus Varro, welcome to my camp." The seated man smiled, again with warmth and kindness unsuited to an enemy. "I am Athenagoras, the general leading this army."

Unsure of protocol, Varro stood mute. He expected to be shoved to his knees, be made to grovel, or otherwise abused for his insolence. Yet the soldiers surrounding him did not act, nor did anyone else. The silence expanded until Varro felt as if he must speak.

"You know my name, sir? And you speak Latin well."

"I am educated," he said with a wry smile. "Contrary to what you may have been taught about our people. As for your name, I believe you announced yourself to your former countryman."

Varro narrowed his eyes at Paullus, who remained smiling.

"Then what do you want of me? You know why I am here."

"I do. Marcellus has now demonstrated his loyalty most admirably."

Surrounded as he was by spearmen, Varro considered leaping

through them to throttle Paullus. It seemed the traitor knew it, for his smirk only widened.

"There is the matter of your two companions," Athenagoras said. "And the fact that you murdered several of my guards. It would be best if they could all face judgement. I've considered offering you as bait to lure them back for capture. Would they try?"

"I've no doubt they'd fall for that sort of trap." Varro tilted his head back. "But I did not think a mighty general of King Philip's glorious army would be so petty. We're just three common soldiers, all of us expendable, none of us expected to actually return. If we could grab Paullus, then it would be our way back into the graces of our officers. I don't believe they expected us to succeed."

Athenagoras laughed and it seemed genuine. He appeared as a man at ease in every situation, unable to become agitated. Yet the scars on his face and hands told the story of a man versed in combat.

"You really came this far and faced such dangers to rescue Marcellus?"

"Of course, sir. We either return with him or do not return at all."

The general's smiled faded and he shifted on his chair, rubbing his chin through his tight beard.

"I'll make you the same offer as I did Marcellus. Join me. You will have to prove yourself, of course. And there will be men eager to avenge the deaths of their friends. But you must be highly capable to have accomplished this much. I never turn away talent."

"I would never betray Rome as lightly as Paullus has. I would never disgrace myself and family."

He sneered at Paullus, whose smugness smoldered into anger.

But Athenagoras laughed and clapped his hands together as if settling the matter.

"I expected as much. But I felt I must ask. So, Optio Marcus Varro, I will fulfill the wishes of your officers. You will be executed by beheading. Go to your gods with a clear conscience."

Varro blinked, hoping he had misheard. A wave of dizziness and nausea swept over him, and his knees buckled. Paullus laughed, but no one else followed. Athenagoras settled his hands back on his lap and tilted his head back to stared down his nose at Varro.

Then a woman emerged from behind one of the cloth walls.

And Varro gasped.

It was the woman from his dreams, the one he had thought was the slave girl's spirit tormenting him. But seeing this woman in wakefulness revealed her as his nightly visitor. She was tall and thin, dressed in the manner of Greek women in a flowing tunic of pale blue fastened at her waist with a thin leather belt. Her hair was jet black, completely unlike the slain slave's, and her hazel eyes were a startling contrast. She gave Varro the same long, lascivious look as she had when visiting him in the cage.

Both Athenagoras and Paullus reacted to her appearance, speaking her name in unison, "Alamene."

The woman called Alamene spoke in a chiming, clear voice to Athenagoras. Her words were rapid but not urgent. Her demeanor seemed pleading, for her hands clasped to her chest and her brows joined in an arch. As she spoke, she looked to Varro.

Paullus seemed to reach a hand toward her, but pulled it back into the folds of his toga. He too looked to Varro, but with far less charity than Alamene.

Varro watched the brief exchange between Athenagoras and what must be his daughter and Paullus's so-called true love. The general shook his head twice, and each time Alamene's words grew more forceful. While Varro did not understand—and from

Paullus's confused expression, neither did he— Alamene grew more demanding and less pleading was obvious. At last, Athenagoras sighed and held up his hand for silence. Alamene smiled and lowered her head.

"The gods favor you, Optio Marcus Varro." Athenagoras sighed again, then pursed his lips. "You will be made a slave rather than executed. You die another day."

"But General," Paullus said. "He would make a terrible slave. He is too stubborn."

Athenagoras glared and Paullus stepped back in silence. Whatever kindness had danced in his eyes evaporated. The cold stare of a veteran soldier remained.

A flurry of Greek commands exchanged between Athenagoras, the old man with the strange gray-fringed hair, and Alamene. At last, the general stood up, the old man bowed, and Alamene approached Varro.

She stood before him as she had when he was caged. She studied him now, from foot to crown. He was dirty and stinking, but this did not upset Alamene. At last she nodded with satisfaction then spoke to the old man who now inserted himself between them.

He grabbed Varro's arm while addressing the guards around him. His icy fingers dug into Varro's muscle as he pulled him from the tent. With a glance over his shoulder before exiting, he saw Paullus standing with his mouth open and Alamene smiling with her arms folded.

Outside he again confronted the two guards that seemed to wish his death. The old man snapped at them and they parted. He continued to lead Varro through the camp.

His mind could not process the shifts in fortune he had experienced. The back of his neck still tingled in expectation of the cold bronze that would lop off his head. Yet now he was stumbling through the Macedonian camp to a different fate. Would he be branded or otherwise marked? Now his wrists began to itch in anticipation of iron chains. What sort of work would Athenagoras assign him? He would probably be given the worst and most dangerous tasks. Who would be his master?

The constant assault of fears and questions numbed him to the details of his second trip through the camp. He realized others stopped to watch his ordeal, but he was stumbling through a hazy gray world of crowded tents and grimy soldiers. It was all a smudge until he arrived at what appeared to be a bath area.

A dozen wooden basins were filled with water. The old man with the odd gray fringe shouted in Greek, which he did not understand. At last, the old man shoved him at a basin and pointed at the water. He mimicked removing his clothes.

Being given a bath seemed a strange way to start a life in slavery. But he did not delay. Instead, he splashed into the water and eagerly cupped it into his mouth.

The old man howled with fury, and one of the accompanying guards reached into the tub to stop Varro. He was to clean himself only. Still, even as he did, he gladly sipped in dirty water no matter how bitter its taste. At last his throat burned no longer.

When done, he was dried and presented a clean, white toga and sandals.

The strangeness did not end with this. For he was allowed to shave, though under close supervision by spear-carrying guards. He was fed mutton, bread, and wine. He was allowed to comb his hair.

He felt better than he had in months. When all of this was finished, he was once more led through the camp. This time men scowled at him and some shouted what must be Greek curses. But the old man ordered these soldiers away. They returned to headquarters.

Paullus waited for him here, with arms folded and a deep scowl on his face.

"Well, Optio Varro, are you refreshed?"

"I am," he said as the old man and guard seemed to relinquish him to Paullus. "But I don't understand."

"Are you so stupid?" Paullus checked his fingernails as if this were more important than their conversation. "But of course you must be to find yourself here. Well, let me make it plain for you. It seems you are to be Alamene's slave. Welcome to my household."

19

Varro walked across headquarters bearing a heavy amphora of wine to General Athenagoras's tent. The camp was as busy as it had been over the last three days of his nascent slavery. Yet for all the fine weather and drilling soldiers, it seemed the Macedonians had no plans to attack. He glimpsed pikemen practicing maneuvers in a field as he hurried past with the amphora on his shoulder. The guards at the general's tent knew him by now and allowed him to pass inside.

He set his burden inside the door. Guards here stood where Athenagoras had recently sat to pass judgement on him. They glanced at him, and as long as he did not linger they would leave him alone.

Stealing yet another image of the tent's interior, he turned to duck out. If there was anything of use here, he wanted to remember it. But he had never been deeper into the tent than the entrance.

Stepping outside, he passed between the guards then tripped. One had thrust his spear butt between his feet and sent him sprawling into the dirt. They laughed and kicked dust at him. But they dared to do no more.

Varro collected himself and stood again. He left them laughing as he hurried back to retrieve the last of the amphorae. He would not indulge them in their fun.

Being Alamene's slave meant no one was permitted to harm him, except Alamene and Athenagoras, presumably. Even Marcellus Paullus avoided him and did not dare to give him orders. He had tried to appear frightening and bold. Yet in the three days Varro had chanced to observe Paullus, it seemed he was as much a slave to Alamene as himself. He did nothing without her leave and she seemed less interested in him than Paullus liked.

She was more interested in Varro.

But she lent him to General Athenagoras's staff to help with menial tasks other soldiers could not be bothered to do. He was ordered to remain clean and presentable for Alamene. As he hustled through the camp back to the supply depot where the trader Dimos must have offloaded his goods, he considered his situation. To his chagrin, this was not much worse than life as a soldier. It was considerably less strenuous. But he could not help but wonder at this. For he felt like an animal being fattened up for the slaughter. Certainly a lamb might feel its owner favors it up until the knife is at its throat. What would Alamene do to him when she finally had him back?

He wove through soldiers and tents who paid him no mind. He wore a white tunic and would appear as nothing more than a servant to a casual glance. They mumbled to each other as they went about their tasks, leaving Varro as a white speck in a gray sea.

At the supply depot, the final amphora awaited him. The guard watching the supplies sat on an empty cask and gave him a look of long-suffering boredom. His spear rested against his body and his helmet sat in the dirt. Such lack of discipline, Varro thought. How could these men prevail against Rome?

He hefted the amphora with a grunt. Its rough clay bit into his shoulder. He wondered what might happen if he dropped it. A slave would be whipped certainly, but what of Alamene's slave? In any case, he hoped not to find out. Instead, he threaded the same path back to headquarters.

Despite the height of the mountains, the air was hot and oppressive from the density of troops. Sweat trickled down his brow and back. He had been running since dawn, carrying crates and other burdens wherever directed.

This was his penance, he realized. The gods had magnificent senses of irony. For he had killed Galba's slave, and so they made Varro as she had been. He was now a slave to a powerful woman. While she might linger in this camp at Athenagoras's will, she must soon depart. The frontline of battle was no place for a woman or any civilian family. When she left, Varro would go with her.

Once he left this camp, he would never return to Rome. A life of slavery was assured.

Midway en route to headquarters, gongs rang out over the camp.

His soldier's instincts warned him enemies approached. The Dardanians had to be attacking.

The confusion he assumed the norm for the camp vanished. Soldiers burst from their tents or dropped their burdens. Their officers shouted for order, blew whistles, and raised standards.

Varro bounced around the rush of fighting men flooding into his path. They pressed in a single direction, toward the beating gong. He swam against them, struggling to hold the amphora above the swell. But it was as if wading into high tide. He fought to reach a point off the path to set down the amphora.

It fell from his shoulders, crashing at his feet and breaking open to gush dark wine into the dirt. He screamed in horror. As if to emphasize his defeat, a soldier splashed through the puddle on his way to answer the summons.

He righted the amphora but the lid and neck of it were broken. He could never hide what had happened, but he still had to deliver what remained of it to headquarters. He hefted it again, feeling the wine slosh at the bottom of the large clay amphora.

The entire camp headed to the parade grounds and were assembling for battle. Varro realized he was left unattended.

He had a prime opportunity to find a weapon or something else to aid in escape.

That the gods had made him a slave as penance for his crime was never in doubt. That he would quietly accept this penance was another matter entirely. He would fight. He was a Roman soldier and here was his chance to show the Macedonians what that meant. If the gods agreed, then he would be free and his penance fulfilled.

Continuing past the spill, he jogged along until he found a place to set down his burden. He then went off to explore. Wine stains now flecked his pristine tunic and shed an acidic scent. He batted around the tents, and if no one called out, he ducked inside to see what could be found.

While the camp was rallying to battle, he realized it would not be completely emptied. So he did not dare to be too bold. A half-dozen tents yielded nothing of immediate use. But in one, he found a short knife. It was no pugio, but it could be hidden in his tunic. He pressed it into the folds then left the tent.

He realized he had not paid attention to his path. He was uncertain of where he had set the amphora. Across the tent tops, he saw the Macedonian pikes rise up. There were thousands of these shining in the late morning sun. It made him shudder to think of charing such a formation. He prayed that one day he would be able to do so. Anything would be better than dying in slavery.

His wandering path through the camp had led him back to where he had been caged. The man who had been flogged and thrown into the cages was still there. Looking around but finding no guards nearby, Varro decided to approach.

The man sat despondent against the rusted bars of his cage. His lacerated flesh was now burned red from being under the sun all day. He did not respond to Varro's approach. But he was feeling bold and stepped up to the bars. Still the man did nothing, and Varro guessed he might be dead. Then his head lolled to the side, and he stared up.

Their eyes met and Varro felt deep confusion. He knew this man.

"Roman!"

The man's voice was a dry croak, but filled with urgency. He twisted around and scrabbled to his feet, pressing his face to the bars.

"Dimos? Is that you?"

"Yes it is." He stepped back from the bars. His puff of white hair now lay flat against his skull. The friendly, squinting eyes were filled with loathing and fear. "What are you doing out there?"

"I am a slave. What happened to you?"

"What do you think, Marcus Varro? I was blamed for delivering you into the camp. But I did not. So they whipped me until I agreed. That's what they wanted to hear, yes? Or maybe an officer might be in trouble for letting you in. So old Dimos and his boys were blamed. And now look at me. Look at you!"

"I was made a slave to Alamene, Athenagoras's daughter. What can you tell me? Anything will help. I want to escape, and take you with me. Where are the others?"

"The others are dead or slaves. I don't know where. Only old Dimos has to die slowly and alone. I am so hungry. Food?"

"I will bring you food, and wine." Varro thought of the cracked amphora. At least Dimos would benefit from that disaster.

"Yes, wine. I am so thirsty, Roman."

"Now what about Athenagoras's daughter? Do you know when she will leave? Have you ever dealt with Alamene before?"

Dimos gave a hoarse laugh.

"I know all about Alamene. She is not Athenagoras's daughter. She is Philip's cousin."

"What?" Varro stepped back from the bars, touching his chest. "Then why is she here?"

"I don't know," Dimos said. "But she loves Roman soldiers. That is well known. So she dressed you nice, yes. Made you her slave? Ah, and you still don't know what she wants?"

Varro felt heat rise to his face as Dimos laughed, dry and coughing.

"I haven't been taking orders from her, but from Athenagoras's old man. The one with the weird gray hair. But I will be sent back to her. How many soldiers does she have escorting her? She must have hundreds. And she must be costing Athenagoras to stay here. So he will be eager to send her away, especially with the threat of the Dardanians."

He listened to the assembled army marching out to meet their Dardanian foes. He glanced back, too distant to see the pikes over the tops of the tents. But he knew the northern gate was now opened for them to exit. Would Marcellus Paullus be with them?

"She is a royal woman," Dimos said. "So many guards, I would guess. What does it matter? You will kill them all yourself?"

"No, but if I can get you out, will you swear to me one service? I mean before all the gods and on your life, an oath made with your own blood."

"If you get me out, I will swear to worship you as a god for all my days. I will do all you ask."

Varro looked around for a way to break Dimos free. The bars were rusted, but without tools they could not be pulled apart. He rattled the door, drawing a pained smile from Dimos. Without a key, he doubted be could find another way to get him out of the cage.

"I will fetch the wine now, before I am missed. I have some time with the battle called, but not much."

"I'll wait here," Dimos said with a smirk.

Rushing back along the main path, for he saw no reason to hide with the camp emptied, he considered how Dimos could help him. Varro's own escape seemed impossible, unless he fled this moment. But fleeing would do him no good without Paullus in tow. A short, brutal life of wandering and banditry awaited him if he could not return to Tribune Sabellius without Marcellus Paullus.

But it felt that the moment the amphora fell and spilled its wine into the dirt, Varro's fate had changed. It expelled the germ of a plan, one that was desperate and fraught with uncertainty. Yet as it solidified during his run to fetch the broken amphora and return to Dimos, he believed it was his best and only hope to escape with Paullus.

And the plan required him to remain a slave a while longer.

He jogged back across the field with the half-emptied amphora sloshing at his shoulder to reach Dimos still pressed against the bars. He laughed when he saw what Varro carried.

"I will be too drunk to escape!"

Varro tipped the shattered clay rim to the iron bars and lifted so the wine flowed out. Dimos bathed his face in it, slurping it down.

"That's enough for now," Varro said, placing the amphora down. "Is it the same three guards that come to feed you each evening?"

"Only the boy comes with his pail of water and handful of hard bread. He has come later and later every day, and I think soon he will stop coming."

"That is well," Varro said. "The gods may well be watching you. The plan to escape is simple enough."

He produced the knife he stole from one of the tents and fed the wooden handle through the bars. Dimos gasped.

"Hide this," Varro said. "When he comes with the water, he will want to strike you in the face with the ladle."

"The little bastard has broken my teeth!"

"I know it, and we'll use it against him. If you judge no one else is watching, do not accept the water. Hang back as if you are afraid of the ladle. Try to get him to lean up against the bars. I assume you have no hesitation in killing him. Try to be as quiet as you can."

Dimos shook his head, his narrow eyes squinting to nothing. "No hesitations, Roman. Only pleasure. So I kill the boy. I'm sure he does not have the key to my cage. He is a fool."

"When he doesn't return, the real jailer will come looking for him. Kill him too, and you'll have your key."

"There is much luck involved here, Roman. What if he does not come himself but sends another fool like that boy?"

"These are not officers. They're lowly men given the lowly task of keeping prisoners at the edge of death. He won't have another fool to send. They are all fools. So he will come himself. Of that I am certain. Of what comes after, less so. As you say, it involves much luck."

"You cannot get the key yourself?"

"I will be fortunate enough to arrive here in time. My only hope is that today there will be enough confusion for me to slip away. The Macedonians will return with their injured. They may have won their battle, or lost it more likely. I cannot see pikes of any use in the mountains the Dardanians have forced them to endure. I am set to return to Alamene tonight. This will be my moment to sneak back here. I want to find dead guards and an opened cage when I do."

"As do I." Dimos turned the blade over in his hand, tested its edge with this thumb, then slipped it into the tatters of his pants. "But if I get out, where do I go?"

"Where you parked your caravan. All your wagons must still be there. Hide among them and wait for me. If I do not show, then find something to scale the wall. Take your freedom and you owe me nothing. But don't be too fast to leave."

"Scale the wall?" Dimos chuckled and slapped at a fly circling his head. "Was there a ladder?"

"If I join you, I can boost you up. Once you grab the top, haul yourself over. You are not weak for an old man. I've seen you wrestle those wagons out of ruts."

"I do not feel strong. But a chance at escape will renew my strength. What have I to lose? If I fail, maybe I will be tortured and die. If I succeed, then I will never return here."

"If you succeed, then you owe me service. You swear to carry it out, even if it seems too dangerous?"

"Escape death just to die for you? I don't think so, Roman. But I will do all I can, if you will tell me what it is."

"I will tell you," Varro said. "Just before you go over the wall. If this fails, I do not want you to be forced to tell the enemy my plan."

"But I will tell them you aided me, and that you had a plan."

"Fair enough. But let's pray that never comes to pass. Now, I've been gone overlong. I will be here tonight. If the boy does not come, or you cannot kill him, we will set a plan for another night. We must act in unison."

"The gods bless you," Dimos said. "I have cursed your name a hundred times since I've been locked here. But if you free me, I will be your servant. But my men, you cannot help them if they live?"

"We cannot help everyone, as much as I wish we could. This is a huge camp and I cannot say where they might all be, or if they are dead, or if they betrayed you."

Dimos nodded, patting the knife hid at his back.

Varro hoisted the amphora and trotted back toward headquarters, certain that he ran both toward punishment and freedom.

20

Varro's head plunged into the cold water once more. Strong hands forced his face to the bottom of the wood basin, crushing his nose. He thrashed and struggled, feeling as if his head were expanding and his eyes were about to explode from their sockets. The bindings around his wrists pinned his arms behind his back. Terror overcame reason. The fight for life surged through him and he bucked against the man holding him under water.

Bubbles escaped his mouth. He screamed through his sealed lips, fighting the urge to inhale. At last, he could not stand it and gasped.

In the same instant, the hands yanked him out of the water.

The dark tent was lit only with clay oil lamps. His vision was hazed white. His coughing and gasping overcame the hard, chiding voice of Athenagoras's advisor, the old wretch with half black and gray hair.

He spit out the water and coughed. How long had this gone on for? The burly soldier holding his dripping body in hand let him hang like a wrung-out cloth.

Slowly he realized the old man was staring at him, judging whether he could endure yet another round of nearly drowning in this basin of water. He slid a thin finger along his bony nose and tapped as he considered. Varro continued to cough and sputter, letting himself slump in the grip of his enemy.

At last the old taskmaster clicked his tongue as if disgusted. He waved a finger in the air and spoke words that sounded watery and muffled to Varro.

But rather than be dunked underwater again, the soldier who had tortured him now hefted him off the ground and dragged him toward the tent exit. The floor was pounded earth, and Varro's knees dragged across it. He had been stripped naked, and another man waited with his wine-stained tunic.

The broken amphora sat beside the tent entrance. Varro's blurry vision came to focus just as the soldier dragged him past it.

Outside, he was in headquarters again where other slaves were setting timbers to create the bonfire. Athenagoras's tent rose high above the others, and Varro looked to it but saw only two guards idling at the entrance.

His own guard dropped him into the dirt, flung a brown linen at him, then the other man threw his clothes over his naked body. Both shouted at him, but Varro had not learned any of their tongue other than the smattering of useful and polite words he had gleaned during his time on the Macedonian farm.

Though he had no strength, he understood he was to pat himself dry and wear his tunic. They had been careful not to leave marks while torturing him for the loss of the amphora. He had to return to Alamene unscathed, since Varro was now a prized possession of hers.

The sun set over a sullen and dispirited camp. Initially Varro had thought he might escape punishment for the amphora. But when he returned with it broken, he found himself confined to that tent until the weird old advisor to Athenagoras had been ready to punish him. That had taken most of the day, since the Macedonians had returned in what Varro assumed was defeat. They had none of the bluster of victorious men. They carried scores of injured, most of them through with arrows. He now understood how they could have fought the Dardanians all summer with no progress. They would not yield their formations and adapt to the enemy's style. And so they suffered stalemate and defeats.

But these were the thoughts that had passed Varro's afternoon. Now he lay breathless on hard earth, dripping water from his exhausted body.

Once he wore his tunic, the strong guard ordered him up with a curt wave of his meaty hand. He tramped Varro across the parade ground, past the stacked logs for tonight's bonfire, and to a tent where Marcellus Paullus awaited outside.

He dressed in his Roman toga, regarding Varro with hooded eyes. The guard deposited Varro at the tent entrance and left without a word to either of them.

"You look well cleaned." Paullus smirked, tilting his head as if in challenge.

"And you look like a traitorous piece of shit. Didn't you ride out with the enemy to fight Rome's allies? You look well cleaned yourself."

A dark wave rolled across Paullus's face, but he simply tilted his head back.

"What I do and where I go is not a slave's business. My lady is most pleased when I am clean and dressed as a proper man. She makes the same demands of her slaves."

"She is Athenagoras's daughter?"

"I've told you as much," Paullus said. "But you country boys are too stupid to remember anything. Listen to me, slave. Alamene had to attend her father tonight. So I am here to show you where you will live for now. You'll find that if you are obedient—and don't drop things—life here can be pleasant. Far better than army life, even as a slave."

Paullus gestured to the tent behind him. He pushed open the flap and exposed the dark interior.

"In you go. Don't come out unless summoned. I'm afraid you missed the evening meal while you were cleaning up from spilling all that wine. Don't worry. You'll eat again tomorrow night. I'm certain you got a belly full of water to hold you over."

Water still clogged Varro's nose, and the exhaustion of hanging over the edge of death still clung to him. Nevertheless, he squared up to Paullus.

"The gods have no mercy on traitors. It is not too late to change. These are not your people, and Alamene is not your wife. Do you think you are really an officer here? Do the men you command," he twisted the word into mockery, "even understand what you say? Think hard, Paullus. In Rome you are a member of one of her most powerful families. Here, you are a foreigner at best, and one of the enemy at worst."

Paullus raised his hand as if to slap Varro, but held it overhead and glared at him.

"You don't know what it was like at home. Here I am free to be with the woman I love, the woman I am destined to marry. We both know it, even if spoken words fail us. The true language of love speaks between hearts. You will never know this, you poor slave. Now, into your tent. Don't think to leave it. A guard is set here every night."

With a rough shove from Paullus, Varro tripped into the interior. He stood in shock at the scene before him. The gods were especially cruel, for the interior was almost identical to the tent where he had killed Galba's slave. Paullus must have considered his reaction as despair, and laughed as he snapped the flap shut.

Three small cots had been set up, and a man lay on his side on the leftmost one. The other two appeared to have never seen any use. The man seemed asleep, but he mumbled at Varro's entrance.

"Take the far bed, and don't get close to me."

"You speak Latin," he said, rushing to the man's side. He wore only his loincloth, a white toga hanging by a peg from a nearby tentpole. He was in good shape with a neat beard much darker than his sandy hair. He lay with arms folded and eyes pressed shut. His shoulders were speckled with fat freckles.

"What did you expect? The whore loves us Romans. Now let me sleep."

"So it's true," Varro said, squatting beside the man and ignoring his request. "I'm Optio Marcus Varro, First Legion Tenth Hastati Tenth Century. Who are you?"

"A fucking slave like you, sir. If you keep talking, sir, I'm going to ram a cloth down your throat."

Yet he continued to lay on his side, eyes shut and brows furrowed.

"Listen, what do you know about Marcellus Paullus? What is his relationship with Alamene?"

Now the man's eyes flicked open. They were pale green and unsettling in their clarity. He stared at Varro before answering.

"You ask a lot of questions, Optio Marcus Varro. He's new here. He thinks a great deal of himself. I guess he's allowed to since he's the whore's latest plaything. But I expect she has fucked him enough by now. You'll be taking his place for a bit. She goes in rotations like that."

"But how can she behave like this right next to her father's tent?" He asked the question with deliberate innocence. As expected, the man sneered at him.

"She's not his daughter. She's part of the royal family, and a real troublemaker for the lot of them. She's Philip's cousin and why she's here is her own business. She doesn't tell her slaves and doesn't let us overhear much."

"Us? Are there more than just we two?"

"Three," the man said. "Marcellus is one, but just doesn't realize it. Then again, he's different being a rich man. It seems Athenagoras would like to keep him around too. But the whore gets what she wants. And, no, right now it's just us. But there have been others. Most men go away when they bore her. If you don't want to go away, then I suggest doing everything she asks and don't make her bored."

Varro sat on the bed next to this man, considering how deluded Paullus was about his situation. Such a man was beyond reasoning. He would have to drag Paullus away from here. But then that was his plan. He needed to be certain that Dimos had spoken the truth.

"Look, do you have a name I can use? We can forget about rank and whatnot. Maybe you're a tribune, for all I know. We're both slaves now."

"Will you let me sleep if I give you a name?"

"Eventually."

The man rolled onto his back. "Call me Lucius. I'm not a soldier, at least not when I was captured. I've done my six years already, not that I'll ever see Rome again for it to matter."

"Lucius," Varro leaned forward lowering his voice. "Don't speak like that. There may be a way out of here."

But Lucius raised his head and cocked his brow. "Why do you assume I want to leave? Can't you see me sleeping in a clean bed, with clean clothes, and nothing better to do than serve a beautiful woman? I've been with her longer than I was in the army and like it much more."

Now Lucius narrowed his eyes and smiled knowingly.

"Ah, all the new ones think they can escape. After all, where are the guards and the chains? She's just a woman. Easily duped, right? You won't get any help from me, Optio. And if you try anything funny, I'll be sure to let her know you need to be used up quickly. So that you too can go away once she's bored."

"You fucking traitor."

Lucius laughed and folded his hands behind his head. "It's a better life for me, if not for you. I didn't want it at first. I might've said the same thing myself those years ago. But Alamene is most fond of me, and has lots of uses for a loyal man. Maybe one day I'll also go away. I don't know. But in the meantime, it's not a bad life. As long as you can perform, anyway."

Varro sat back on the bed, wondering what to do about Lucius. He had hoped for an ally, but now had another guard to defeat.

"I guess you're right. I'm sorry for cursing you. You didn't deserve that." But Varro cursed him harder in his thoughts. He lied to lower Lucius's suspicions.

"Never mind it. It's a hard thing to lose your freedom. But if you can learn to accept a smaller world, it's not a bad place. Not like if you were a regular slave. Then there's branding and beatings, and gods knows what else. But Alamene wants her Roman men in fine form."

"How long will we be here? Does she live in a palace? Do you think I'll get to see it?"

"She drags us all over the countryside whenever her father is away, which is often, especially now with the war. If he goes north, we go south. That kind of thing. But she always returns home sooner or later. This fight over who owns Paullus has kept her here a while. But I think she's won it. She is the king's beloved cousin, after all. I expect we'll be moving on soon enough."

"To a palace?" Varro put on his best wide-eyed country boy impression. Lucius seemed to believe it and chuckled.

"Most likely. We've been gone overlong. And living in tents only appeals to the whore for a short while. She'll want her baths and grand bedrooms now. You'll love the palace in Pella. The slave quarters are probably better than your old home. Just be obedient, stay in good form, and please the whore. You'll learn to enjoy it."

Varro nodded and wiped his face.

"I'm sorry to have disturbed your sleep. No one is telling me anything. Do you speak Greek? Maybe you can teach me?"

"Sure, we'll have time on the road back. Now take that far bed. You stink."

He had a dozen more questions to ask, but knew he would draw suspicion again. So he picked across the dark space to lie upon the bed and consider his next steps.

The sun was setting and soon Dimos would be murdering his tormentor and grabbing a key to his cage. He was in a forlorn part of the camp, where prisoners rotted, animals drank at troughs, and carts waited to be filled. No one would miss him, possibly until this time tomorrow. So Varro only needed the cover of darkness and less than an hour to aid Dimos's escape. From there, he had to trust that his plan would work on its own and the gods would favor it. He had nothing more to offer in return than his continued devotion to the goddess Fortuna, courted by every living man but favoring only a handful. Varro counted on her continued attentions.

Or he was going to die in a palace in the heart of Macedonia and never see Rome again, as Lucius had so pointedly noted.

When darkness settled over camp and the voices beyond the walls of his cloth prison faded, he studied Lucius. He was a dark shape against the bonfire light glowing through the tent wall. His sides rose and fell. He was as good a guard as any posted outside.

Now was the time to act. If he waited longer, Dimos would leave and his plan would fail. He slid his feet off the bed with exaggerated caution, and slipped them into his sandals.

21

His sandals crunched the pounded earth floor of the tent. To Varro it sounded as if he had stepped on pottery, and his eyes bulged at Lucius's shadow. His fellow slave appeared asleep, but Varro held still long enough to confirm it. Daring a second step, he moved closer to the rear wall of the tent. Each footfall grated on him, but Lucius remained unmoved and lying on his back. Varro looked to the tent flap. A shadow wavered outside, outlined by the bonfire at the center of headquarters.

Taking a lesson from Curio, he crouched beside the rear tent wall and ran his hand along the bottom. Stakes pinned the cloth to the earth, but he pulled these up. It was slow work, and sweat beaded on his forehead. The night was hot even this high in the mountains, but the sweat rolling down his face was cold. If he brought the tent down on himself, the plan would end in failure before it began.

Yet the stakes rose up, and the rear of the tent allowed enough slack for him to slip beneath. Before he did, he waited and listened. The rear wall did not benefit from the bonfire light. If someone guarded the back ways, Varro would not know unless they made noise. He held his breath, but found it was harder to do after having so recently been on the verge of drowning. So he tugged up the length of tent wall then stuck his legs beneath it.

For a moment he was bisected between tent and freedom. He had the strange sensation of being cleaved in half, as if the gods would slay him in this moment of vulnerability.

But he slid beneath, the tent edge flipping across his lips and nose, until he was wholly on the outside of the tent.

The Macedonians did not expect Alamene's slaves to flee, or so Varro surmised. Based on Lucius's attitude, maybe her slaves preferred their condition. While he enjoyed the fresh air of freedom, in practical terms he had escaped nothing. He was in the center of eight thousand enemy soldiers. There was no real need to guard his tent.

He reminded himself of his comparisons to mosquitoes. As long has he remained small and flitting, like a nocturnal insect, he could move through the camp unchallenged. He was part of this camp now, and men had seen him crossing all day long on tasks for the general. Granted, the Macedonians were in their tents at night, and slaves penned for the evening. But knowing if he were cornered, he might be able to convince a guard he was on official business granted him courage. Not speaking the language would make it a challenge, if not impossible. But what mattered to Varro was belief that he was somehow safer than his last failed attempt to navigate the camp at night.

He crouched low and zipped along the edge of the tents. He knew this part of the camp best. Once beyond the track that separated headquarters from the common ranks, he was less certain. But he had established a sense of direction over the days running around the camp. He followed landmarks and knew where there was more space between tents. In his last run with Falco, they had plunged into the heart of the camp by letting the natural paths guide them to where most men gathered. Now he knew to follow a different track to lead toward the ever-thinning edge of camp. Men did not like to be next to the wall, for in an attack or breach they would be most vulnerable. Also, garbage tended to accumulate there and it smelled even worse than the heart of the camp.

So he darted through the night, listening for the approach of guards or the cough of a soldier still awake after dark. He only moved when he judged it safe. When he felt panic rise at the approach of a shadow or the sound of a voice, he held still and waited. Patience repaid him with safety.

At last he emerged along the southern edge of camp where Dimos's carts were still in a semicircle. His oxen had been taken away, most likely put to work elsewhere but possibly butchered for their meat. The goods had all been off-loaded and the carts sat empty, outlined by the faint light of stars and a half-moon.

Dimos was not visible, but Varro was glad for it. Guards patrolled the camp, even at its most forlorn edges. So he bent low and rushed to the first of the carts. He then worked his way around, hugging the edges until he found Dimos.

His white hair betrayed him. He was huddled in a gray cloth and crouching between two carts, looking at Varro with wide eyes.

"You did it," he said, rushing to the old trader's side. "Was it difficult?"

"The boy died easily. The man, not as much. I was hurt, but he is dead."

Varro crouched down between the carts then pulled away the dirty cover from Dimos's shoulders. He hissed at the ragged cut that ran from the old man's left nipple to his belly button. Blood leaked in a bright stripe.

"It's not deep," Dimos said. "But there was much blood. Flies will come to the bodies with the sunrise. So I must get out, Roman, or they will do worse to me."

Varro looked around for anything to bind the wound, but beside his own tunic he had only the dirty cloth.

"This will have to serve. Let me bind this, at least to protect it while getting over the wall."

Dimos raised his arms, sucking his breath against the pain and spilling more blood from the cut. But Varro worked with speed and care. He had seen worse wounds than this, though not on an old man. He hoped Dimos would be able to endure all he was about to ask of him after losing blood in an already weakened state. All of Varro's hopes rested on this one man. It was as if he were placing his life into a clay cup then throwing it into the air, hoping it would not shatter on the ground and spill his life away.

When he tied off the wound, Dimos lowered his hands and nodded thanks.

"All right, I am going to give you a boost to the top of the wall. Get over it, hang from the other side, and drop. Be careful of your ankles. You're strong but not young."

"I will be careful, Roman. Get me to the top, and I will not lose my one chance at life. Now, tell me what it is you want me to do."

"Listen carefully. When you are free, go to the Dardanian camp. They must be in the mountains a fair distance from here, but not too far."

"I know where they are, Roman. I am a trader. It's my business to know where the coin is."

Varro gave him a crooked smile. "And you made such a fuss about bringing me into this camp? I thought you had family here?"

"Maybe," Dimos shrugged. "My nephews went somewhere. Why not here?"

Waving his hand to dismiss the topic, he continued. "Then go to the Dardanians. I am certain Falco and Curio went there. They would have nowhere else to go. They have a letter from our tribune that should at least guarantee their safety if not outright aid. When you get there, find the Dardanian leader. Do you know him?"

"Bato? Of course. He's a tough old warrior and knows how to bargain."

"Then go to him. Ask for Falco and Curio. You tell them how I aided your escape and about my slavery to Alamene. Now this is the most important part. You must ensure Bato will act on what I tell you next."

Dimos leaned in closer, his squinting eyes widening in expectation.

"Alamene, cousin to King Philip, enemy of Rome and her allies, will be leaving with her escorts for Pella within the week. Possibly as soon as tomorrow. I cannot be certain. But it is a journey of several days, if not more through the mountains. I'm sure Athenagoras will assign her escorts at least part of the way. Bato can capture a royal prisoner while she is exposed on the road home. Such a prize should not need further explanation. He could bargain his way to victory against Athenagoras with Alamene as his captive."

"I am a Macedonian, Roman. Will Bato believe me or believe I have been sent to trap him?"

"That is why you get Falco and Curio. You can prove yourself to Falco. Just tell him that I have done my penance for my crimes, and that we're bringing Paullus home. And if he still doubts you, tell him I caught him rolling the barley fields with Old Man Pius's granddaughter five summers ago. He doesn't even know I saw it. That'll end any question of where you got your information."

Dimos chuckled. "Spying on your friends, Roman?"

"We weren't friends then. Now, do this and you will have paid me back a thousand times for tonight."

"Thank you, Marcus Varro. You are a good man. I will do this for you. For I was certain old Dimos had driven his last caravan."

"Not yet. Now, over the wall and away with you. I wish I

could've brought you supplies to aid you on your way. I can only ask the gods keep you, if they even listen to me anymore."

Dimos reached around his back, then presented the knife Varro had stolen. It was dark with blood, but he held it forward.

"This isn't going to help me if I find danger on the way. I'm better off throwing rocks. Plus, I know where I can go to get my own things before continuing on. So you take it."

It slipped easily into Varro's hand, sticky with blood and not good for anything other than a thrust into soft flesh. He tucked it into his tunic, feeling the hard warmth of it against the flesh of his hip.

They approached the wall with exaggerated caution. As Dimos winced and fell against the wall, Varro realized just how exhausted the old man must be. Days of deprivation and a bad cut must have stressed him to his limits, and only nerves were carrying him now.

Dimos set his foot into Varro's interlaced hands. After balancing himself against the wall, Dimos grunted to signal he was prepared. Varro hefted up and Dimos pushed off.

He slapped his hands onto the wall and hung there.

It seemed as if the entire camp must spot Dimos. Surely guards would see such an obvious figure.

Yet the old trader groaned and pulled himself up, his wiry muscles standing out on his back. He struggled. But even in his degraded condition he still mounted the top of the wall, then disappeared over the side.

Varro rushed to the wall, pressing his ears to it. He heard the bump of Dimos's body vibrate through the wood. He sighed, glad the old man dangled on the opposite side. Then he heard a softer thump, and Varro knew he was away. He rapped the wood wall with his knuckles, hoping Dimos would answer. Moments passed and Varro wondered if he were hurt. But the return knock came, and Varro knew Dimos had his freedom. Realizing he was in the open still, he ducked back between the wagons.

An overwhelming urge to follow Dimos swept across him.

If he moved a wagon into position, he might be able to jump from its platform and grab the top of the wall. He could take his own advice, find Falco and Curio with the Dardanians, then lead an attack on Alamene's escort himself.

He could be free now. Maybe he didn't need to return with Paullus, and just tell Tribune Sabellius that he had died. After all, Paullus was enslaved even if he didn't realize it. Eventually Alamene would make him go away, as Lucius had described what must be a euphemism for death. Such a report would not be a lie for long.

However much this temptation built in him, and despite how it seemed now, he realized remaining with Paullus was a far better plan.

If he did reach Falco and Curio with the Dardanians, he would still have to attack Alamene's escorts to capture Paullus. He realized that whatever deals Athenagoras and Alamene had made for the valuable hostage, it would never include Paullus's death. When Alamene made Paullus go away, he would be ransomed back to his family. If she did not want to bother with it, then Athenagoras would. Sabellius would know he had been deceived, and as Falco had once said, they would all be reduced to body parts thrown into the Tiber for that lie.

He could escape and live the life of a deserter, which he had already ruled out as impossible. Death was preferable. So if he had to attack, he had to guarantee Paullus's capture. Being at Paullus's side when the attack occurred would ensure success. With Dimos's blood-crusted knife, he could take Paullus hostage and lead him to the Dardanian lines. If attacking from the outside, he might yield Paullus an opportunity to escape or do something even more rash like die defending Alamene. Perhaps carrying his head back would serve Sabellius's purposes. But Varro did not want to chance such an outcome. Too much had been sacrificed to let Paullus die at this point.

So he emerged from the wagons and followed the same path back to the slave tent.

And found a flurry of activity surrounding it.

Lucius's light hair was clear and obvious against the bonfire blazing at the center of headquarters. The bright lines of his clean toga drew harsh shadows as he loaded an elaborately decorated cart with heavy baggage. Paullus worked alongside him.

A score of other soldiers also worked to load two other wagons, one outfitted with an empty cage where its door hung ominously open.

Another score of soldiers scratched their heads and stretched as if just awakened. Bonfire light sparkled off their bronze helmets.

Varro crouched behind a tent on the other side of the track that demarcated headquarters. His heart raced and his breath drew short. He searched between the soldiers and spotted Alamene. She stood before the bonfire, her jet-black hair rimmed with brilliant orange. The intense light shined through the many layers of her Greek dress, revealing her winsome shape.

It seemed as if she stared right at him.

He ducked back and again closed his eyes like a child. But curiosity overcame his fears, and he peered from behind the tent where unsuspecting soldiers slept. The slave tent billowed down and Lucius now assisted soldiers with folding it up. All the contents seemed to have been removed already.

He realized they were not searching for him. It seemed as if they were packing up and preparing for travel.

The cage, he realized, must be for him and Lucius, and possibly Paullus depending on the outcome of the negotiation between Alamene and Athenagoras.

Dimos had no time to reach the Dardanians. Alamene was

leaving tonight, under cover of darkness. Athenagoras must have loaned men to escort her, yet their numbers fell short for a royal escort. Perhaps traveling in a smaller band was easier and less obvious. But those wagons spoke of wealth which would make it a target. This made no sense.

If Alamene left with Paullus now, his plans would be ruined.

Voices echoed out of the darkness behind him. He turned to find a band of soldiers marching up the track between tents. They rubbed their eyes and grumbled, their shoulders slumped and heads lowered.

With no time to spare, he jumped to the front of the tent, exposing himself to view from headquarters. But he pulled open the flap and ducked inside.

Seven men curled up on their blankets. The air was thick with the odor of sweat and buzzing with their snores. Varro nearly stepped on one of their dark-haired heads. But he snapped the flap shut and held his breath. His heartbeat could have been heard in Rome. He trusted the ordinary soldier's love of sleep, believing it a universal condition of all fighting men. He guessed these Macedonians were exhausted from their day of battle, and nothing short of an officer screaming into their ears would wake them. Thus far he was not wrong.

The complaining column of soldiers passed outside as he stood one toe's breadth from waking a tent full of enemies.

The darkness inside the tent was incomplete from the bonfire light across the track. With the flap loose from having been hastily torn open, a thin line of illumination filled the interior. His eyes fell on gear. Helmets, harnesses, daggers, shields, swords, all of it laid out beside each man's space.

His feet grew cold, but what other plan did he have?

Picking up the bronze helmet was simple enough. It slid atop his head, ill-fitting but passable. He worked over the prone form of a man with a fresh-shaved beard. A thick cut had scabbed under his eyes, but both eyes remained closed in slumber.

His body shook with the effort of holding himself arched over the sleeping man. But he picked up a belt with dagger still attached.

Someone snorted and coughed, then rolled over to press against another who growled in his sleep at the intrusion.

Varro might have fainted, but he held still as sweat rolled off his head and into the collar of his tunic.

Dragging the sword away was hardest. It was longer and heavier than the gladius, and probably not something a pikeman often had cause to use. It was a single-edged blade, pitched forward at the front. It seemed more like an ax than a sword, yet he was grateful enough as he looped it around his waist. Finally, he grabbed a round shield.

He stood over the sleeping men, smiled, and nodded to them.

Then he strode out of the tent into a plan he was making up with each step forward.

If the gods needed entertainment, he was prepared to provide it.

22

"Marcus Varro, you will be found. Better to surrender yourself now than be dragged to my feet!"

Paullus cupped his hands to his mouth as he shouted in Latin into the surrounding tents.

Varro stood thirty yards away with a knot of sleepy-eyed Macedonians outfitted as he was. Most squatted on their haunches, while others folded their arms and appeared to be sleeping while standing. The roaring bonfire cast heavy, defined shadows that masked men from each other. The oversized Macedonian helmet slipped over his brow and cast his face into shadow. He smiled within it as Paullus stared forlornly after his shouting.

Alamene oversaw the proceedings with both arms crossed over her chest. When Paullus's shouting did not yield results, he turned as if to explain something. He offered words Varro could not hear, but received a sudden slap across his face. The sharp crack of it drew looks even from the score of tired soldiers. Some laughed softly, hiding their faces from Paullus, who stood back in shock.

Alamene screamed into the night, probably curses and dire warnings for Varro to reveal himself. But unlike Paullus, she did not wait for an answer. She spun on her heels, flung what seemed a flower into the bonfire, then stormed back toward the carts.

Paullus chased after her. His desperation was sickening, and Varro joined the others who now laughed more boldly.

A nearby man muttered something to Varro then snickered. He returned the laugh and nodded, moving away casually though his heart pounded him breathless.

His only focus was to follow this procession out of the camp. He could break away later and attempt to reach the Dardanians then urge them to action. But he had to find them first, and every hour Paullus would be traveling east to Pella. The Dardanians would be unlikely to catch up before reaching the Macedonian heartland.

Unless Varro could halt the column's progress.

Somewhere along the path, he might be able to get ahead and create a roadblock. He had learned how effective that could be from Philip's own troops. It seemed an appropriate turnabout to use against Alamene's escort. Perhaps then the Dardanians might still have a chance.

More and more of his plan began to feel as flimsy as butterfly wings. Yet the only other plot he could imagine was taking Alamene hostage right now, then bargaining for Paullus in exchange. Of course, he would die the moment after any exchange. Athenagoras would ensure it. Even as mad as his current plan was, going for Alamene now felt even more deadly.

So he watched as carts were packed up and tied off. Drivers sat on their seats and horses were readied. The soldiers began to shift, responding to the orders of a lone figure black against the blazing fire. Varro followed along, head down and as forlorn as the others of his group. These men were not part of a regular unit. For none of them seemed to converse with each other except for short exchanges. It was easy enough to understand the mission. They would surround the wagons to protect Alamene and her attendants as they traveled to Pella.

Athenagoras remained in his tent or otherwise hidden. But the shadowed figure in black turned out to be his advisor, the man with the strange fringe of gray hair who had spent the evening plunging Varro's head underwater. As he passed, he wished he could shove the bastard into the bonfire.

Varro stalled so that he assumed a spot in the rear guard. The cart with the cage waited before him. Lucius happily climbed into the cage and made himself comfortable against its bars. To Varro's surprise, two other men climbed inside. Athenagoras's adviser shoved these unfortunates into the cage, shouting at them then finally slamming the door shut. The bars reverberated and the adviser glared at them before finally stepping off the cart.

At the rear of the column, Varro could see nothing beyond the slave cart. Men ran to and from the lead carts, and Alamene along with Paullus were escorted to somewhere in front.

The men around him shifted on their feet and rubbed the back of their necks. The man directly before him spit on the ground as they waited, then shifted so that his profile faced Varro. The bonfire outlined him in orange and he began to chat amicably.

While he did not understand the words, he guessed it was grumbling about their late-night duty. Varro nodded at pauses and tried to reflect the man's expressions. Such mimicry succeeded a short time, but his friendly partner seemed to be growing suspicious. Varro hummed and grunted, but never spoke an actual word.

To his relief, someone at the lead shouted an order and the man spun around. Torches were lit and held at intervals along both sides of the escort. The carts rattled into life, and began to roll forward.

They marched ahead, gaining speed as the carts trundled

along the track out of headquarters. Varro glanced behind, seeing nothing but a clutch of soldiers against the bonfire. Two tents were now absent from the wide circle, like missing teeth in a giant's grin.

The iron bars of a cage that should have contained Varro now rattled ahead of him. The three men imprisoned inside sat quietly, only the tops of their heads visible. Varro matched the pace and posture of the man in front. He had learned this from his own time as a recruit. Roman officers demanded uniformity and discipline. Every man had to match every other man. There was no excuse for the slightest deviation, and any deviation was acknowledged with a sharp and stinging crack of a vine cane across the shoulders. Pain made a good teacher, and Varro found it simple enough to look like a trained Macedonian soldier.

At least to his own eye.

The eastern gate yawned open. The carts rolled through and Varro followed. His heart pounded with the thought that he was walking away from eight thousand enemies while disguised as one of them. If he survived this, he would have stories to tell his grandchildren.

But thoughts of future progeny swept aside before the cold reality of the task that remained ahead. Had he been simply trying to save himself, within the hour he could safely slip away and claim success. Yet Paullus was likely in the middle cart. The two carts looked identical in their ostentatious decor. The lead one probably held Alamene's belongings. The middle would be most protected and so likely held her, her attendants, and Paullus.

If he shadowed the escort, he might find an opportunity to nab Paullus. He would eventually have to relieve himself. Varro would be there.

He smirked at the thought of leaping upon him while he crouched behind a bush, pissing his pristine toga. A few good punches to his handsome face, and he would quiet down.

Everyone knew cavalrymen had nothing on the infantry when it came to brute strength. At the height of his training, Varro felt he could lift Paullus and his horse overhead with one arm. He was weakened and hungry now, but he still did not worry for overcoming Paullus.

These dreams led him a fair distance from the camp, such that the campfires and bonfires were just orange glows in the dark distance. They had been following a road for two hours, and Varro never found a chance to peel away. Yet now the lead called a halt. The horses would need rest as well as the escorts. Varro's feet were callused from his journey north, but nothing like they were from regular marching. Still he felt the ache as keenly as anyone.

As the wagons rolled to a stop, their wheels crunching and thudding over gravel and ruts, the soldiers relaxed their pace. The moment to sneak away arrived.

But the man in front of him spun around the moment the rest was called.

A frown creased his face. Clearly, he had time to consider Varro over the first leg of their march, and his doubts had grown.

He started in with a long sentence that sounded accusatory. Varro smiled and nodded, but the man suddenly grabbed his wrist. His hand was hot and tight around Varro's hand. He repeated himself, his eyes flashing.

Varro tore out of the man's grip and mumbled a curse, or what he hoped sounded like a Greek curse. He tried to imitate Dimos and his brother when they had been upset. It seemed to work, for the man let him go and Varro turned his back to head toward the others who now stepped off to the side of the road.

But his new friend was insistent. He called after him, and Varro just raised his hand as if to wave goodbye. His eyes scanned ahead to terrain where he could escape. But in the darkness, there was only grass and scattered trees. The land was rocky and undulating, being in the mountains, and most of it was obscured in the faint moonlight.

Now the man shouted to others in their small group. Whatever he said, a dozen eyes shifted to Varro. Many narrowed in suspicion. One man stood and spoke low to Varro.

They were demanding his identity. He did not understand the words, but taut postures, staring eyes, and set jaws all indicated challenge. He was caught between his so-called friend and the line of rear guards, eight by swift count.

No way to flee from this.

One of the Macedonians leaped to his feet and pointed at Varro's tunic, shouting excitedly.

All eyes focused on his stomach, and Varro looked down as well.

Dimos's blood had smeared him while he had worked on binding his wound. Now, as someone brought a torch to bear, the light revealed more blood than a mere accident would yield.

He drew the wedge-shaped sword from his belt. It was heavy and unwieldy, and his training had caused him to hold it like a gladius. Yet this was a slashing weapon with a single edge. His miscalculation cost him the benefit of surprise.

The guards shouted together, and none of them fumbled with their swords. A wall of round shields sprang up before him, backed by blades flashing moonlight.

He hurled forward, seeking the open field of high grass. Skirting the wall of round shields, he shouted as a sword swept past the side of his head. His helmet bobbled as he ran and his feet pounded into hard, uneven earth.

The Macedonians recovered the brief advantage Varro had in running first. The entire escort column was now roused. He heard the warning shouts spreading behind him the way fire runs along a roofline. Armed and armored, carrying a foreign shield, he still had no chance to fight his way free.

The closest man behind him screamed as something like the sound of a snapping branch reached Varro's ears. He heard the pursuer collapse, likely having snapped his ankle bones stepping into a rut. Yet Varro's own feet carried over the dark grass as if the earth itself rose to meet his sandals.

Though the clump of trees and scrubby bush would not provide any advantage, it was at least a target for Varro to flee toward. His mind raced with possibilities, yet none of them seemed helpful.

But the hard edge of a shield slammed into the back of his shoulders.

The bright line of pain shoved him forward, unbalancing him and causing him to wheel to the side. The momentum of his pursuer sent the Macedonian sprinting through where Varro stood.

Looking back, a cluster of four shields pressed at him, bowling him over so that he slammed to the hard earth on his back. He drew his own shield over his body and head. Swords clanged on the bronze edging and central boss. But the shield battered down on him, striking his face.

Someone grabbed his legs. His shield tore aside. A foot stamped on his sword arm.

The brief battle was over. A half-dozen flushed and angry faces glared down at him.

Swords raised and the soldiers growled with fury. Even if he could twist out of their grip, one of the blades would strike home.

To his relief, a shouted order halted further violence. The Macedonians remained with their strangely canted blades overhead as if ready to hack Varro to bits. But they gritted their teeth and held. Behind them other soldiers shouted, orange torchlight bobbed closer, and the man who had broken his leg screamed into the vastness of the sky above.

Varro stared up at the stars. Near the half-moon they vanished into its silvery brightness. How he wished he could fly now. It was the only way out of this circle of enemies.

Their swords lowered, but they remained pinning Varro to the ground where a rock dug painfully into the base of his back. At last, someone forced into the tight group and glared down at him.

A stream of invective followed, and Varro tried to see who it was.

Athenagoras's adviser, or whatever he was, stared down at him. His black hair with the even rim of gray fell across his angered face. But the brightness of his evil eyes was unmistakable. He extended his thin arm and pointed with a shaking hand. A stream of words flowed, but Varro only understood one.

Roman.

He closed his eyes in defeat. The Macedonians hauled him from the ground. They kicked him as they did, and twisted his arms painfully behind his back. Their swords remained poised for a quick blow, but Varro was no longer a threat. Even if escape was possible, he was in the middle of a field with not a single hiding spot. He allowed them to prod and push him as they would.

They knocked off his helmet, then stripped his weapons. Men handed these around, staring at them as if unbelieving a Roman could have possessed them. At last they unbuckled the harness for his weapons. One man struck him across the face with it, a sharp flash of pain across his cheek.

The old adviser mumbled low threats through his gritted teeth. He snapped orders at the surly soldiers who surrounded him. They shoved him back toward Alamene's wagons. As the Macedonians kicked him ahead, he saw his so-called friend had broken his ankle. He smiled at the bastard's fate.

He arrived at the wagons, where additional torches had been lit to create a wide pool of golden illumination. Alamene and Paullus stood in the center, surrounded by guards with raised shields and readied swords. The two were at ease. Paullus smirked as the soldiers flung Varro before them. He had a moment to offer a snarl in return before someone stuck the back of his knees and sent him crashing to the ground.

The old adviser circled around, arms folded and face creased with a frown worsened by the wavering torchlight. He spoke softly to Alamene as he stood over Varro.

Her hazel eyes now glowed yellow with the torches. Her beauty had vanished into a contortion of rage. Paullus chuckled and pretended to hide his face as if embarrassed. The old adviser continued on until Alamene raised her delicate hand to silence him.

A hush fell over the circle of torchlight. In the distance, the broken-legged soldier cried out in pain. Varro lowered his head and stared at the grass. A black ant crawled over a long blade, dangled at the end as if deciding what to do. It then fell down into darkness, vanishing beneath the long grass.

Alamene knelt before him, cupping his face in both hands. Her skin was soft from never having lifted anything heavier than a silver cup. Her fingers were smooth and cold, and trembled on his cheeks as she raised his eyes to hers.

The rage had vanished, replaced with what seemed intense sadness. She was beautiful. Yet there was something wrong about the cast of her features, something that revealed a deeper ugliness that Varro did not like. She said nothing, did not shift her expression, but simply stared into his eyes. Her lips parted, and she ran her tongue along the edge. This was the same animal yearning he had seen from her when she visited him in the cage.

At last, she released him then stood. Varro remained staring at the grass. He feared if he looked up, his predicament would worsen.

She spoke to the adviser, who seemed to disagree. This elicited a frustrated puff of laughter from Alamene, who appeared to repeat herself. The old adviser once more restated something, and now Alamene shouted. Paullus tried to interject himself here, speaking in Greek so horribly mangled that even Varro knew it was incomprehensible.

Nor did it seem to matter, as the old man and Alamene devolved into shouting. At last he dared to look up. Paullus was on the outside of their disagreement as Alamene and the adviser faced each other. Both of them balled their fists and stood rigid. The guards around them stared ahead, the plain look of terror at being torn between two leaders clear on their faces. Even as enemies, Varro felt a tinge of sympathy for their plight.

The shouts bounced back and forth, with both pointing to Varro at different times. Paullus raised a tentative hand, then dared to touch Alamene's shoulder. She rounded on him with the fury and speed of a surprised cat. Paullus snapped back under her tirade. The old adviser simply waited for her to return to the real argument. Paullus was like a child put outside while the adults speak.

In the end, all Varro could do was kneel in the grass and await judgement. The old adviser who had him tortured seemed to prevail. Varro noted he carried a long knife at his side in a sheath that vanished into the black robe he wore. It dangled above Varro's head as if mocking him.

Finally, Alamene stamped her foot and retreated to her wagon. Paullus appeared as shocked as Varro, and he simply looked to him before chasing after his beloved.

The old man turned a murderous eye to Varro.

He pointed out two soldiers and growled angry words.

They seized him off the ground, wrenching his arms behind him, then dragged him to the rear of the column. Another man had already opened the cage, and the old adviser pointed wordlessly at it.

Rather than be dragged onto the cart, he mounted it himself then ducked into the cage.

The door slammed behind him. The lock clicked.

Two forlorn men stared up at him. But sandy-haired Lucius relaxed against the rear of the cage, arms folded comfortably over his stomach. He smiled then laughed.

"The new ones always think they can get away. But they never do."

23

The iron bars of the cage rattled as the line of wagons rolled through the night. Varro looked out from the cage on the rear guards he had hid among. His so-called friend with the broken ankle now sat on the cart's edge. At every rock and rut the cart jarred, sending the Macedonian into another explosive round of curses. The soldiers following hushed him with impatient curses of their own. Varro's erstwhile friend would then glare at him, mimicking a knife slice across the neck.

"He wants your blood," Lucius said, laughing every time the soldier groaned with pain.

"He'll have to wait his turn." Varro refused to look at Lucius, or the other two male slaves who curled away from him as if he might infect them by his presence. Instead, he watched the night falling victim to the dawn as a thin white haze appeared on the eastern horizon.

"I don't know about that," Lucius said. "You're still Alamene's man. I'm not sure how she feels about you, though. She'll want one good ride before you're done. So maybe you'll reach the palace alive."

Varro sighed and rested his head against the hard iron of the cage. He remained a slave, as the gods intended. If he had to endure a period of slavery so that when he passed to the next life his guilt would be lessened, then so be it. He had intended to reunite Paullus with his family, imagining a distraught mother and sisters weeping daily for the fate of their brother. How glad would they be to have him returned? But now he wondered if anyone missed Marcellus Paullus. He was an ass and a fool. Perhaps his family privately celebrated his fate. Inflicting the foolishness and stupidity of a man like Marcellus Paullus on Rome did not feel like a good deed done as penance. It felt like a crime. Perhaps this was why the gods turned against his plan.

As the iron bars vibrated against his head and the wagon wheels crunched the dirt road, his eyes began to droop. His stomach growled and his mouth was thick with woolly spit. In the space of a day he had labored for Athenagoras, been nearly drowned, and still had come this far without sustenance or rest. He was spent. Even knowing death must come soon, his eyes inexorably closed and dreams visited him.

It was a strange dream, for he realized none of this misty visage was real yet he could not act as he would in wakefulness. He was in camp, a common soldier sharing a tent with men he did not recognize. They did not speak to him, but interacted with him as they readied for the day. One handed him a stone which was cool and smooth as if it had been in a fast-running river for centuries. He slipped it into his tunic as if it were the most natural thing he could do.

Outside the tent, Centurion Fidelis waited for him. Varro felt instant fear at his snakelike grin.

"You're coming with me, Varro. No one to help you this time."

A soldier who may or may not have been with the centurion now hauled Varro through camp, though it seemed more like the Illyrian bandit camp where he had once been held captive.

Roman soldiers moved about their duties as if this ramshackle collection of tents was a true Roman fortification.

"You've got a lot to answer for," Fidelis said as they followed the irregular paths of the dream camp. "I know what you did, but I just don't know why. Tell me, Varro. Why did you kill Consul Galba's slave?"

"It was an accident, sir."

"Yet you had drawn your pugio. Why?"

"Because she had the necklace, sir. We wanted it back and things got out of control. She died, sir."

"She died," Centurion Fidelis said flatly. "And that's the whole point, isn't it? The consul will take it from here."

And suddenly he was in Consul Galba's tent. The man whom he recognized as Galba was actually his father. But in the strange dream logic, Varro accepted him as the actual consul. He waited with his head bowed, but his father-as-consul just stared at him, drinking wine from a silver cup. Varro felt the weight of the stone pulling his tunic down to his belt.

When he looked up at last, the consul had been replaced by his murdered slave.

Now Varro was certain of her. No mistaking Alamene for this woman. She wore a long, white stola that was stained brilliant red at her neck where Falco had accidentally stabbed her. She glared at him, but more chiding than hateful.

"Roman, do you have it?"

He answered that he did, assuming she meant the chain. This seemed to appease her and she nodded. She then touched his arm and beckoned him to follow her from the tent.

Stepping outside, they came to a stream he recognized as being near the camp. He had been on teams to bring water back from this place to supplement supplies. The slave dripped fresh blood from her opened throat, brilliant scarlet pattering on the small swell of her chest. Yet she smiled sweetly and extended her hand.

Varro knew to withdraw the gold chain, which had a moment ago been a stone hidden in his tunic. It was whole as the day he had claimed it, not cut in half to share with Falco. The golden braid was as thick as a man's thumb and long enough to fit a strong man's neck. She weighed it happily in her hand, then knelt to scoop mud by the flowing stream. When she had dug deep enough, she plopped the chain into the hole and plowed mud back over it.

"There," she said with a small sigh. "All is well."

She looked up to Varro, beaming, though her ravaged throat revealed white bone through the flow of gore splattering into the mud.

Then she laughed and splashed Varro with stream water, spraying it into his face. He jumped back with a shout of shock.

And awakened.

Dream and reality collided, for indeed cold water rushed down his face. He sputtered and pushed back, finding the cage bars resisting him. An intense brilliance glared into his eyes and a wave of heat assaulted him. As be blinked away the water, he realized men were laughing at him.

He was alone in the cage. It was late afternoon somewhere far from the Macedonian camp, yet still in the mountains. He saw their purple tips against the brilliance of a blue sky. The sun was low but struck his eyes.

"Good morning," Lucius said with false camaraderie. He was outside the cage and held an empty bucket that dripped water. Your big moment is here."

A group of soldiers stood a distance behind Lucius, and they laughed darkly while pointing at Varro.

"How long did I sleep?" He flicked the water from his eyes, but licked up every drop that rolled into his mouth. Had he less pride, he might have lapped the tiny puddles trapped in the divots of the wagon bed.

"Through the night and most of the day." Lucius let the bucket fall and extracted something from under arm. He drew closer to the cage and his face grew serious. "This is for you, Optio. I'm not a cruel man, really. I enjoy my life and don't want to see it changed. But that doesn't mean I like to see you suffer. You remind me of my brother when he was still alive."

He held forward a loaf of flat bread. Clearly this was not allowed, for Lucius searched about as he dangled it through the bars.

Saliva sprang to Varro's mouth instantly, and he snatched the bread away before it could be taken back as a cruel joke. But Lucius withdrew his hand only after Varro had the bread.

"Lie down so no one sees you eating it. Sorry, Optio, it was the best I could do for you. I don't know what you're trying to do, but you were a fool to follow if you hoped to escape. Now that chance is gone."

Varro stuffed his mouth with the bread, which was not fare for slaves. This must have come from Alamene's table, for it was soft and delicious. It was warm, too, though probably from being held under Lucius's arm. Such a thought might have revolted him before, but hunger ruled today.

Lucius picked up the bucket and slammed it against the bars, running it back and forth as if teasing Varro. He laughed, looking back at the soldiers who joined him and added their own curses. Then he left as Varro lay on his side and swallowed the last of the bread. With his mouth already dry, it went down hard and felt as if it caught in his chest. He remained on his side, staring at the gray side of the wagon through the bars of his cage.

A short time later, another Roman called his name. He cringed at the happy note in Paullus's voice.

"Optio Marcus Varro," he said, singing the title and name. "My lady and I have allowed you to pass the day at rest rather than in complete terror. It is the best we could do for you, seeing how your antics have left us no other recourse."

Varro peeled himself off the rusted bars and sat up. Paullus dressed in his toga, though it was no longer as pristine as it had been. His smug, carved face was bright even against late-day sun. While Varro could not see lower than his chest, it seemed as if Paullus was nearly dancing with anticipation.

"I came to take you back to Rome," Varro said. "And I'm not surrendering that mission until I am dead."

"Then your rest is at hand in more ways than one," Paullus said. The glee in his voice was sickening. "While my dear Alamene regrets your loss—for what I cannot say—I do not. I've no wish to go home ever again, but intend to live every day with my one and true love. Watching your beheading will be a joy, for cutting off your head also cuts me off from boring Rome and my miserable family. Such an economy of action, don't you think?"

Varro could not think.

Beheading?

He touched his neck as he considered the word. Paullus doubled over with laughter.

"You heard me correctly, Varro. You've been deemed too much of a threat to indulge any longer. Also, you injured a guard in your escape, and who knows if you killed a soldier to steal his gear. Your tunic is smeared with someone's blood. So, you're to be executed before we move on."

Varro did not answer, but his mind raced over what to do next. All the while, his hand rested at the base of his neck as if to hold his head in place. With so few options, he needed little time for consideration. Dimos might have been able to bring help if Alamene had departed even a day later. But that choice vanished the same moment Dimos escaped. Varro could attempt to break free and flee. At least here the land was rugged and full of folds and enough trees to form a small woods. That was a nearly impossible chance. He would be struck down before he could reach freedom. He needed an ally, someone to aid a stealthy escape. Lucius might be a Roman, but he was too well trained as Alamene's toy.

He looked to smirking Paullus and realized this man was his only hope.

"Listen to me," Varro said, pressing against the bars. Paullus flinched back and his smirk wavered. "You are just as much a slave as I am. You're Alamene's fascination of the moment. When she is finished with you, you'll find yourself in this cage or worse."

"You don't understand what you're saying." Paullus folded his arms and looked aside, frowning.

"But I do know. Look at Lucius. She still sleeps with him, and he's been with her a long time. He told me all of this. He doesn't think you'll last as long as he has."

"So what if she chooses to have a slave entertain her?" But Paullus's face had shaded red and his eyes were wide in surprise. Varro guessed he had confirmed something he had suspected about Lucius.

"If you would abide her sleeping with you only on her whim, then you are truly her slave." Varro leaned closer. "Do you know she is not Athenagoras's daughter? I don't know why you thought that."

"Because he told me so."

Varro chuckled. "How good is your Greek? Maybe he claimed she was like a daughter and you misheard. No, she is cousin to King Philip. And if that means nothing to you, then it will to everyone else. Be certain that your little romance with King Philip's relative will get back to Rome. Do you hate your family enough to ruin their reputation?"

"I don't care about my family's reputation!"

The shout drew looks from others around them, but the nearby soldiers shook their heads and laughed. Varro pressed on.

"She has a fascination with Roman men, soldiers in particular. That's why she saved me. To take me to her bed, to be her possession, like you. There is no great love between the two of you. Maybe your passion for her enhanced this fantasy, but she will tire of you. Then you will be remembered as a fool. Your family will disown you or else their shame be unbearable. Ah, but of course when that day comes you won't care. You will be remembering my head staring up at you from death, and that I foretold you would share my fate."

"This is enough." Paullus drew himself taller and Varro had to admit he made an imposing sight. He was not physically large, but he radiated the power of old Roman families. It was in his blood, after all, as the scion of great leaders.

"Get me free, Paullus, and free yourself. A royal Macedonian will not marry a Roman man, especially one who has spurned his family and brings her no benefits. Think clearly. This is the last chance we both have to escape. The only difference between us is when our heads fall. Today it's mine, but when does yours follow? She's already hungry for another and her patience with you is less than it was when you first met, or am I mistaken?"

His last jab landed as cleanly as a sword thrust against an unarmed opponent, and it drew blood. For Paullus bit his lip as he must have realized his fantasy crumbled. Varro backed away from the bars and let the wound bleed.

Paullus ran both hands over his head, settling at the back of his neck. His head turned aside and his eyes pressed shut. Varro expected him to at last concede.

But when his eyes opened, they were cool and distant.

"I've done it," he said. "I've resisted your lies. You were very convincing. You would have made a fine orator back in Rome. But you shall not live to return."

"Check all I've told you with Lucius. It is all true."

Paulus shook his head as if trying to shake off any remaining doubt.

"Just unlock the cage, then leave. I will sneak away myself, and while they search for me you can make your own escape. If you've no desire to return to Rome, then I will not seek you. I'd rather live life in the wilds than be dead today. I swear that I will not interfere with you again. We can both live our own lives."

Varro lied, of course, but he found lies easy while his life was at stake. If he did regain freedom, he would bring Paullus's head back in a bag if he must.

"I am living my own life today," Paullus said through gritted teeth. "Your lies will not destroy it. I will not be swayed. You will die today. I'll do it myself if I must."

He spun on his heels and marched away.

Varro followed him in the confines of the cage, jumping to the bars and shaking them as he cried out.

"Don't leave me to die, Paullus. We are fellow Romans, fellow soldiers. Have pity, for the love of the gods!"

But Paullus left his pity along with Varro, who now slumped in defeat against the cage. Soldiers laughed at him, and one even shook the cage to mock his despair. Varro turned his back and sat facing a wagon wall. Soon, an officer shouted at the men and moved them off. He was left in peace for what he considered his final hours alive.

Despair had no place in survival, he knew. Once a man gives up, not even the gods may save him. But he had made his last failed attempt, and knew of no other way to escape the end that awaited him. What was left but despair?

Attempting to flee would be undignified and still end in death. He refused to be struck by a sling stone in the back of his head while he ran for the trees. If death must come today, then he would face it bravely.

Yet his eyes stung as he sat staring at the gray wood of the cart.

He hoped Falco and Curio escaped, and even wished they would somehow return with Paullus and live out their lives with honor. What else could he think of with the cold touch of death upon his shoulder? He could dwell on the thousands of regrets he accumulated in his short life. He could cry for all that he would never do.

But none of that would change the future where his head would look up to his own body. Would he wonder at what happened? How much pain would he feel? He hoped for a strong man with a sharp sword. He had unfortunately witnessed men attempting to claim heads of hated enemies on the battlefield, and necks did not cut easily.

The tears did eventually fall. He tried to be quiet and not to shake with weeping. But he gasped and at last bent in despair. If the Macedonians were eager for his death, none of them teased him in these final hours.

Then, as the sun burned blood red and birds sang in their distant nests, his cage door rattled as the lock clicked open. He turned, hoping to find a convinced Paullus there to offer him an escape.

But he met the dour face of Athenagoras's strange advisor flanked by a half-dozen soldiers with drawn swords. He gave a bitter smile and beckoned Varro from the cage.

24

Tears had dried on Varro's face, but his eyes still felt puffy and irritated. He wished to appear unafraid and dignified to Athenagora's adviser. He stood in his black robe, awaiting Varro to exit the cage and step from the cart. The six soldiers with drawn swords each had a grim cast to their dark faces. Most were simply following orders, but two gave Varro vicious grins behind the advisor's back.

He straightened his shoulders and extended his chin. He jumped off the cart to land close enough to the adviser to startle him. Varro had an inspiration to grab the advisor's dagger from his side then plunge it into his neck. He would achieve only the satisfaction of having killed his enemy as his final act in life.

But he had his vow to consider. His life as a soldier was finished. Any life at all would be finished soon enough. There was no sense in violence now, particularly when it would not save himself or another. Six swords surrounded him against the wagon bed. The black-clad old adviser narrowed his eyes in disgust and spoke words Varro did not understand. But he followed the old man's pointing chin and saw the crowd gathered for his execution.

"You are lucky, old man," he said, knowing he said would not be understood. "Or I'd ram that carelessly held dagger of yours through your yellow teeth and out the back of your head. But I am sworn to peace."

The old adviser must have assumed he had been cursed, for he spit at Varro's feet and made some sort of ward with his left hand. One of the soldiers shouted at him, then kicked him forward.

The sun was blood red, a fitting color for a bloody end to the day. As he walked among his captors, he looked upward and to the black dots of birds shooting into the sky. There were so many birds, all screaming and swirling in a huge flock. He took it as a sign of the gods' mockery. For they even sent the birds to watch his ignominious end.

Alamene sat under a canopy with Lucius fanning her with a plume of blue feathers. Paullus stood beside her, as did the two other hopeless male slaves that had shared the cage with Varro for a short time. Paullus grinned at him, and Varro returned it. The fool could not even see he was lined up with the other slaves. His betrayal was no loss to Rome. When he was eventually ransomed back, he would be a disgraced laughingstock. The Paullus family might even refuse to pay, and then stupid Marcellus Paullus would be sent away to die in misery.

He realized he had taken his last steps, as now he had come to the fresh-cut stump prepared for his beheading. He had wasted his final walk on vengeful thoughts. He should be focused on the next life now, not the affairs of life here. This was all done, all meaningless.

The crowd cheered when one of the escorts shoved him before the stump. There were scores of armed soldiers, a mix of Alamene's men and Athenagoras's. Varro noted that she patted a delicate cloth to her eyes as she watched. Lucius's feathered fan waved quietly behind her, like a bird flying in place. He let his eyes slide across Paullus. He had seen enough of him for this lifetime.

The old advisor began to address the crowd, probably reciting Varro's crimes and why he had to die. Across the stump the Macedonian with the broken ankle sharpened the strangely canted blade that would be used to lop off Varro's head. When their eyes met, he smiled and again mimicked slicing his neck. This drew laughter from his friends.

Varro looked down at the stump.

The calm that he armored himself within now began to crack. A guard pushed him to his knees while the old advisor prattled on in an irritating, proud voice. This was really the end.

He was going to die.

The guard wrenched his arms to the small of his back and bound them with heavy cord. It seemed a pointless exercise since his head would soon be rolling at this bastard's feet. But he followed procedure as all soldiers must.

With surprising gentleness, the soldier guided Varro's head to the stump. The rough, white wood touched this right cheek and the scent of sap filled his nose. He faced Alamene and Paullus. He thought to close his eyes, but soon his eyes would see no more. So he held them wide to see all he could of this world, even as tears began to leak.

The old adviser ended his recitation to cheers. The soldiers Varro could see in this position raised their fists as if they had won a great victory.

"I'm one man," he muttered to himself. "What do you celebrate? Fools."

The adviser leaned down to fill Varro's view with his lined, evil face. He grinned and clicked his tongue. Then he said more words that meant nothing. He heard "Roman" in that mix of gibberish.

Oddly it gave him strength. That single word, a reminder that he was and always would be a proud citizen of Rome. The tears stopped and his breathing slowed.

"I am a Roman citizen," he said with all the calm he could muster.

The old adviser grinned again, his strangely rimmed gray hair hung like a curtain. When he pulled back, he revealed Paullus. He was staring with a creased brown and his smirk was gone. Lucius continued to wave his fan, looking into the distance as if bored.

Alamene wept openly now.

Why should she care? Varro wondered. But it was enough that at least one person cried at his death. There were too few otherwise to shed tears for him.

So he waited, knees painful on the hard earth, head pressed to the stump of a tree. It seemed more occurred behind his back, as the old advisor spoke to another. The soldier with the broken ankle handed the sharpened sword to the executioner, who then assumed position over Varro. His long shadow draped over the stump, casting him into darkness. He could feel the executioner's proximity through the body heat radiating against his right side.

The cold touch of the blade at his neck made him lurch. Some men laughed at this. It had been merely the executioner finding his mark.

Varro closed his eyes, then forced them open so that when his head fell he might still have a glimpse of the sky before he passed into the next world.

But the blow did not fall.

Instead, the black-robed advisor suddenly halted the strike.

A ripple of confusion flowed through the crowd. The men in scope of Varro's sight frowned and cursed at their spoiled entertainment. Alamene and Paullus both looked on in surprise, and even Lucius's fanning had stopped.

The old adviser began speaking rapidly to the crowed, almost as if he were nervous. But as the words tumbled out of him, more and more of the crowd began to nod in appreciation. Someone called out what sounded like encouragement, and soon half the crowd was shouting merrily.

He had devised some new torment, Varro thought. Some greater spectacle than his head falling to the grass and a gush of blood and fluid to follow.

Yet Alamene leaned forward, a look of intrigue on her face. Paullus seemed confused, shaking his head and searching between the adviser and his lover. He spoke frantically to Lucius, who resumed halfhearted fanning. Varro heard an exchange Latin, but he could not hear the specifics. Apparently, the old adviser's idea had frightened him enough to seek confirmation of his understanding the Greek words.

Now Alamene nodded and the entire crowd cheered. The old adviser left Varro at the stump.

And he guided Paullus back to it.

"I don't see why this is necessary." Paullus's voice quivered with fear, and he spoke Latin to the adviser. He was so frightened that he even forgot to speak the correct language.

The executioner left his position, circling around Varro's head to join Paullus and the adviser. Paullus leaned away in revulsion. This drew jeers and laughter from all around.

Conversely Alamene leaned forward, chin resting on both hands like a child watching her favorite play. Lucius shook his head and fanned her.

"I am loyal," Paullus said in reply to something the old adviser said.

His face had turned white and sweat beaded on his forehead as if he had just run ten miles.

Now the Macedonians began to chant and stamp their feet in time. Varro did not understand the chant at first, but it sounded like a mangled pronunciation of Paullus's name.

The executioner laughed and clapped the sword into Paullus's grip, then shoved him toward Varro.

"They want you to cut my head off," Varro said. Strangely, he no longer felt any fear. He simply confirmed what he guessed.

Paullus nodded, staring at the sword in his hand. He then looked plaintively to the old adviser, who simply clapped his hands in time with the chanting crowd. Lacking comfort there, he turned to Alamene.

But she clapped her hands as well, her tears vanished and gleeful expectation shining on her wicked but beautiful face.

He turned back to Varro, mouth hanging open and sweat dripping onto his toga.

"You promised to execute me yourself," Varro said, head still resting on the stump. "Looks like you got your wish."

Paullus adjusted the sword in his hand, and this drew instant applause and whistles from the crowd.

"You see how little you mean to your beloved?" Varro lifted his head to better see Paullus. "I'm telling you this now, not because I'm going to save myself. But because you might still save yourself. You clearly do not want to kill a fellow citizen and soldier. What kind of lover would ask such a thing?"

"Shut up!"

This elicited greater excitement from the crowd, and Alamene erupted into a flutter of clapping. But Paullus frowned at the blade in his hand.

"Of course I can do this." He announced his resolve loudly, raising the sword higher. Then he repeated more tentative, "Of course I can do this."

Varro closed his eyes, his whole body tensing and arcing with the blow that would soon fall.

But it did not, and he looked back up to Paullus frozen in place.

Jeers flooded over the field. Some soldiers threw small stones that bounced around the stump.

"It seems they want to see a Roman kill a Roman," Varro said. "But you won't do it, will you?"

Paullus blinked, then raised the sword higher with a scowl. But Varro knew he was defeated, and that the final blow would not come from him.

With that thought, Paullus lowered the sword along with his head. More jeers followed and Athenagoras's adviser began screaming at Paullus, pointing to Varro lying across the stump.

But Paullus threw the sword into the grass. Men howled and laughed. Some cursed in anger. A dozen stones flew at him, falling short or wide. He ignored these and walked back to Alamene who now stood.

Her fists were balled and her face tight with anger. Paullus stood before her with his head lowered. He spread his hands and said something Varro could not hear, and likely would not understand in any case. But he understood Alamene's response.

The crack of her slap defeated even the raucous calls of the Macedonians. His head spun aside and a tirade of curses streamed from her. Lucius simply retracted his blue feathered fan and watched with a raised brow as she tore up her erstwhile true love.

For all his pleading, she was in a fury. At last, the old adviser appeared between them. Whereas the two had once seemed at odds, now both seemed agreed that Paullus had crossed a line. The adviser waved forward two men, who leaped to the summons with lusty glee.

Paullus backed away, but they seized him by both arms and easily wrestled him into submission.

The rest of the soldiers jumped up and cheered as Paullus was led away from his former lover. He called after her, but she sat down under her canopy with an expression of intense dissatisfaction. She folded her arms tightly and looked at no one. Lucius resumed fanning her.

Varro remained forgotten. He might have stood up and walked away as the soldiers were absorbed in the rapid downfall of a man they must have universally detested. What could be worse than a foreign traitor? While he might have proved useful to Athenagoras for a short time, certainly no one loved him. They followed his slow progress toward the cage where Varro had been held. He dug his heels into the ground, but the guards dragged him ahead with no mercy.

The old adviser had not forgotten Varro. He ordered other men to fetch him from the stump. No one seemed to consider than another man might easily resume the execution. Yet the adviser snapped at these new soldiers and pointed toward the cage. These men did not need to drag Varro. Having his head on the stump and expecting death, he was glad for life even if it meant living in a cage.

If able he would have run to the safety of that cage, and his escorts had to haul him back. The old adviser followed, and when they reached the cart, he grabbed Varro by the chin and searched his face with lusterless old eyes. Whether he saw what he wanted, Varro did not know. His creased face crumpled under his frown and he shoved Varro's face away. He then spun him around and cut the binding at his wrists with one fluid motion, scooping away the bindings then shoving him at the cage.

Once inside, the door slammed shut and left the bars quivering.

Paullus sat ashen-faced and silent.

Varro took the opposite wall of the cage and slumped down. The fear of death had exhausted him as well.

The festive atmosphere dissolved and soon soldiers were back in line. With some daylight remaining, the wagons rolled forward. Varro and Paullus alone remained in the cage. Perhaps Alamene needed the comfort of her three most loyal slaves after Paullus's disappointment.

The two remained in silence as the escort pushed forward,

neither looking at the other. All Varro could do was wonder what came next. Why had he been given a reprieve because Paullus would not execute him? A hundred different fears bloomed in his mind. Perhaps they suspected the two of them were cooperating toward a greater betrayal? So he was spared execution for torture and confession. But what could he confess to? They might break his bones, flay his skin, burn him, poke out his eyes, pull out his teeth. The list of terrors did not stop. He would have to confess to something or else the tortures would never cease. A skilled torturer could keep a man alive indefinitely, or so he had been told.

"There's something worse than death," he said to himself, imagining a leering Macedonian touching a hot brand to his cheek.

"What did you say?"

Paullus did not look up but hung his head to his chest. He pulled his knees in so that both arms hung over them in an overall posture of limp defeat.

"Why didn't they finish my execution?"

"How should I know? Why? Aren't you glad to be alive?"

He placed his hand at the base of his neck and pressed the flesh there. "You don't know how happy."

"Ah, well, good for you. I'd trade places with you now."

"You wouldn't say that if you knew what it was like." He shivered at the memory of the executioner's blade skimming the back of his neck.

They fell to silence again. The sun was now fully set, and they halted on a section of the trail lined with woods to one side and a steep hill to the other. It seemed a poor spot for making camp, and their prior location had been better. But perhaps they were deep enough in their own territory now to no longer fear anyone.

Varro shifted his feet forward over the rough bars of the cage floor and touched Paullus's leg.

"We have a new chance to escape," he said, whispering though no one else would understand. No one was even paying them any mind, and instead groaned as they set about making camp on the road.

"Don't bother me with your mad plans. Besides, you seem more talented at being caught than evading capture."

Though he did not want to laugh, he did. "You've got a fair point. But we're Roman soldiers, and we don't know when to surrender. We've both got arms and legs, so we can fight. My old optio used to tell us it only takes one hand to hold a sword."

"Do me a favor and fall on that sword."

"Listen, there's two of us now. I've no idea how to escape. But we'll have to watch for opportunities."

Now Paullus raised his head. His eyes were puffy and bloodshot. Varro had not even noticed his crying, so absorbed was he in his own fears. But now Paullus scowled and shook his head.

"This is not when we become friends, Varro. Just because I am principled enough to not kill a fellow citizen does not mean I wouldn't enjoy another killing you. Everything was perfect until you arrived in camp with your misguided mission to bring me back. Ever since that day, you've made a mess of everything. And here I thought I was finally rid of you. But like a fool you followed along and now look at me. Look at me, Varro. I'm in a fucking cage with you."

"Exactly," Varro leaned forward, rapping his knuckles to the cage floor for emphasis. "Exactly like me, a slave to be thrown away. You mean nothing to Alamene."

He turned his head aside. "She only is teaching me a lesson. She would not harm me."

"A lesson?" Varro cocked his head. "She is mad. Is that not obvious to you?"

Paullus answered only with the most hate-filled expression Varro had ever seen. Beyond narrowed eyes and furrowed brows, something unearthly emanated from him. Such loathing quelled all further talk. Varro retracted his leg into his own space.

They did not speak again. No one approached their cage. No one provided food or water. Neither he nor Paullus asked for any. At least for Varro, he did not want to be seen again lest they remember to cut off his head.

So night fell and watches were set. Soldiers crawled into tents. At the rear of the escort, Varro saw a tent with guards and the long path winding into the folded landscape. With Paullus wrapped in unyielding silence, he rested against the bars. Exhaustion and hunger dragged him into slumber.

He awakened just before dawn.

The sky was still splattered with stars above, but the horizon glowed with new light.

Something had made a noise. A metallic click.

He did not move, but held his breath until he saw a dark shape leap from the cart. It landed softly, with only a faint thump on the earth track.

The figure was built like a man and dressed all in black, with a hood covering him. He leaned down to fetch something from below the cart. It was a bundle wrapped in dirty brown cloth. This he set on the cart to the side of the cage. Varro heard the faint clink of metal as the bundle shifted to rest.

The black robed and hooded man glanced back up at the cage, then darted away.

But as he did, Varro glimpsed the unmistakable fringe of gray hair and craggy face of Athenagoras's advisor.

He waited until he was sure the advisor had left, then crept forward.

And an alarm horn sounded from the front of the escort.

25

Varro froze. He believed the horn had sounded for him, though he had done nothing more than crawl toward the cage door. Yet in the next instant he heard the war cries of hundreds coming from the woods lining one side of the road. A steep stone incline pressed the encamped escort on the opposite side.

He stood, kicking Paullus awake.

"We're under attack."

Paullus snorted and recoiled from the kick as he awakened. His expression shifted from surprise, to anger, then back to surprise as he heard the shouting and sounding horns.

The tent at the back of the escort opened and the eight soldiers of the rear guard jumped out with shields and swords in hand. They looked across the morning twilight to where the enemies shouted beyond Varro's vision. With a shout of their own, they ran toward the developing battle.

"Come on," Varro said. "We're free. Let's go."

"What do you mean?" Paullus got to his feet, wiping sleep from his eyes. "What's happening?"

"I don't know." He pressed on the cage door, and it swung open with a creak. His eyes widened, unbelieving.

"How did you do that?" Paullus pushed him aside then stuck his arm into the open space as if testing whether he dreamed.

"Athenagoras's adviser did it." Varro leaped through the opening to land on the ground. More horns sounded and throaty shouts echoed. But he turned to the dirty brown cloth that the adviser had stuck between the cage and the cart wall.

"Who is attacking us?" Paullus leaned out the cage, but did not jump down. Instead, he craned his neck to see farther up the caravan.

Varro put his hands on the bundle, and with a single touch he knew what was beneath the cloth. His heart slammed against his ribs as he tore the cover away. He shouted with joy.

"Swords!"

Lying atop the dirty cloth were not just swords, but a Roman gladius for each of them. They were in perfect condition, with an edge honed white. The blades reflected Varro's astonished face. He lifted one, amazed at the feel of it in his hands.

"Where did you get that?"

Paullus now jumped off the cart and grabbed a sword for himself. He looked between it and Varro, eyes wide.

"Athenagoras's adviser left these for us after he opened the cage. But I don't understand." Varro stared toward the sound of men joining battle down the row of wagons. He lifted his sword and weighed it. Was this some trick or another test for Paullus?

Then everything made sense.

"He freed us and provided swords. He made sure I was not executed, and that you and I ended up alone and together. Then he moved the escort here to be ambushed. By the gods, Paullus, he's an ally. He must have told the Dardanians that Alamene would be vulnerable."

Varro regretted speaking the name, clamping his mouth shut.

But he had already galvanized Paullus.

"Then she is in danger!"

Despite his voluminous toga, Paullus dodged out of Varro's attempt to grab him. He then slashed backward with his new blade, and had Varro not collapsed against the edge of the wagon bed he would have been cut across his throat.

Paullus took two strides before Varro recovered.

He snared a trailing cloth of the toga, then yanked Paullus back, causing him to stumble. With fluid ease, he hauled Paullus into the fall and sent him sprawling on his back. He then leaped atop him, turning his sword so that he could use the pommel to strike.

"Get off me, you bastard!"

Paullus struck up with his gladius, and Varro had to roll aside or else be impaled. His momentary advantage vanished. Now Paullus sloughed off his toga down to his plain gray tunic. Kicking it away, he sprinted forward.

Varro had jumped up then attempted to tackle Paullus, then landed with his face in the dirt track. His fingers brushed Paullus's ankle as he ran ahead.

Scrabbling to his feet, he rounded the corner of the wagon.

Paullus had vanished.

Ahead were two lines of men drawn up before the wagons. He recognized the Macedonians from their helmets and shields. The others must be the Dardanians, but otherwise looked so similar to their enemies that Varro would not know who to support when the lines broke.

With no time to care about the main battle, he guessed Paullus had ducked around the front of the wagon to shake him. So he followed, and popping out on the side facing the steep rock incline, he found nothing.

He screamed Paullus's name in frustration. With only a moment's lead he had shaken Varro's pursuit. Growling in frustration, he at least knew where Paullus would go. So he ran along the back of the escort to reach the lead wagon where Alamene must be guarded.

It was a short run even with the wagons spaced out along the path.

As expected, the wagon door facing the rock wall hung open and a clutch of soldiers emerged with shields held overhead to shelter the woman at the center.

"Alamene!" Varro shouted, and she glanced through the gaps in her bodyguards. Her face was pale white and stricken with terror.

Paullus held her along with Lucius, both pressed to her like plates of human armor.

The awkward but tight cluster of armored guards bumbled down the short steps set at the door. Varro made to rush.

Ambushers on the ridge above emerged, leveled short curved bows, then released.

Varro screamed in terror along with Alamene. Paullus cannot die now, not so close to capture.

"You fools," he yelled up to them, waving his gladius. "That's Alamene! Don't you want her alive?"

But the arrows fell around her guards, most shattering or impaling the raised shields. One soldier collapsed out of the cluster with an arrow in his neck. The others closed the gap and pushed ahead.

Varro's shouting drew the ambushers' attention.

As well as their arrows.

He dove behind the second wagon just as a shaft cracked against its corner, spraying splinters over him. Without a shield of his own, Varro knew the Dardanian ambushers would make short work of him.

Cursing, he slipped out the other side to avoid the foolish

bowmen. Perhaps they did not care to take Alamene alive, in which case Varro had even less chance to save Paullus now.

The main battle was the chaos he knew too well. He had never seen the rear of a Macedonian line, and he was unimpressed. Each man was attempting to shove into the one before him. Yet without their sarissa pikes they were hopeless. All they did was trap the men ahead of them against the Dardanians who seemed to be shoving them back against their wagons and the rock wall.

They would not hold much longer.

Varro rushed past them.

Then he saw the feathered helmets.

Two black feathered helmets, with three feathers each, their shining bronze catching the growing morning light, bobbed along the end of the Dardanian line.

"Falco, Curio!"

He called across the lines, momentarily forgetting Paullus. His heart raced as he saw the two helmets turn toward him.

Yet the Macedonians in the rear turned toward him as well.

Joy turned to fear as the dozen enemies at the rear of this line had nothing to do but attack Varro.

He fled and they followed.

But it could not have been a better plan. For the release of the pressure they exerted on the Macedonian line weakened that section. Varro heard the shrieks of the defeated and the cheers of the victors as the Dardanians won through.

He rounded the front of the wagon in time to see the testudo-like formation sheltering Alamene and Paullus climbing into the rocky higher ground. He did not see the archers, but glimpsed figures picking through the rocks above.

His pursuers caught up with him, not as many now that the Dardanians had broken through. But he faced four of them with shields and canted swords. They drew together in mutual support, becoming as one giant against Varro's shieldless defense. If he turned his back to run, they would hack him to death.

If he could loop through them, he might live.

His headlong charge and fierce cry stunned them. They seemed like four boys creeping up on an injured bird intending to torment it. But rather than lie on his side and flap broken wings, Varro burst forward with his gladius leading.

The first stab shot beneath the shield of the nearest enemy. A true gladius, it was sharp and accurate and nearly an extension of his own hand. Unlike Macedonian swords, which needed wide arcs to deliver any damage, the gladius killed with the barest effort from the wielder. A puncture no deeper than a finger length was fatal and took little strength to deliver.

So the first man screamed and bent over his popped guts, expelling blood and foul breath as Varro grabbed the shield of the next closest man.

He yanked it aside and gave a quick jab to the enemy's face, gouging out cheek and eyeball to send him falling away with a terrible screech. If not dead, he was no longer a threat.

But momentum and efficiency only carried so much. The two remaining enemies had recovered, though they hid behind their round shields. They lunged at Varro, who without his own shield lacked any defense except intense indignation and anger.

Yet their lunges faltered and both collapsed.

A light pilum each hung out of their backs. One died instantly, having taken the missile through his kidney. The other crabbed along the ground in agony. Varro wasted no time in ramming his sword into the enemy's neck to finish him.

When he pulled up, Falco and Curio were charging across the short distance.

The three Romans crashed together in jubilation despite the panic and murder surrounding them. Varro felt tears rise to his eyes as they celebrated their reunion, only he found the scutum shields impossible to manage.

"Where did you get this gear?"

Varro backed up, staring in amazement at how well provisioned Falco and Curio both were.

"From our allies, of course," Falco said. "There's some Roman advisers with them."

"Glad you're both here. Now, we've got to catch Paullus," Varro said. "He's gone up into this ridge. Follow me."

He snatched a round shield from the ground, then dashed off after Paullus. As he ran, he explained the situation between gasps to Curio and Falco. Both flanked him, and would outstrip him if they knew where to go. Both were better fed and rested.

Gaining the narrow path, he pulled through rocks and jumped up small inclines. He kept looking ahead into the brightening light, certain the armored men could not gain much distance in this terrain.

His expectations were correct, for he spotted the dark cluster of soldiers up a sharp slope. Two of the archers that had ambushed them hid behind rocks, and upon seeing Varro and his two Romans they smiled.

"Don't shoot, you fools!"

But Varro's command, if they even understood it, had no effect. Two more popped up where Varro had not seen them and let their arrows fly at the retreating Macedonians.

"They don't want Alamene alive?" Varro shouted at Falco as they scrabbled up the slope.

"I thought they did."

Cursing, Varro realized the arrows covered their path forward. The archers were at an angle and the Macedonians had to position themselves to block the shots. Two already lay dead along the path. Varro sprinted past their lifeless faces staring up at their final dawn. Only two more blocked the path ahead while

Paullus and Lucius escorted Alamene deeper into the craggy ridge.

"For Rome!" Varro shouted and pointed to the enemies with his sword. He charged the final distance at his grim-faced opponents.

They were black shapes against the rising sun, thick with armor and shield. But Varro felt the momentum of Falco and Curio at his sides, shouting the same war cry.

He rammed his round shield on theirs. They held the higher ground and shoved back, causing Varro to slip. Curio met the same fate. But the sturdier and larger Falco clung to his enemy.

None could doubt the Macedonians were dead from the moment they chose to block the way forward. Varro did not look behind, but heard the archers chirp commands and knew they moved forward. He slid on his knees, skinning them against the grit, but got up and rejoined the fight.

Sword and shield clanged together. Grunts and curses flowed with blood from both sides. Varro took a gash to his right shoulder. Falco's nose rained blood on his chest.

Yet in the end, the two Macedonians lay dead in the path. Blood flowed down the gritty slope, forming a gory mudslide.

"Bastards put up a fight," Falco said, wiping his nose. "Should've let the archers handle them."

"Come on, we've got to get Paullus before the archers do."

The archers shouted victory and raced past Varro through the chokepoint the Macedonians had defended and into the clear path up the slope. He followed on their heels, and seeing Paullus's gray tunic vanish over the top of a ridge gave him a flash of strength.

He shoved into the midst of the archers, knocking them aside with his shield. Falco and Curio did as well, and with their larger and heavier shields had more success. The archers cursed and shouted, but Varro led his group like a wedge through their midst.

His feet slid on the scree, but both Curio and Falco wore their hobnailed sandals, caligae, and enjoyed better footing. They each grabbed his arm and prevented him from falling behind.

At last, he mounted the ridge and found Paullus with Lucius and Alamene.

They had trapped themselves against a vertical wall of stone. A single tree grew atop the ledge above them, casting a thin line of shadow that cut between Alamene and Paullus.

Breathless, Varro ran the final distance with shield forward. Falco and Curio flanked him to cut off escape. The archers followed on, shouting at them in irritation. But Varro did not care. He looked to Paullus who stood with his gladius extended. Neither Alamene nor Lucius held any weapon.

They stared at each other, hair matted with sweat, faces red, and cheeks puffed from their labored breathing. Alamene cried and clung to Lucius. But the sandy-haired slave simply stared at Varro.

"It's over, Paullus." He stepped forward, gladius set to the edge of his shield. "Put down your weapon. The Macedonians are broken. There's nowhere to go."

"I'm not going back." His voice trembled along with his extended sword. His face flushed red. "I'm not going back as a prisoner."

"You're not a prisoner." Varro calmed and steadied his voice. He stared only at Paullus, ignoring Alamene in her soiled blue dress and Lucius who clung to her as if she would protect him.

"Don't get closer, or I'll make you regret it."

Tears showed in Paullus's eyes. Varro knew he had won, and only needed to remove the gladius.

"Put the sword down. We're taking you back. If we fight, you will die. I don't want that to happen and neither do you."

Alamene began to plead with Paullus. He did not face her, but searched Varro's eyes as if looking for assurance. They hung locked in this strange silence as Alamene continued her stream of foreign words. Even the archers, who had crept forward, now halted as if awaiting Paullus's choice.

"No one needs to know what happened here. You will return to camp as a Roman soldier. There's a whole life ahead of you there. On this ridge, there is only death. I think you know what to do."

Paullus shook his head as Alamene's pleading increased. He began to weep.

And his sword lowered.

Alamene shrieked in indignation. But Varro stepped in to disarm Paullus, handing the confiscated sword to Falco. With tenderness he did not feel in his heart, he guided Paullus away so that he stood enfolded in his and Falco's shields.

The archers rushed forward. Alamene hurled curses at Paullus, who hung his head in silence. Curio joined Varro, placing Paullus in an inescapable triangle.

Looking over his shoulder, Varro witnessed Alamene's capture. The archers shouted with joy as they peeled Lucius from her. She reached out to him as two men wrestled her toward the others.

Lucius looked over the heads of his captors to Varro. His eyes were wide with fear and begging for help. Yet before he could do anything to aid Lucius, Varro cringed as one of the archers slit the Roman slave's throat. He collapsed with a gasp and Alamene shrieked. An arc of bright blood pumped into the air to spray the wall where they had been trapped. Varro turned away.

"What are you going to do with me?" Paullus asked, sniveling.

"We're going to ensure you won't escape. Just until your mind is settled." Varro patted his back as he guided Paullus toward the path off the ridge. He would rather have beat him unconscious, bind him in chains, then throw him at Tribune Sabellius's feet for the traitor he was.

"You're not going to tell my mother?" He looked up, eyes wide and glassy.

"Gods," Falco growled. "Is he five years old? Don't tell his mother?"

Silencing Falco with a glare, he looped his arm around Paullus as they approached the path off the ridge. "You are a Roman citizen from a proud family. We're just three simple farmers. We won't say anything to anyone, and no one would believe us even if we did. Be at ease."

This appeared to assuage Paullus, and he climbed down the ridge with them in silence punctuated with violent sniffling. Behind, Alamene shrieked and cursed. She wrestled with her captors, who likely would have enjoyed beating her to submission. But for all their careless shooting, they appeared committed to returning her uninjured.

The escort was in process of being looted when they reached the bottom. Dardanians swarmed over it, hauling away whatever they could. A standard comprised of a bear's head and its hide flew at the center of the escort. The sun appeared to be shining on this spot.

"That'll be Bato," Falco said. "He's the Dardanian chief. This was so important, he led the attack."

"You've got to have a good story for me," Varro said. "As to how you came to be here."

"We heard the Roman slaves were going with Alamene. So it's just natural you'd be here and so would we. But there'll be time for sharing stories. We need to get Alamene and Paullus to Bato."

"You look like shit," Curio said. "Did she mistreat you?"

"No, that'd be Athenagoras's adviser. But let's go."

Paullus no longer seemed to have a mouth. He hung between the three of them silent and dark, looking like an old log dredged up from a mucky lake. They waited for the archers to catch up. Despite Alamene's violent resistance, their smiles and laughter were contagious. They shouted something to Varro and the others, probably congratulations. He nodded back to them and they headed for the bear standard.

As others realized Alamene had been captured, shouts of victory followed their path. When they arrived at the standard, almost all of the Dardanians not guarding captives now surrounded them.

The bear standard and the name Bato led Varro to expect a giant, hairy man. Yet instead he found Bato to be average height with a thin beard and hair shaved close to his round scalp. He wore a mail shirt and rested on a heavy sword. His mail was splattered with blood which he wore like red jewels.

He let his sword fall and began clapping as the archers wrestled Alamene before him. The entire force, Varro estimating about one hundred men, clapped as well. This seemed to quell her violence, and she at last lowered her head in defeat.

Varro watched for Paullus's reaction, but he seemed as if nothing could break into his dark thoughts. Even Falco and Curio raised brows, and as the crowd celebrated Alamene's capture, they allowed him more space. He was clearly defeated.

"Romans!" Bato shouted, pointing to Curio and Falco, then raising his brows to Varro. "You found your officer?"

"We did, sir," Falco said, then turning to whisper to Varro. "He speaks Latin."

"I wouldn't have known," Varro said. Then he inclined his head to the Dardanian chief.

Bato joined them, looking to Paullus and then the others.

"You found your friend, too? He looks sad."

Varro nudged Paullus, but nothing roused him. This drew a warm chuckle from Bato.

"He has been through much," Varro said. "I am grateful for your arrival. I think we both might have died without your timely aid, sir."

Bato clapped his hands. "This has been long planned.

Alamene is a prize worth the patience. But you had help from a friend, yes?"

Here Bato twisted aside to reveal Athenagoras's black clad advisor. He gave Varro a wicked smile that made him feel as if he were drowning again.

"Optio Varro and I have met several times," he said. His Latin was heavily accented but fluid.

While the advisor's sudden appearance shocked him, it seemed to engulf Alamene in a blaze of fury. She began screeching and jabbing her finger at him. Whatever invective she hurled at him, the adviser with his strange rim of gray hair simply closed his eyes to it.

Anger revived, Alamene now pointed at Paullus. This drew laughter from some of the Dardanians. She made a fist to emphasize each new curse. Bato cocked his brow at this.

"It seems the woman has a problem with your friend?"

"There is some history," Varro said, unsure of what he should reveal to Bato.

Then Alamene struck with catlike speed.

She shot forward, snatching a carelessly sheathed dagger from the advisor's hip. The very one Varro had seen dangling there during his failed execution.

In one step, she was at Paullus. Her beautiful face was now the visage of an attacking lioness.

The dagger flashed.

And it plunged down into Paullus's chest, collapsing him to the ground at Varro's feet.

26

The days following Paullus's stabbing saw Varro recovering from his enslavement. He lay on his back on a comfortable bedroll in a typical Roman tent. If he could stopper his ears so he did not hear the Dardanians chattering outside he might imagine this as his own tent back in camp. The presences of Falco and Curio only enhanced that illusion. For the moment, he blinked away gritty sleep from his eyes which watered as he did. Cool mountain air filtered into the dim tent from the opened tent flap. He heard Curio and Falco speaking as they cleaned up their breakfast in front of the tent.

He shot up, thinking of Paullus once more. Bato's best doctors were still uncertain if he would live or die. What if he had died during the night? Why hadn't someone fetched him?

Falco popped his head inside the tent.

"How long are you going to act too weak to do your part? I'm not rushing you, sir. But I would like to know if I must wipe your ass for the next week or if I have the pleasure for only the next few days."

"It's good to be back together." Varro reclined again, realizing that even if Paullus had died overnight his presence for it would not change anything. He closed his eyes.

"Thank you, sir," Falco said. "Let me wash your feet, sir."

Falco shuffled inside then delivered a sharp kick to Varro's leg, drawing a surprised shout.

"I didn't eat for days. I barely drank any water, except when I was drowning. What do you want me to do?"

"It's not obvious?" Falco sat beside him, pulling off his sandals to inspect the hobnails. He used a twig to begin picking at the soles. "I'd like you to get off your back and take us home. We've earned it, haven't we? If you fully recover, I think that so-called adviser is going to put all three of us to work rather than let us go."

Varro chuckled. Rome had sent a small contingent of twenty men to the Dardanians to act as envoys and advisers. The leader of this band was not of any military rank Varro understood. He supposed the man considered himself a tribune or something like it.

"He's got nothing to say about us," Varro said, folding his hands over his chest. "We have Sabellius's letter. That's all he needs to see. When we're ready to go, we leave."

"As you say, sir. He's a self-important prick, though. He sniffed at the letter first time he saw it."

"I'll stick it right up his fucking nose and give him a good whiff of it next time. We're taking Paullus home."

"Yes, sir!" Falco then laughed, replacing his sandals as he did.

Curio now entered, dropping his bronze patera into a corner, having cleaned it out after breakfast.

"Doctor's going to check on Paullus," he said. "Maybe he'll be safe enough to move now."

Varro sat up again, yawned as Falco rolled his eyes at him. "Let me get ready. As long as he's alive, it's good news."

After dressing and eating a bit of bread soaked in undiluted wine, Varro followed them on the short walk across the Dardanian camp to find Paullus. Over the few days he had been recovering, he had no chance to explore the camp. However, he recognized the organization and discipline of the Dardanian soldiers. Unlike the Macedonians, there was a pattern to the camp that Varro understood. Bato and his leaders, though they called themselves chiefs, appeared to live as consul and tribunes in an established headquarters. Falco said they held regular drills and marches and shared a camaraderie that matched Roman armies. In short, they were not mountain barbarians like Varro had thought but skilled soldiers using modern techniques of battle.

The hospital tent was a Roman contribution to the camp, or so he believed. For Roman soldiers surrounded it. This was probably more for Paullus's protection rather than any chance of his escaping. Alamene was being held as Bato's "guest" and might still want revenge on her former lover. Yet her tent was also heavily guarded all around, Varro noted. It was her actual tent, recovered from the escort.

Inside, they found the doctor and his assistants hovering over Paullus so that only his feet were visible. For a moment, Varro had the sinking feeling he had died. But then his toes flexed and he coughed softly. Varro and the others waited until the doctor had finished. He sat back, then noticed Varro at the entrance.

"Good news," he said. "His lungs are clear now. The bleeding has stopped."

A pile of bandages with rust-colored stains were heaped on the floor. Varro winced at the sight. Paullus had paid a heavy price for his foolishness. But he had been warned.

"Is he talking?" Varro took a tentative step forward.

"He's weak," the doctor said. "Don't push him. But if he rests and eats well, he will rebuild his strength."

"Strength enough to travel?"

"Depends on the method of travel. He won't be marching or riding a horse for a while. The poor man nearly died."

Varro nodded, then looked past the doctor.

His pale skin shining with a glaze of sweat, Paullus appeared even more like a marble statue standing outside the Roman Senate. His eyes were closed and rimmed with heavy black circles. A doctor's assistant drew a sheet over him, but Varro saw the thick wrappings and the spot of blood still spreading on it.

"I thought you said he was not bleeding?"

"Not significantly," the doctor said. He stuck a finger into his ear and rotated it violently. "It should stop completely by tomorrow. He is healing well, trust me."

The doctor, being Greek, spoke with a mild accent. But somehow this imparted assurance to Varro. The best doctors were all Greek.

He stepped aside to allow Varro and the others to stand beside Paullus's bed.

"Is he asleep?" Falco asked.

"Are you asleep?" Varro asked, gently tapping the side of the bed with his leg.

"Have you come to laugh at me?" The words were thin and weak, but full of the arrogance Varro had grown accustomed to.

"Nothing to laugh about. I'm glad you're alive."

"No thanks to you."

Alamene had surprised everyone with her murderous strike. Varro had covered Paullus with his body the moment he realized what had happened. Bato himself restrained Alamene, protecting anyone else from harm.

"I warned you about her. Look, the doctor says you need to rest and get strong enough to recover. We'll take you home where you can recover as long as you'd like.'"

"I need to complete my service," he said weakly, raising his left hand. "Can't hold public office otherwise."

Varro gave both Falco and Curio a grave look, but said nothing of his fervent hope that Rome would not have to suffer under his incompetence.

"My duty is to return you to camp. From there, the consul will decide where you go."

"Remember your promise, Varro."

He opened his eyes, his lids peeling back as if they had been glued shut. He shifted his glassy eyes at him. Varro nodded.

"Rest up. I'm taking you home as soon as you're able."

Outside the tent, he pulled Curio and Falco together.

"I'm feeling good today."

"Gods, I thought you were going to lie on that bed for a year." Falco slapped his shoulder with a smile.

"It was comfortable." Varro smirked. "Now, you two can take me to Bato and his adviser. Let's make arrangements for travel. I want to depart the instant that doctor says Paullus can move again."

Both Curio and Falco offered their hearty agreements.

Over the three days Varro had been recovering, he had heard the stories of their escapes. Apparently neither of them found each other after scaling the camp wall. It was too dark and chaotic. But both had the idea to locate the Dardanian lines and seek aid. Both spent time trying to pinpoint the location, but it was not hard to follow the signs of battle.

The Roman adviser threw Curio in a cage for being a deserter. Falco arrived the next day with Sabellius's letter, explaining their reasons for being so far from anywhere a Roman soldier should be. Apparently Bato was aware a Roman cavalryman had become involved with Alamene and so their stories made sense. Varro knew this meant others knew of Paullus's treason, but he could do nothing about it now. It was a mess Paullus had made from himself.

A traitor in Athenagoras's camp had informed Bato of Alamene's presence and offered to aid in her capture in exchange for safe passage to Rome, where he planned to start a new life. Falco and Curio learned of the plan through the Roman adviser, and insisted they accompany the attack in order to find Varro.

Now they met with Bato and his Roman adviser inside the Dardanian command tent. Of the two, Varro found the smiling, nearly bald Bato preferable to his unsmiling countryman. Yet their discussions were succinct and open.

"My men will take you east through our lands to the Illyrians," Bato said with a smile, then extended a hand to the Roman adviser. "I'd let your own people do it, but I need them in negotiating terms with Athenagoras. I'm sure he'll send his response any day."

Bato radiated confidence, while the Roman stood expressionless with arms locked behind his back.

According to what Varro had learned from Curio and Falco, the adviser had been against capturing Alamene. He considered it a distraction at best and possibly a fatal mistake at worst. Apparently King Philip had no great love for his cousin or her father. Certainly Athenagoras must negotiate for her return, but Bato did not hold the Macedonian throne by the neck as he believed. The lack of response from Athenagoras suggested he did not care as much as Bato hoped, or that he still reeled from the betrayal of a trusted adviser.

"As soon as Paullus can travel, we must leave." Varro inclined his head to Bato. "And I am grateful for your aid."

"Of course!" Bato clapped his hands in delight. "You'll bring word to your consul of what has happened here. Tell him I have a royal hostage."

"And I will have letters for you to carry as well." The Roman adviser gave a short-lived, sharp smile to which Varro nodded in agreement.

Bato raised his arm and mimicked a ship going over waves. "You must travel overland to the Illyrian coast, then take a ship south to Apollonia. From there, you can find your consul without difficulty."

"We are not camped far from there," Varro said.

"Consul Villius has moved south to engage Philip," the adviser said. "Your old camp might be there, but your leaders may be elsewhere."

"Thank you, sir. I'm certain once we are close to camp the army will find us. It always does."

This comment might have ended their audience, but a soldier rushed into the tent and saluted Bato. The chief spoke a few words and the soldier rushed out a stream of explanations. The Roman adviser sighed with impatience and looked away. Whether he understood or not, Varro certainly had no idea what was said other than it appeared urgent. Bato's head tilted side to side in debate, until he finally made a gesture and statement that appeared to be agreement.

The soldier called back to the outside of the tent. Another guard escorted an older man with wooly white hair into the tent.

"Dimos!"

Varro spoke his name in surprise, and it shocked not only Dimos but everyone else in the tent.

"Roman! How did you get here ahead of me? I came with all haste!"

"Haste? It has been nearly four days." While Dimos had taken too long to arrive, he was glad to see the Macedonian hadn't betrayed him.

"You know this man?" Bato asked. "He has an urgent message for me?"

Dimos pulled free of the guard holding him, who seemed unsure of whether this man was a captive or guest. He bowed stiffly to the chief.

"I have news of Alamene's movements. She is going to travel to

Pella, and will be vulnerable during this time." He gave a sly smile to Varro. "But I suspect my news is late."

"Late, but it heartens me to hear it." Varro then explained how he had freed Dimos to look for help while he stuck close to Paullus. When finished, the Roman adviser bent his mouth in appreciation.

"I admire your dedication, Optio Varro. Your plan was quite dangerous."

"Failure to secure Paullus was more dangerous, sir. But thank you nonetheless."

Dimos was allowed to share Varro's tent while they waited for Paullus to recover. He insisted he was Varro's servant for life. For his part, Varro smiled politely and thanked the old trader. But he knew the Macedonian had no place in the Roman army, and knew it himself.

One week became another waiting for Paullus to recover. Alamene was ransomed back with an agreement that the Macedonians would withdraw toward the mountains at their backs. However, the exchange was still to be made nearly a month later when Paullus was ready to travel.

Varro and the others drilled with the Roman soldiers accompanying the adviser during this time. They were back into fighting form and feeling strong and confident when the day to depart arrived.

They loaded Paullus into a cart, and with final thanks to Bato, and taking on stacks of missives from the Roman adviser to either go to Rome or to Consul Villius, they set out for the Illyrian coast. It was not the end of summer, nearly six months from the time they had set out to bring Paullus back.

When they finally reached the coast, Dimos helped arrange a ship to Apollonia. Their Illyrian and Dardanian escorts ensured the shipmaster understood it was his duty to transport Varro at no cost. While this smacked of intimidation to Varro, he was grateful as he had no more coin left.

At the docks, he made his farewells to Dimos, who made a show of insisting he travel with him.

"And where will old Dimos go? I go with you, Roman."

"Go and find your brother," Varro said. "And if I come back this way again, we will find each other. You can repay me at that time."

Dimos gave a wide smile, the sea air blowing his wooly white hair.

"As you say. If we meet again, I will be glad. I owe you my life, but maybe you put it in danger. So this is fair."

They laughed and clasped arms.

Falco and Curio had already loaded Paullus onto the ship. Per the doctor's orders, he was to be carried on a stretcher and limit his movements. He was also ordered to eat meat and fish three times per day, and as his strength recovered so did his imperious demands for well-cooked food.

Now they had settled on the deck and cast off. Dimos waved from the pier while the Illyrians and Dardanians parted ways, having dispensed their duties.

"There was a time I thought we'd not even go back." Falco stood beside him at the rails, watching the dockside workers milling about their business.

"Especially after that bear attack," Varro said. "I still have nightmares of it."

"The list of things that bring nightmares gets longer every day."

Varro grunted in agreement. He looked back to Curio who stood apart, looking from the opposite side toward the open sea. He pulled a dry flower from within his tunic and studied it. He then crushed it in his hand to let the dust of it blow out across the waters.

"He'll feel better when he gets his share of the gold," Falco said with a chuckle. "He was never going to see that girl again. I told him so."

Varro's stomach tightened at the mention of the gold necklace. He had been waiting for a chance to discuss this with Falco. Now was as good a time as any, particularly while Paullus was quiet.

"About that necklace," he said with a nervous smile. "I think we need to give it back."

27

A week after setting off from Illyria, Varro, Falco, and Curio returned Paullus to Tribune Sabellius.

The camp was as it had always been, but not as it was when they set out months ago. The rebellion of the Punic War veterans had ended. The camp was made whole again. The regularity of it, the order, the trumpeting of elephants, the Latin spoken all around, jarred Varro. He had become accustomed to life as a foreigner, where customs and language were different. He had also grown used to speaking his mind without fear of anyone else understanding. That would have to change immediately or else land him in trouble.

Their arrival did not elicit any extra attention. They gave Sabellius's letter to the gate guards and waited until the tribune arrived to welcome them.

And from that moment, they were all back in the army.

They were to immediately deliver Paullus to Consul Villius, who had failed to bring Philip to battle and therefore remained in camp.

"It is an amazing feat," Sabellius said. "You were gone so long, I thought you all dead."

"Most of the men you sent are dead," Varro said, looking to Paullus.

He reclined on his stretcher, now appearing more like a Roman god to be carried about than a wounded soldier. He turned away as if he had not heard. During the final days of their journey, Paullus constantly reminded Varro to make a careful report and that his family was powerful.

"It is a sad fact of leadership that I must order men to duties that will surely kill them." Sabellius lowered his head. "I will ensure their families are taken care of."

At last they were allowed to meet Villius in his command tent. Both Curio and Falco carried Paullus, and all of them followed Sabellius.

Inside the consul's tent, Paullus underwent an incredible transformation. Now he lay flat on the stretcher. He closed his eyes under furrowed brows and folded his hands over his bandages, which were prominently displayed and not entirely needed at this point. But he had insisted this morning Varro wrap him in an older bandage that still had spots of dried blood.

"Is it true?" Villius was nothing like Varro remembered him. He had spent so little time under this consul's command that now was as good as a first meeting. Dressed in a brilliant white toga, he seemed much as Paullus had when he was Alamene's slave. He had to suppress a smile at the thought.

The consul rushed to Paullus's stretcher and took up his hand as if finding a lost son.

"Marcellus Paullus at your command, sir."

His voice was weak and tired, as if he were fighting back from death to greet his superior.

"Set him over here," Villius said. He was about the same age as

Tribune Sabellius. He had a narrow head and narrow eyes which Varro disliked.

When Falco and Curio set Paullus down on a long table, he cried out as if in great pain.

"Be careful, you fools!" Villius stabilized Paullus as if he might break in half. "You didn't bring him so far to kill him now."

Sabellius cleared his throat. "Paullus endured quite a bit, sir. I'm certain he will survive to the end."

"How was he injured so gravely?" Villius again took up Paullus's hand and looked down on him with a strange expression. "I have had no end of requests from Rome on his condition."

Heads turned to Varro for the explanation. Paullus looked at him with hooded eyes, his marble-like face stern and expectant.

"The enemy stabbed him in the final moments of our escape, sir. He nearly died."

"But thanks to you three, he did not." Villius finally smiled, as if he had only just thought to award it to them.

Sabellius again cleared his throat and spoke more quietly. "Sir, I've mentioned these men before."

"Ah yes." Villius narrowed his eyes as if wrestling with a difficult choice. "Well, here is Paullus, wounded but alive. A good battle scar is worth it, though. In any case, his family will be delighted at this news. Ensure these men are rewarded, Tribune. And you three have my gratitude."

Paullus raised his head with a wheeze, straining his voice past believability. "And the gratitude of my family as well."

"This is wonderful," Villius said. "Now, I will ensure that Paullus continues his recovery. Unless there is other business, Tribune?"

"No, sir. I will see to these three fine soldiers."

Dismissed, Varro turned to exit after the tribune. Before he did, he looked over his shoulder. The consul knelt to Paullus at eye-level, smiling and speaking in encouraging whispers. Paullus nodded, wincing as if even this much caused him agony. Neither man paid any more attention to anyone else. Varro shook his head and exited the tent, glad to be done with Paullus for the rest of his life.

Sabellius escorted them through the camp. If their reappearance meant anything, no one showed it. Across the headquarters he saw Centurion Drusus watching him with folded arms and an inscrutable expression. Varro did not know what to do, wondering if he should salute as he trailed along in a disorganized group behind the tribune. Drusus solved the issue by offering short nod, then turning aside.

So much for the welcome home, Varro thought.

Once within Sabellius's tent among the Second Legion troops, the tribune relaxed and gave them a wide smile, offering them chairs set out in the cool and dim tent.

"Tonight you will dine with me, and eat well. You three have rendered a great service to Rome and to me. Not to mention you have saved the consul's political career. There is cause for celebration."

Varro shared the smile with Curio and Varro, but he still needed closure.

"Sir, pardon me for speaking so bluntly. But I want assurance that the consul will not pursue any more actions against us. We are free of any threat of death?"

Sabellius rocked back with gusty laughter.

"Of course! Had he wanted you dead, you wouldn't be here. I appreciate your fears, but he owes you a great deal.'"

"I'm also afraid of powerful men feeling like they owe me something, sir."

This halted all laughter, and both Falco and Curio stat up straighter as if realizing the same fear. But the tribune simply nodded.

"You are growing in wisdom, young Varro. That is good."

A servant entered with cups filled with wine and distributed them to the gathering. They drank to their success and to the future, then fell to a companionable silence. At last, Falco cleared his throat.

"With respect, sir, you were holding our valuables while we were away."

"The necklace and your other things," he said, smiling. "Once I knew you had returned, I prepared them immediately. They are with your other possession, which I have had stacked over there."

He pointed to their packs and other belongings. Falco looked to the tribune for permission, then began going through the packs until he found the chain and the two rings stolen from King Philip's hands. The sack with the rings he palmed aside, but held forward the gold chain.

The two halves slid out onto his palm, as thick and lustrous as Varro had remembered.

Curio whistled. "I finally get to see what this was all for."

"You'll get your third," Falco said. "You've more than earned it."

Sabellius watched with a bemused smile. Could such wealth be meaningless to him, Varro wondered? It must be, for any other man would have stolen the necklace and rings for himself.

They admired the necklace a short time and gave Sabellius an outline of their journey to find Paullus. But he insisted they go into more details during dinner, where a wider audience would appreciate the adventure. Apparently, Centurion Drusus would attend as well.

"Now, you three should go about cleaning up and resting. I will find a time to integrate you back into your maniple. But before then, you can share my tent."

"That is generous of you, sir," Varro said, and the others agreed.

Sabellius stood, prompting the others to as well. But Varro

paused and considered his next words. Now was the time to speak, or he may never have the chance.

"Sir, you should know the truth about Marcellus Paullus."

"Varro, shouldn't you rest before getting into this?" Falco laughed and tugged at his tunic sleeve. But he would not stop. Sabellius raised his brow.

"Paullus is a traitor. He took up with Alamene, King Philip's cousin, and worked with Athenagoras against the Dardanians. He resisted returning to camp. He made me a slave and would have done the same to Curio and Falco had he the chance. He wasn't wounded in battle. After we forced him to surrender, Alamene stabbed him out of anger."

The words had flowed with more passion than he wanted, and he realized Sabellius might not even understand the context. He looked to the tribune, who remained staring at him with his brow cocked.

"Sir, Rome was better off if Paullus never returned. We haven't done any good bringing him back."

The tent suddenly felt darker and warmer, though Varro understood it was the embarrassment shining on his face. Sabellius said nothing, did not shift his expression, and finally Varro accepted nothing would come from what he had said.

He exited the tent to return to a world without justice.

28

They stood by the stream's edge, Varro, Falco, and Curio. It was all like he remembered from the dream the night of his foiled execution. The water gurgled through a muddy bank just like the dream. The only difference being the slave girl was not present, and sour-faced Falco and Curio stood beside him instead.

"Lily, I cannot believe you've convinced me to do this. Curio, how is this happening? How is this stupid optio making me do this?"

Curio shivered and shook his head.

"I want her ghost to leave me alone," he said. "She just sits beside me while I sleep, staring at me. Only when I was at the farmhouse with that beautiful girl did she not haunt my nights."

"So just get another girl," Falco said. "Then you won't be bothered by ghosts. We don't have to do this."

Varro looked at the chain halves in his palm. Sunlight dappled him, flaring links into brilliant yellow. He closed his hands around them.

"Falco, I understand how you feel. But this is our penance. I've been wrong this whole time. It wasn't just about me. I might have restrained her, but Curio bumped you and you held the pugio that ultimately killed her. We all did it. We all have a crime to pay for."

With a long sigh, Falco turned aside. He had fought Varro on this decision since their sea voyage from Illyria. At first he flatly refused. But Varro promised he could keep both of King Philip's rings as compensation for the lost half. This had comforted him, and eventually led to his agreement.

Curio did not even need to hear the complete plan. He was overjoyed to think he could be free of his guilt. No one had known he suffered for the slave's death. But he had and now was eager to divest himself of it.

"Just do it," Curio said. "Don't listen to Falco."

Varro knelt beside the stream and, just as the slave girl had done in his vivid dream, he scooped out the mud to create a deep hole. His hand hovered over it with the chain sitting on his palm.

"So much blood has flowed from this chain." He dumped it into the mud with a plop. "It carries a curse. But now we return it to its owner, who guided me to this spot when I stood between life and death. I never learned your name. We were not friends in life. But let us not be enemies in death. Take back your chain. Bring it to your brother, and leave this world. Be at peace."

He plowed mud back over the hole then patted it flat. He crouched over the spot, expecting to feel something. But he only felt the fall breeze against his back.

"How dramatic," Falco said. "All we really did was make ourselves poor again."

"The Paullus family might send a reward," Curio said brightly. At dinner the prior night, Sabellius intimated there could be something more tangible than gratitude to follow from the Paullus family. While it excited Curio and Falco, Varro considered it a distraction.

"They should buy our silence about dear Paullus," Falco said. "They should make me a senator."

"Let's forget about him. And forget about gold." Varro stood and clapped mud from his hands.

"If anyone followed us, they'll be the rich ones." Falco said.

"No one will ever find that chain," Varro said. "When the moonlight falls on this spot, it will pass into another world."

"It's going to sit in the mud," Falco said. "But believe what you want. We've paid our price to the dead slave. And we'll be free from now on. But I'm sure someone will find the chain one day."

"Maybe a hundred years from now," Curio said. "Or maybe in a thousand years. We won't be alive when someone pulls it out of the mud. But they'll get the curse that comes with it. So good luck to him that finds it again."

They followed the path back to camp, carrying buckets of water as their excuse for having visited the stream. Whether the gate guards believed such a feeble excuse, they offered no challenge as long as they gave the proper passwords on return. Passing beyond the gate and back to camp, they headed for the cistern to dump their buckets.

Varro found Centurion Fidelis waiting for him along the main road.

This paused all three of them, but the centurion had eyes only for Varro. With a curt nod, he sent the other two off.

"Go on," Varro said. "I'll catch up with you two soon."

Falco gave a dark look to the centurion, but left without a word.

"Walk with me, Optio. I've just a few questions."

He and Fidelis walked the perimeter of the camp where no one would hear them. Neither spoke until they had crossed halfway between the western and southern gates. Fidelis called a halt to their walk.

"I had heard you were three deserters. You were gone quite

some time. But now you're back, and heroes at that. Congratulations."

Fidelis's eyes offered anything but congratulations. A feral gleam shined from them and his smile was tight and crooked. But Varro no longer feared him.

"You heard wrong. We would never betray Rome."

"I believe that," Fidelis said, and this seemed sincere. But the gleam remained and he leaned closer as he dropped his voice. "Look, I know you killed her. I wasn't wrong. But I still don't know why."

"You weren't wrong, Centurion." Varro met his surprised eyes with confidence. "Killed but not murdered. It was all an accident. We tried to frighten her into returning a gold necklace she had stolen from us. But we were three fools acting like toughs. It was bound to failure, and that failure cost the poor girl her life. We bumped around and knocked her onto a pugio held against her neck. She died instantly. I would have given anything to undo that moment. Now you know the truth."

Fidelis rubbed his strong chin and considered what he had been told.

"A gold necklace she stole from you? War spoils?"

"Exactly, I took it from her brother's neck myself. He was an Illyrian brigand chief, and I killed him. She stole it when I was in the field, and did not hide the fact. I swore to get it back. You know how it ended."

"Did she have the necklace?"

"It was never found," Varro lied smoothly, not even pausing. "Wherever she hid it, it remains there forever. If you find it, Centurion, you might want to consider all the bad luck that has followed it."

Fidelis leaned back as if surprised. "I don't want the necklace. I wanted to know I was right and why you did it. All for a gold necklace?"

Varro closed his eyes and nodded. "As shameful as it is to admit, it was all for a gold necklace."

When he opened his eyes, he found Fidelis holding a sheathed pugio. He spun it by the point on his palm.

"So this was yours? It's a fine weapon. Well cared for."

"It was a gift from my mother when I joined the legion." He tried to act unperturbed, but his hands itched to snatch it back.

"Well, I've kept it warm for you. Here you are, Optio. Good job with Paullus, too. I'm sure your future is bright."

The pugio passed between Fidelis and Varro, slipping easily into his palm. The centurion flashed a brief smile, then left Varro standing alone by the camp walls.

He began to laugh, holding the pugio in both hands. He was free. He was forgiven. The gods had denied him the blessed weapon when he smeared it in shame. Now they returned it.

Slipping the pugio onto his belt, his steps were light as he walked toward a bright future.

HISTORICAL NOTES

In 199 BC, the enterprising Dardanians under the leadership of Bato took advantage of Philip's preoccupation with the Roman forces arrayed against him to the south and west of his kingdom. They crossed through the mountain passes and inflicted heavy damage on the Macedonians. Once Philip received news of these predations, he sent his general, Athenagoras, to deal with Bato and his allies.

Athenagoras caught up to the rear of the Dardanian forces and several skirmishes ensued. But to the Macedonians' surprise, Bato turned his army around and offered Athenagoras a proper battle line. This turned matters into a formal war between the Dardanians and Macedonians that would not be settled for years to come.

Marcellus Paullus is a fictional character, though the Paullus family is not. Lucius Aemilius Paullus was consul during the Second Punic War and died in battle. His daughter, Aemilla, would marry Rome's newest star, Scipio Africanus. I've loosely fit fictional Marcellus into the Paullus family. Placing him in the cavalry would be the exact location for a wealthy, young patrician to serve in the military, which was required to hold any public office.

Alamene is likewise a fictional character. Philip V had an elder half-sister but no other siblings. His other relations did not play a part in history, except for his son. A character like Alamene represents a fair bit of artistic expression, and would be unlikely in actual history.

The troubles facing the new Consul Publius Villius Tappulus upon assuming command of the Macedonian theater were real. The Punic War veterans under his command rebelled, claiming they had been forced to continue fighting illegally. It took Villius the entire summer to settle their disputes, thereby preventing any real action against Philip. While I have fictionalized Galba's hand in this rebellion, it does seem opportune for the revolt to have occurred after Galba departed. Many considered him to have squandered a chance to end the war, and it would not look good for his successor to do exactly that.

This brings real history up to the timeline represented in this story. A new consul will soon be elected and replace Villius in Macedonia. Varro and Falco, maybe richer or poorer for their exploits, have a long march ahead before the war is over.

IF YOU WOULD LIKE to know when my next book is released, please sign up for my new release newsletter. You can do this at my website:

http://jerryautieri.wordpress.com/

If you have enjoyed this book and would like to show your support for my writing, consider leaving a review where you purchased this book or on Goodreads, LibraryThing, and other reader sites. I need help from readers like you to get the word out about my books. If you have a moment, please share your thoughts with other readers. I appreciate it!

ALSO BY JERRY AUTIERI

Ulfrik Ormsson's Saga

Historical adventure stories set in 9th Century Europe and brimming with heroic combat. Witness the birth of a unified Norway, travel to the remote Faeroe Islands, then follow the Vikings on a siege of Paris and beyond. Walk in the footsteps of the Vikings and witness history through the eyes of Ulfrik Ormsson.

Fate's Needle

Islands in the Fog

Banners of the Northmen

Shield of Lies

The Storm God's Gift

Return of the Ravens

Sword Brothers

Descendants Saga

The grandchildren of Ulfrik Ormsson continue tales of Norse battle and glory. They may have come from greatness, but they must make their own way in the brutal world of the 10th Century.

Descendants of the Wolf

Odin's Ravens

Revenge of the Wolves

Blood Price

Viking Bones

Valor of the Norsemen

Norse Vengeance

Bear and Raven

Red Oath

Fate's End

Grimwold and Lethos Trilogy

A sword and sorcery fantasy trilogy with a decidedly Norse flavor.

Deadman's Tide

Children of Urdis

Age of Blood

Copyright © 2021 by Jerry Autieri

All rights reserved.

No part of this book may be reproduced in any form or by any electronic or mechanical means, including information storage and retrieval systems, without written permission from the author, except for the use of brief quotations in a book review.

Printed in Great Britain
by Amazon